BITTER
WATER

Other books
by Douglas Clark

THE BIG GROUSE
JEWELLED EYE
PLAIN SAILING
STORM CENTER

BITTER WATER

DOUGLAS CLARK

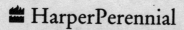 **HarperPerennial**

A Division of HarperCollinsPublishers

Published by arrangement with John Farquharson, Ltd.

FIRST EDITION

ISBN 0-06-081024-6

90 91 92 93 94 WB/OPM 10 9 8 7 6 5 4 3 2 1

For
James Richard

1

Kent was living up to its reputation as the garden of England. The early morning sun was already warm even though most people had not yet breakfasted. June had been bountiful. More than a week of glorious weather had reassured even the most cautious that French windows and patio doors could be opened wide at so early an hour without fear of cold blasts entering houses to chill and disturb the inhabitants. There was a busy stillness all about. Bees and other insects noising their activities pianissimo; birds done with the dawn chorus and quietly settling down to the never ending chore of feeding themselves and their nestlings; shadows cast by trees and bushes marching silently round the arcs prescribed for them by the sun; the sky cloudless, the blue unbroken even by vapour trails and, momentarily, no noise of aeroplane engines as background music for the idyll.

"The trouble with builders," said Margot Carlyle angrily, "is that they never seem to do anything as you really want it done. You can envisage it and explain in minute detail, but builders, in spite of all their protestations of being prepared to carry out your instructions to the letter, always change the specifications or wilfully misunderstand them, so that one finishes up with what can best be described as an abortion."

Her husband, Hugh Carlyle, laughed aloud. A big throaty laugh, coming from a big heavily built man in his prime. "My dear girl," he said, "you have made that speech, or one strikingly similar in tone and burden, every day on which the sun has shone warmly for the past two years. And, let's be honest, the object of your wrath is not a builder. It's nothing more than a ramp of concrete six feet long."

"That is exactly my point," retorted Margot, steadying his wheelchair as it took to the slope. "It is much too steep for you to manage comfortably on your own. And why? Because it is six feet long and not the eight feet I stipulated."

"They had their reasons, my dear. The extra two feet would have taken me too close to the edge of the pool. They thought it would have been unsafe for me."

"Nonsense," said Margot severely. "They could have taken the ramp at an angle from the French window to get the necessary length."

"It would have been awfully difficult, old girl."

"Not in the least difficult." She strained against the gathering momentum. "They could have built a level platform and then led off downwards at right angles."

"There's a manhole cover in the way."

"They could have bridged that quite easily," she said as she brought the chair to a halt.

"Certainly they could, but it wouldn't have left enough clearance for raising it should the need arise."

She made no reply as she turned the chair onto the path round the pool. "Now, are you going by yourself, or do you want me to hang on?"

"I'll manage, Mags. The brakes will hold me. I'll be out in time for breakfast."

"A quarter of an hour?"

"Make it twenty minutes and you're on. Can we eat out here? It's a beautiful morning."

Margot Carlyle stood by the chair and looked up at the sky, shading her eyes with her hands. She was a handsome woman. Not big. In fact, small-enough-made to emphasise an excellent figure. In her early forties, she looked no more than thirty-two or -three. Her hair, skin, eyes . . . all were those of a woman in her prime. But she was a bundle of strength. Hugh Carlyle had

2

often been surprised at the power of the small hands and slim wrists.

"I don't see why not," she said at length, having satisfied herself that no errant breeze was likely to blow to do him physical harm. "I'll bring out the infrared grill and the toaster." She put one hand on his shoulder. "Will kidneys and mushrooms suit you? I find eggs are difficult out of doors."

"Anything, my lovely." Briefly he laid one hand on hers and said: "Now, if I don't get in there smartish my twenty minutes'll be up and I shall miss my grub."

She left him to it, knowing his spirit of independence and his preference for managing things himself as far as possible. Various additions had been made around the pool to help him do so. The chair could be steered between tubular steel banisters which allowed him to raise himself on his arms and edge slowly onto a small seat that could then swing out over the water and, at the touch of a button, lower him down almost to the surface at the shallow end. He did it competently. Slowly, but with the facility which comes from practice.

In the water he was a different man. Here, the malaise which affected his legs on dry land was no longer so apparent. The buoyancy of the water and the strength of his great, muscular arms allowed him to swim quite adeptly. But first, the exercises for the near-useless legs. Using the buoyancy to lift them, he flexed the flaccid muscles. Bending, stretching, massaging. He doubted the value of the daily drill, unsure whether it improved matters or prevented them from worsening. But his physiotherapist insisted on the hydrotherapy and he enjoyed the water, aware that in this medium he was nearer to normality than on land.

Because he was wealthy enough to build and equip the pool, Maisie Firth, his private physiotherapist, had been able to plan his routine carefully to suit his specific disability. It was up to him to execute the exercises in accordance with her wishes. The spasticity of the leg muscles caused an increasing weakness which Maisie was sure only exercise could stem. She had explained how the muscles, too weak to work against gravity, could only be aided by hydrotherapy or slings and counterweights slung over pulleys. For this reason the pool had been adapted for his use. For the winter months, when bathing outside was impossible, he had installed the biggest domestic bath available so that he could continue unrelentingly with his underwater exercises. In addition, there were the passive movements Maisie had prescribed. Margot had been taught how to massage his legs and move them so that the affected muscles were stretched smoothly and rhythmically. It was during these twice-daily sessions that he had come to realise and appreciate the firm but gentle strength of his wife's hands and wrists.

He had finished the course of exercises and was dog-paddling about the pool, using the strong arms as his only motive power, when Margot again appeared to plug in the toaster at the guarded external power point.

"The kidneys are done," she told him, as he came to the rail close to where she was standing. "I cooked them indoors, after all, but I'll bring the grill out, just the same, to keep them hot until you're ready."

"Coming out now, Mags."

"You must towel off and change before you have breakfast."

"Must I? It's warm enough just to put on a robe."

She insisted. "You must be dried and in proper clothing. I'm not letting you take the risk of catching even a summer cold. Come along. I'll help you." She sounded firm rather than dictatorial, but it was a firmness born of anxiety. Hugh's doctors had been adamant. Every precaution must be taken against any chance of infection. Even minor illnesses, such as colds, could be much more troublesome for him than for others. She intended to play her part conscientiously and without fuss. She had done so now for some years, ever since the need arose. She realised that probably she was sometimes a little short on cheerfulness. Usually when she remembered the whole man too vividly to accept willingly this handicap: a progressive disease which had turned the young lion she had married into a physical cripple.

Mentally, Hugh Carlyle was jovial, although the doctors had told her that this cheerfulness could be pathognomic, specifically characteristic of sufferers of this particular disablement, the presence of which went some way towards confirming the diagnosis of the disease. Certainly Hugh did not give the impression of viewing his condition as seriously as she did. But this attitude was so like the attitude of the man of earlier days: cheerful, witty, good-humoured, good-tempered and as energetic as it was possible for a human to be.

Mentally she was the cripple, because she grieved constantly. Her knowledge of his disease caused her to question fate as much as any man or woman who wonders why his or her loved one should be stricken in the prime of life by any serious disabling or fatal illness. The cause of his condition, according to the doctors, was unknown. Margot knew from her reading that there were several schools of thought. Some said infection was the cause, others that it was due to an allergic reaction of the nervous system, whilst another opinion, quite widely held, stated that it was the result of a metabolic upset or even a deficiency disorder. Not to know exactly was painful, because Margot was an intelligent woman liking to know about whatever concerned her, particularly something as closely as this. Perhaps wrongly, she felt that ignorance as to the cause prevented her from taking some comparatively simple remedial action and this, in turn, engendered a feeling of helplessness. She had read what she could, but found it all little more than background information: the disease is more common in temperate climates; sixty percent of patients show the first manifestations between the ages of twenty and forty; onset is exceedingly rare below fifteen or over fifty; the incidence is much more common in women than men. And so on.

She went indoors to fetch the little portable grill and

then, having plugged it in, waited at the chair as he swung himself easily out of the water. She had carefully draped a bath towel on the seat to stop it getting too wet and then put a bathrobe round his shoulders. He propelled himself to the ramp, and might have been able to manage it himself, but she helped him up and across the threshold of the French window.

The room had been turned over to him. Not as a bedroom, though it did contain, against one wall, a divan on which he could rest should he need to. Desk, two armchairs, even filing cabinets specially built on stilts so that no drawer was below the height of his knees and so that the footrest of the chair could go underneath to make reaching the contents easier.

"I'm almost dry, Mags, and I must say the kidneys smell good. Amazing how a swim sharpens the appetite."

"Your trunks are still sopping."

They came off easily. A tie at each side allowed the garment to open out so that it could be flicked from beneath him.

"Ups-a-daisy." He looked at her closely. She had never said that before when she needed him to shift his weight. It was unlike her. Not her sort of expression.

"Something is bothering you, Maggie. Is it because I'm putting on weight? Getting to be too much for you?"

She kissed him on the forehead. "Never that, my darling. And your tummy is as flat as a pancake, much to my great delight and surprise. I suppose it's all the exercises which keep you . . ."

He lifted an arm and put it round her shoulders, drawing her down to him. "You're burbling, Mags. Running on, in fact, so what is it that's bothering you? And don't say nothing is, because I know the signs too well."

"I'm worried lest you are doing too much."

"Too much, old girl?" He removed his arm and looked up at her as she straightened. "In my condition?" He laughed. "How can I? I don't do a quarter of what I'd like to do."

"No, perhaps not." She heaved the elastic of his pants up at the back and then eased his trousers up his legs, leaving him to wriggle his backside into them and fasten the belt clips. She did not expand on her reply. Silently she handed him a pale blue, freshly laundered bush shirt, made to order, with pockets on both breasts and both skirts so that he could carry all his impedimenta on his person without recourse to trouser pockets.

"I'll serve breakfast. Be careful coming down the ramp."

The little table, placed on the grass to the left of the ramp, was exquisitely laid, and the trolley carrying the grill and toaster was pushed close so that he could reach to feed more of the thick-sliced bread into the pop-up machine should he want it.

After manoeuvring himself to the table he took the vitamin pills she had put by his plate and drank the fresh orange juice. Then she put the kidneys and mushrooms in front of him.

"Good grub," he said, after a moment, obviously enjoying it. He looked across at her. "You not having any?"

"Toast and honey will do me."

He put down his knife and fork. "Come on, sweetheart. Something's bugging you. What is it?"

"I am a bit worried," she confessed.

"About me? Why?"

"You're looking strained. Tired."

"Am I? Surely not."

"You are doing too much."

"No, no, Mags. The doctors have told me to keep on the go."

"Eat your breakfast while it's still hot."

He ignored the instruction. "They said it is dangerous not to. What was it, exactly? Inactivity could lead to urinary infection, constipation and probably pneumonia? Or some such catalogue of ills."

"I know all that. Now, eat your breakfast, Hugh. It's getting cold."

He speared a segment of kidney and then put his fork

7

down. "I know what it is, old girl. You need a holiday. A real one, I mean. Without me. For years now you've never been away anywhere except to the cottage. You refuse to leave me and we only go to the cottage because it has all the aids for me installed there. You need a complete change."

She shook her head and smiled gently. "I don't want a break away from you, my darling. Always, when you're not here, I'm longing for you to get back."

"Even when your pals come to keep you company for the day?"

"Even then."

"You seemed very happy to entertain Wanda Masters and her little boy on Tuesday. I've not seen you so full of vim, vigour and verve for a long, long time."

"Wanda is one of my oldest friends. We've always been very close. And look at the fuss you made of her. And of young Michael, when you came home in the middle of the afternoon." She smiled again. "Honestly, Hugh, you enjoyed their visit more than I did."

"Nonsense, old girl."

"You mean you didn't like them coming?" She smiled.

"You know exactly what I meant. I think the world of Wanda and I like the little chap. But to say I enjoyed their visit more than you did is nonsense. You revelled in their company."

Margot laughed aloud. "And who was it who didn't stop at giving Wanda two complimentaries for tonight's opening of *Round the Barley?* Who was it who not only papered the house, but actually gave her a residence?"

"Gave her one?"

"You offered her Housmans for about half the price it would fetch on the open market."

"And who promptly took her to look it over?"

"I couldn't do anything else but take her. I wanted the poor girl to see what you were offering before she felt she needed to give you an answer, however conditional."

"I noticed you were full of its praises and running on

about how nice it would be to have her living nearby and how good the country air would be for Michael."

"Of course, and I meant every word. I'm not complaining about your offer. I'm delighted that you thought of it. But I can understand why Wanda was a bit taken aback."

"She told us she and George were thinking of moving out of their little place in London because it wouldn't be big enough much longer. From that I deduced an increase in family. I've got a nice oast-house, converted into a domestic dwelling, but standing empty. As it has been for over a year now. Nobody has offered what you and the agents call the market price, so it seemed reasonable that I should offer it to a friend in need at what, I reckoned, was a realistic price. That is, the price they would want, and could afford, to pay."

"With ten thousand knocked off after that?"

"It will need a bit of decorating and the garden has gone to pot."

"Wanda loved it."

"So I gathered. But she was a bit cagey..."

"Wouldn't you be? Wouldn't you be wondering whether there wasn't some hidden snag attached to such an offer?"

"Of course. And to show I meant what I said about it I spoke to George yesterday morning."

"At the Yard?"

"Just to reassure him that it was a good property and that he could have it surveyed at any time. And to re-iterate the price, of course."

"You didn't tell me."

He grinned widely. "I've been too busy, old girl. You know, as you said a few minutes ago."

"Oh, you idiot."

"I thought Wanda would ring you and tell you all the developments. My idea was to leave it strictly to them from now on. Don't want to seem to be steamrollering them."

"I expect she'll ring today. If you spoke to George

9

yesterday morning they'll have discussed it last night and she'll ring as soon as she can this morning. Anyhow, we'll probably see them tonight."

"Maybe. But to get back to your holiday."

"I don't want a holiday alone. Would you like another cup of coffee?"

As he handed his cup over to her, he said, "Then we'll have a break together."

"What do you mean?" She put two sweeteners into the cup of black coffee before handing it over to him.

"A cruise. If we were to book a deck cabin so that I could push the chair in and out, use the lifts for the dining room as long as we make sure that the ship has promenade cabins—and have a handhold made for beside the bed. You know the sort of thing. Two lengths of strong metal tubing, one fitting inside the other. Ideal for ships with steel decks. The tubes, with endplates fitted, could be extended hard up against the deck and ceiling. A simple screw-type locking device in the middle to keep it absolutely rigid, and I could haul myself in and out of bed as I do here. At the end of the trip we just unlock it, telescope it down and bring it away with us for next time. I'll get somebody on it today and..."

"No, no, darling."

"No cruise?"

"Of course a cruise would be lovely, but..."

"You've just said I've been doing too much."

"You have. You go to business every day."

"From ten to four—at the latest."

"You still drive yourself there and back. That in itself is a strain in London traffic."

He laughed again and then, pushing away his plate, he leaned forward in mock severity. "No it isn't. The car is specially adapted so there are no foot controls. The steering is power-assisted. And as for the risk of accident... well, you insisted that I should have bumpers fore and aft built of quarter-inch solid steel and that the bonnet and engine bulkhead should be strengthened so that the engine can't be pushed backwards.

10

Darling, if I had any sort of shunt, the other chap involved would think a tank had hit him."

"You haven't drunk that last cup of coffee."

He lifted the cup. For a few moments there was silence and then Margot got to her feet and pushed her chair under the table. As she did so she said, "You don't always get home by four o'clock. A day or two ago you stayed in town for a stage party."

"A very mild affair. Everybody was just a bit sad at reaching the end of the run. No high jinks. Just chat. You know that. You were there."

"But it was still a long day for you, and a strain."

"You drove me home."

"I know all that. But you won't be coming home at four this afternoon, either."

"No fear. Opening night of a new show. But there again, Mags, you'll be with me to take the strain."

She sighed in exasperation, pulled out her chair and sat down again. "And on Saturday you have insisted on having a party here."

"It's my birthday."

"I like you to have a party on your birthday. But that will make three occasions in one week, and that's too much for you."

"Eight days, actually, but you must admit it's a very exceptional eight days. We often go for months without attending any evening function."

"Quite right, too."

"Darling, remember I've been told to keep active. Don't the doctors threaten me with all sorts of bumps and blains if I sit back and don't move?"

"They do. But they don't suggest you should overdo it, which is what you have been doing just lately. Or are about to do."

He smiled at her. "I'd rather carry on, Mags. I can still run the business successfully, and as for the stage . . . well, it's my hobby. It always has been. Oh, I know I've made a bit of money from being an Angel, but that's not the point. I love being involved. Always have done, from the moment I first put a hundred and twenty-five quid into *The Diarist*. That was well over twenty years ago, and let's face it, my sweet, that was how I met you. So I haven't done too badly from supporting the Arts. Made a few bob from time to time and got the fairest flower in the bunch into the bargain."

"What you got," she replied, rolling her napkin for the ring, "was a girl totally disillusioned by her inability to act, who was, if anything, slightly better at painting scenery for a repertory company than making a success of any part she was given, and who was financially on her uppers when you met her." She looked up at him. "Your flower, as you call her, was ripe for the picking."

"So what are you saying?"

She got up and came round to him. With her arms round his neck and her cheek against his, she said: "That I think we were both lucky. I know I was."

"Me too. And it's damned nice of you to say so, Mags, with me in this state. That was something we never bargained for."

She straightened up. "No, but if it had happened to me ... well, you'd have carried me about in your arms and cared for me like a baby."

"True." He eased the chair backwards. "And I do know why you are frightened, really." He took her hand. "These damned demyelinating diseases are progressive. You think if I do too much I'll precipitate further deterioration."

"No, darling, no."

"Maggie, I know you too well. You're edgy. Frightened."

"You've got it all wrong, Hugh. Of course your condition worries me, but I'm optimistic about it, really. You're so cheerful, and your mental attitude reassures me. So often your ..."

"Disorder?"

"Yes. So often there are remissions. I've read a lot about them happening. And even if there is none in your case, in many patients like you, with the will to make the best of things, the condition remains mild and doesn't interfere with ordinary life any more than it does initially. I'm sure things won't get worse. Sure of it."

"Then why the jitters, my love?"

She said, a trifle wildly: "If you must know..."

"Yes, please."

"I know you've been getting threatening letters. Anonymous ones."

This time he really gave way to mirth. "Oh, my sweet! Those?"

"I saw one on your desk. You'd left it lying there. And since then I've made sure I've taken in the post in the mornings. I've seen two more in the same sort of envelope."

"Don't pay any attention to those. I don't. If I'd taken them seriously I'd have shown them all to you and told the police."

"But besides threatening you, they called you names."

"The most repeatable of which, if memory serves, was Ruthless Bastard, with capital initial letters."

She shook her head. "But what does it all mean, Hugh? What are they referring to?"

"Haven't a clue. I assume it refers to something to do with the business. But I can't guess what and I certainly haven't the time to try to find out. And I don't suppose you want me to expend any energy on a witch hunt, do you?"

"I confess I found them frightening."

"Don't worry. They'll stop as they began, and they'll be forgotten."

"I hope so."

"They will. Now I think it's time I made a move. It's nearly nine o'clock and here's Mrs. Hookham coming to clear the table." He waved at the middle-aged woman plodding down the ramp. "Morning, Mrs. H. Lovely day again."

"Beautiful. My hubby says it's set fair for another few days yet."

"If he's right," said Margot, "we shall be able to hold

the party out here on Saturday evening."

"Good idea," said Carlyle. "We'll have the fairy-lights strung in the bushes. Are you coming, Mrs. H.?"

"I'll be here, Mr. Carlyle. Washing up and the like and keeping an eye on those outside caterers you've got coming in. I know them of old. Full of horsey-borsey, they are. Think they own my kitchen. They use every dish we've got in the house and just pile them up. Mucky tups! No order, that's what I don't like. Me, I like a tidy kitchen, and so does Freda. I've taught her my own ways and I'll have to warn her to watch her tongue, Saturday, or there'll be ructions out back."

Carlyle laughed. "Don't you worry, Mrs. H. We'll all have a splendid time. Freda included. Don't forget to bring your old man along."

"He'll come for a bit of supper in the kitchen, I expect, sir. But only after closing time."

Detective Chief Superintendent George Masters ushered his wife, Wanda, out of the door of their little house behind the Westminster Hospital and into the cab that had backed its way down the narrow road and was now waiting for them.

"The Victory Theatre, please."

"Right, Super. Going to the first night, then?"

"That's it."

"Foyer entrance, then, if we can get near it. You might have to flash your card to clear the way." The driver closed the window behind him and concentrated on turning out of the little street into the mainstream traffic.

"The cabby obviously knows you, darling," whispered Wanda. "Do you know *him*?"

"No, but the taxi was ordered by Tip in my name and I suppose she mentioned my rank. But apart from that, these drivers know everybody and everything. It wouldn't surprise me if a good many of them who work this area know me by sight and name."

Wanda smiled. "Fame?"

14

He grinned back. "Hardly. They get to know who to be wary of." He took her hand in his. "Are you feeling all right?"

"Very well, darling, thank you."

"Good. I'll try not to fuss you about it, but are you sure Mrs. Thing will be all right looking after Michael? He seemed a bit boisterous just before we left."

"Molly Howlet will cope with him wonderfully well. She and Michael are great friends. You seem to forget she often sits with him during the day when I'm out and can't take him with me."

Masters shrugged. "If you're happy with her, I am."

"I'm very happy to be able to call on Molly. But you, you're getting to be a bit of an old woman yourself when it comes to looking after your precious son. You could have another to worry about before long. But let's forget all that. We're going out to enjoy ourselves even though *Round the Barley* is not likely to be a show we would have chosen for ourselves."

They were making use of the two complimentaries Hugh Carlyle had given Wanda a couple of days before. Masters fully expected it to be nothing more than a run-of-the-mill farce of the Whitehall-Aldwych variety. He, himself, was very wary of accepting any gift from a member of the public, but these two seats had been given to Wanda. She and Margot Carlyle had been very friendly from long before the Masters had even met, so the DCS had no reason to refuse these particular complimentaries for an opening night. Indeed, it would have been churlish of him to have done so since they were, in essence, not his to refuse.

Nor was this the first occasion on which they had enjoyed complimentaries from the same source. Hugh Carlyle had been a theatrical Angel for so many years that by now he was considered to be something of an Archangel. For Hugh, the business was a hobby and the hobby a business, as he was very fond of telling people who had the time and patience to sit alongside him and listen. And Masters had listened. To the full story.

When the young Hugh Carlyle had just made a tentative offer to an aspiring producer, he had done it out of love of theatre. Not out of love for any particular play, or plays in general, but for the fascination of the buildings themselves. The ambience! Even the smells of an empty house which, in those early times, had often been dominated during the day by the odour of a certain type of raw disinfectant which lingered until overpowered each night by the compounded atmosphere of heterogeneous audiences. Hugh had explained, with some verbal imagery, how he had enjoyed that particular smell and the, to him, tangible atmosphere of an almost dark auditorium, with cleaners passing along the rows, crashing up seats, emptying ashtrays, hoovering, sweeping, mopping, spraying and, or so it seemed, forever singing or humming some current hit from the world of popular music.

This, Masters was told, was what had driven the young Hugh into offering to buy a share in *The Diarist* when he had heard the management was seeking backers. One hundred and twenty-five pounds. A lot of money at the time and a sum which, Hugh readily confessed, he had fully expected to lose. But he had been very happy to buy just one-eightieth of the show simply for the pleasure of being involved, no matter how minutely.

Although he didn't openly discuss the profit he had made, Masters had gathered that the pleasure had been, at least, slightly profitable. Among other qualifications, Hugh Carlyle was a trained business manager. He had had enough sense to keep his hobby separate from all else—an account on its own, making a little very often, rarely losing.

From his track record it had become clear that Carlyle seemed to have the knack of backing shows which, if not wildly profitable, rarely left him out of pocket. But by now each unit he bought in any production was just ten times as big as that first one, and he seldom bought single units. Though offers to managements would sometimes oversubscribe their production estimates, the established fundraisers would usually approach Carlyle. A contribution from him, they believed, would almost guarantee success, and he, still besotted with the theatre world, could generally be counted on to buy at least four units in anything he reckoned would have the chance of breaking even or better. Five thousand pounds was his minimum stake, still coming from the old account set up so many years ago and still thriving gently despite the annual onslaught of tax collectors.

Masters had gleaned that from time to time Carlyle had invested much larger sums, for by the time the two men had become acquainted, the Archangel felt he had developed a nose for real success. It was obviously a conceit, and though he was by no means infallible in this respect, he had gained a reputation for sound business sense not only among the managers, but also among many of the players whose careers he had helped by his activities.

Masters had learned all this by listening to a crippled man with a pleasant obsession and, since his marriage to Wanda, had become friendly with Margot as well as enjoying Hugh Carlyle's company on the relatively few occasions he had met him.

"When Hugh phoned me he said he and Margot would be there tonight."

"Certain to be, at an opening he's got an interest in," replied Wanda, "though whether we shall meet them or not is another matter. I don't know what provisions there are at the Victory for Hugh's wheelchair. I know that at some theatres he goes in through the scenery bay doors and he's then lifted bodily up into a stage box. We are in the stalls."

"At least we'll be able to give them a wave of thanks," said Masters as the driver slowed to approach the theatre outside which was a melée of other cars as well as people on foot. "From the look of this lot the first night at least will be a sellout."

"Hugh usually knows what he's doing. It's obviously going to be a light, frothy piece and I don't think there's one like that on in the West End at the moment. So somebody has seen the gap and decided to plug it and Hugh has backed him. It will run, all being well, until something similar comes along to supersede it."

"Good commercial stuff, in fact."

"With Hugh, everything is commercial. Or he gives me that impression. He's generous to a fault, but with him business is always business."

"My impression, too," said Masters, stretching to reach the door handle as the cab stopped several feet away from the kerb, prevented from getting closer by the throng.

The theatre was beginning to fill up. They had to pass several people to reach their seats in the middle of Row C. Masters handed Wanda the programme he had paused to buy, and a flat pack of plain Neapolitans, no bigger than an old-fashioned box of cigarettes. Wanda smiled her thanks. Neapolitans were a favourite with her and it was customary for Masters to carry a small box in his pocket on occasions such as this. Easy to handle, not noisy to open and not too many contents. At times she had thought that the choice was typical of him. Had even imagined, in fact, that if so convenient a pack had not existed, he would have invented it.

As they had guessed, and as the name suggested, *Round the Barley* was a romp. A sophisticated romp, of course, well-scripted, well-dressed, well-staged and unashamedly supporting the nostalgic belief that all who appear in such things should be good-looking, personable, well-spoken and—particularly in the case of the woman members of the cast—not too old for the parts they were playing.

"Chase me Charlie, round the barley..." Masters thought the words of the old song just about summed up the plot. Reason didn't matter. It was the chasing that counted, and the one being chased most of the time by all and sundry was Carla Sanders, a young and very curvaceous blonde with good legs and the sinuous qualities of an eel when, as so often happened, she was obliged, literally, to avoid capture.

Masters admired the direction. Full use had been made of every stick of carefully chosen furniture as well as the plethora of exits and entrances to make the girl's escapes possible. Her quick, well-timed but natural movements always managed to put a double-decker revolving bookcase or a mobile tea trolley—activated by the same instrument that was used for controlling the television set—bang between her and her pursuer at every critical moment. It was as well-done and as entertaining as one of these modern underwater balletic displays by well-rehearsed teams of bathing girls.

The audience liked it for what it was. They had been entertained, not instructed or made to think, and had showed their appreciation by the number of calls after the final curtain.

As Masters and Wanda got to their feet to file out, Masters asked: "Have you to see Hugh and Margot again before we go?"

"No. As you know, they're up in the stage box and it's a long climb. I said goodbye to Margot in the interval when she came into the bar. In any case, they are going to a cast party."

"So we can go straight home?"

"Oh, yes. I shall be ringing Margot tomorrow. She asked me to, to talk about Housmans, now you and Hugh seem to have come to some definite arrangement."

"Fair enough."

Masters and Wanda wandered slowly with the crowd to the foyer and found their cabby waiting for them.

"You haven't been held up, I hope?" asked Masters.

"We can always get the nod about the time the curtain's coming down, Chief. Give it another ten on an opening night and you're never far out."

He ushered them into the cab and slowly began to pick his way through the crowd. Backstage at the Victory, at about the same time, the cast was percolating off the stage. They were all happy. They had come through the gruelling feat of a first night without any drastic mishaps and it seemed certain they had a success on their hands. There was a lot to talk about, to joke about, to laugh about. After the first round of congratulations among themselves, kissings, darling-you-were-wonderful type splurging, they had begun to leave the set. Carla Sanders, overwhelmed with more bouquets than she could safely carry, and beset by the male members of the cast, moved towards the prompt exit to get to her dressing room. Somebody had once said he knew why the theatre had been named the Victory. On the deck of Nelson's famous flagship was the brass plate bearing the inscription "Nelson fell here." A less than respectful visitor, after slipping on it and then reading the words inscribed thereon, is reported to have said he wasn't bloody surprised Nelson fell at that spot. Anybody treading on it would measure his length just as he had done himself. This, claimed the one who knew, was why the Victory Theatre had been so named. The dressing rooms were all below stage level, and the descent thereto was by means of a short but wickedly spiralled metal stairway. From time to time, various actors had emulated Nelson and had fallen there. Which is just what Carla Sanders did.

It was necessary, when descending this short flight of triangular treads, to hold on to the banister tightly. Carla Sanders, burdened with floral tributes, had no free hand. Furthermore, she was dewy-eyed with success and emotion, and to compound this prescription for disaster, as she started to descend she was chattering over her shoulder to one of her male colleagues. It was a near certainty that what did happen would do so. Carla, in high heels, missed her footing. The middle-aged male actor who was preceding her, apart from being showered with cellophane-wrapped blooms, fortunately took most of the brunt of her fall. He, himself, staggered but managed to hang on, so the girl did not finish up in a crumpled heap at the bottom of the flight. She did, however, do some unsightly damage to the famous legs which formed so great a part of her visible assets. In short, not only did she severely twist her right ankle, but she suffered a nine-inch abrasion on the same leg, wide enough to damage the skin and the outside part of the calf. The edge of a metal step had done its bit exceedingly well, because not only had it taken the skin off this area, it had also caused two long, fairly deep scratches which immediately started to well with blood.

This accident caused turmoil. Apart from Carla's sobs of pain and fright, there were her screams of anger when she realised that the damage done to her legs was not only unsightly, but would almost certainly cause her to miss the second night—and probably quite a number of subsequent nights—of the success in which she had achieved so much personal triumph. The piece demanded great agility and much showing off of the famous legs. Both requirements could no longer be fulfilled by Carla. Her fears were confirmed by the doctor who had been called to attend her in her dressing room, and she was in a hysterical rage when Hugh Carlyle propelled his chair through the door.

It was he who quietened her down, first with stern, commanding language and then with more soothing, sympathetic words. When he left her, she was quiet if tearful, and allowing her dresser to get on with the business of preparing for her to be taken home by Howard Collier, her current live-in boyfriend, who was also an actor, but in a different play—*Mirror Writing* at the Leader—from which theatre he had just rushed in order to attend the stage party at the Victory as Carla's guest.

This post-farce drama was unbeknown to Masters who, at about the time Hugh Carlyle was quietening Carla Sanders, was gently ushering his own wife into their little house behind the Westminster Hospital.

"I shall be sad to leave it," she said as they entered the hall. "It has been a lovely home, hasn't it, darling?"

He smiled and nodded, but said nothing as they relieved Molly Howlet who was all ready to leave in the cab which was still waiting to take her home. After that they had much to discuss and, to the delight of both of them, they discovered that they had each had the same idea about an important step they were due to take.

The next evening, about an hour after he had arrived home from the Yard, Masters was interrupted as he was drawing the cork on a bottle of what he hoped would be a dark, vigorous red wine. He had never before served Madiran, but he had been assured that the '78 would be to his liking, so he had bought a quarter of a dozen, of which this was the first. He answered the door as soon as he could lay down the opened bottle and the corkscrew. Wanda was in her kitchen doing wondrous things to the food she was preparing for her small supper party. The ring of the bell suggested that their two guests, DCI and Doris Green, had arrived, well up to time as usual.

It was a very small house, tucked away in its little narrow street, but so well-maintained and tastefully furnished that all who knew it referred to it as Wanda's Palace, a name originally used by DCI Green, who now stood on the doorstep, slightly ahead of his wife who was staring upwards at the first-floor window above her head.

"Good evening, Bill. Nice to see you, Doris."

"Don't mind the missus, George," replied Green. "She's taken up astronomy and she's looking for the evening star."

"In broad daylight? At seven o'clock on a summer's night?"

Green shrugged. "She's a bit early, perhaps..."

"Idiot!" said his wife. "George, I think I saw Michael at the window. He must be out of bed."

22

"Come in and make yourselves at home while I go up and see what's going on." He turned and went up the stairs, taking the risers in pairs.

"What did you want to split on the choker for?" Green demanded as he shut the door behind his wife.

"Because I didn't want him to fall out. There are no bars on the windows. Now he's big enough to get out of bed on his own and he's finding it difficult to drop off to sleep on these bright nights we'll have to start taking precautions with that young man."

"His mother watches him like a hawk."

"I know that, but even Wanda has to let him out of her sight sometimes. Ah! There she is. Hello, dear! Is there anything I can do?"

"No, thank you, Doris. Hello, William. Where's George?"

"Settling the heir-apparent who apparently decided he'd like to look out of the window rather than stay in bed."

"It's a new habit," sighed Wanda. "It started a day or two ago. But come into the room and sit down."

Masters joined them a few seconds later, in time to pour the drinks.

"What's all this?" asked Green as he accepted a glass.

"Gin and tonic. Isn't that all right for you?"

"The booze is bang on, thanks." Green gestured with his free arm. "But this? The place is full of house catalogues. *Dalton's Weekly*, agents' blurbs and free newspapers. What goes on, George?"

"Bill! You can't ask questions like that," protested Doris.

"Can't I, love? I have done. And if the answer isn't the right one, you and I are going to lose our home from home. How would you like that?"

"Wanda, you're not thinking of moving, are you?" asked Doris anxiously. "Not out of this beautiful cottage."

"Sit down, Doris," replied Wanda gently to the older woman. "And you, too, William."

23

"That sounds bad," grunted Green. "As if you were preparing us for a shock."

"I hope not, but George and I have something to tell you. And to ask for your help and advice, perhaps. That's the main reason why we invited you round tonight specifically."

Green looked across at Masters who raised his glass in silent salute. Green responded and then said to Wanda, "Right then, poppet, let's have it."

"As I'm going to have another baby . . ."

"Wanda, how lovely," cried Doris. "Oh, I am glad."

"What?" screamed Green at the same time.

"Another baby, William."

"I got that bit. But where does the 'as' come in? Does it mean you're actively taking steps to achieve it, if you'll pardon my way of putting it, or does it mean it is actually on its way?"

"On its way," said Masters. "But only recently suspected, and confirmed just yesterday, so we couldn't let you know much before now. We didn't hold out on you and Doris, Bill."

Green stared at Wanda for a moment. "I knew," he said airily. "Have known for the best part of a fortnight, in fact."

"You liar," snorted his wife. "How could you possibly have known? There's no sign. Wanda is still as slim as a . . ."

"Wand?" asked her husband, knowingly.

"If you like," she snapped. "So how could you know?"

"Read it in her eyes," said Green. "You can always tell by the eyes. Women go all sort of gooey and filmy round the orbs."

"Filthy beast! You're just making it up to pretend you're not surprised and delighted. Your trouble is you never like to think anybody knows something you don't."

Green shrugged and turned to Wanda. "If I said what I really think, love, I'd break down and cry. As it is, I'm having to try hard not to drop tears in my gin."

"Thank you, William. George and I know exactly how you feel about our news and we're very happy in that knowledge."

"Fair do's, fair do's," grunted Green. "Now, about the advice you said you wanted. Though I'm no gynaecologist or obstetrician or whatever, I do know that the period of gestation is..."

"Bill, will you please shut up," wailed his wife. "We all know you're excited and have to talk nonstop to hide your feelings, but just be quiet now. I want to talk to Wanda."

"And disposable nappies to you, too," snorted Green.

There followed some minutes of women's talk from which the two men were firmly excluded. "So you see our problem," said Wanda at last, "this house will just not be big enough."

"Ah!" grunted Green moodily.

"That is so, Bill," said Masters. "Michael is four now. By the time this next one gets here and grows past the infant stage, Michael will be getting to be quite a big lad. We should want him in a room of his own, not trackled by a much younger child."

"Quite right, too, but you've got the little third bedroom."

"It's only a boxroom really," said Wanda. "Hardly big enough to put a single bed in, and even now if we have anybody to stay, we have to move Michael out of his own room."

Green shrugged. "I know, love. It's just that I don't like the idea of you moving away from here to heaven knows where. I've become quite attached to this place."

"So have we," replied Wanda gravely, "because we've lived all our married life here and been very happy. But the time to move is not yet. It's just that George and I decided we ought to start thinking about it because the delays in buying and selling property are horrendous these days."

"It's a disease," grunted Green. "House agent's tardiness. Symptoms: postponement, putting off, hindrance and the desire for deposits. Signs: loitering with intent to defer and the erection of unsightly notice boards. There should be a TV campaign warning people against them. Don't die from ignorance of subject to contract. Never have anything to do with them without first going to a chemist for a packet of..."

"Bill!" screamed his scandalised wife.

"...itching powder," went on Green, innocently. "You sprinkle it all over them to ginger them up a bit. It's the only way to get any action."

Masters laughed, Doris sank back with a resigned sigh and Wanda smiled. "We think we might have a scheme that would circumvent house agents."

"In that case," said Green airily, "it's worth selling up just to dot them in the eye. By the way, have you had the cupboard under the stairs separately valued? You know, the one that will just take the Hoover and the small ready-for-use stock of booze? I mean, if a broom cupboard will fetch thirty-six thousand, you've literally got a gold mine there, and as for that niche between the dining room and the kitchen—the one that just accepts the reading lamp with the landscape shade— we-e-ell, I reckon you'd at least get an out-of-town cabinet minister to snap that up as his in-town pad."

"Oh, be quiet," said his wife.

"I'm offering the advice I was asked for."

Doris ignored him and turned to Wanda. "Now you've at last got a moment's peace, can you tell us what's going on?"

"William is right, basically," replied Wanda. "We have had this house valued. Just a day or two ago. And what we should get for it would buy us a much bigger property outside London, and leave some over."

"To invest?"

"Perhaps. But as nothing we've got in the way of carpets and curtains would fit a bigger house..."

"Furniture, too," murmured Masters. "Where a couple of easy chairs overcrowd this room... but you know the score. We'd want a bit more of everything."

"All of which will be expensive," agreed Doris. "But you wouldn't have much mortgage to repay, would you?"

"None," said Masters. "When we bought this place we sold up my flat and Wanda's cottage in Little Munny. What we got for both more than bought the house though it was expensive even them. But we preferred to own it outright and I'm very pleased we paid cash down because now, as Bill has pointed out, it is built of gold bricks and they are all ours."

"Meaning, I suppose," said Green, "that with all that cash in your little hot hand you can toddle along and buy the house of your choice without benefit of house agents."

"More or less. Wanda has a friend..."

"Ah! So you know somebody who will take this off you at the drop of a hat, also without any agents poking their noses in. No advertising, no nothing."

"Something like that, but nothing's fixed."

"Then why all the pamphlets and papers?"

"We were trying to get an idea of prices," said Wanda. "They differ so much, even within reach of London. And we have to buy a property as well as sell one, you know."

"Of course, sweetie. I'm getting things mixed up. Pity you haven't got another friend who wants to get rid of a house you'd like."

"Well, as a matter of fact..."

"You have got your eye on something. So the area must be fixed, mustn't it?"

"Oh, yes, but we want to make sure that my friend who might sell to us is asking a realistic price."

"Realistic? You mean he or she is wanting to over-charge you?"

"No, no. Undercharge."

Green sat up. "Grab it with both hands, love. Opportunity knocks but once at a girl's door..."

"It's a question of do as you would be done by, William. Or rather, of taking into account some other factors."

"As yet unmentioned?"

Wanda nodded and said quietly, "Although I must say I was very pleased to hear you advise me to grab the offer with both hands."

Green had no reply to this and there was a short, strained silence, so he said: "Well, go on, poppet. I can't give you the benefit of my advice if I don't know all the facts or factors."

"It's a bit delicate..." began Wanda.

"No it isn't," said Green. "Not when we know what you're going to say."

"You can read the future now, can you?" demanded his wife.

"The past, actually, love. On those occasions in the past when you've been gushing about this house..."

"Gushing?"

"You know what I mean. You think it's the berries, and you've said so in no uncertain terms on three hundred and fifteen occasions. I've counted them."

"Well, I do think it's a lovely house. So do you. Who was it who first started calling it Wanda's Palace?"

"I know, love. We've both broken the commandments and coveted it. We've even gone so far as to say that if the chance ever came our way we'd snap it up." He looked across at Wanda. "Am I getting warm, poppet?"

Wanda nodded.

Green turned to his wife. "In short, love, you're being given first refusal."

"But Wanda has already said she's got a friend who will take it straight off their hands."

"That's what we hope," said Wanda. "But as we've already said, nothing is fixed."

"We could never afford it," wailed Doris. "You heard George say it is built of gold bricks."

Green shrugged and said to Wanda: "There's your answer, sweetie."

"Not quite," suggested Masters. "Perhaps there could be some arrangement, were you really keen to take the house."

28

Green stared at him. "Like underchargement, you mean? To level out what Wanda was saying a minute ago? No thanks. We're not in need of..."

"You were the friend, or friends, we were talking about, William," said Wanda, going over to him and putting her hand on his shoulder. She smiled at his expression. "So don't get on your high horse. There's no question of charity or anything like that. Simply an accommodation between friends. And you did say something a minute ago about grabbing with both hands."

Green looked up at her and put his hand over hers. "Nice one, sweetie. Okay, spell it out."

"George will do that."

"It's this way," said Masters. "If you and Doris would like this house. Really like to live in it, I mean."

"Which we would," said Doris.

"We'll think it over," said Green.

"And so you should. It will need a lot of thought and the whole idea has been sprung on you unannounced. But the point is that Wanda and I have knocked our heads together over this and we think that there are ways and means should you wish to take them. To begin with, you own a house in London."

"A three-bedroomed semi."

"A good solid house which you have finished paying for long since. It's in good nick and so, like this one, it must now be worth a fortune."

"Relatively speaking. Not as much as this."

"Maybe not. Until you've had it valued, you'll not know the size of the discrepancy."

"Big," grunted Green. "Bound to be. Situation's everything."

"Perhaps not," asserted Masters. "For one thing, you have a garage and we haven't. And I think the valuer who came round here put his finger on things when he pointed out that insured value and selling price are by no means the same thing in a house as old as this."

"How do you mean, George?" asked Doris.

"Insured value is for the rebuilding of the property as

it stands. But what you have to realise is that there are a great many features in this house that would be expensive to replace. For instance, our skirting boards are a foot deep and sculptured. The covings are very intricate and would need to be remoulded by a specialist. And so on. Such things shove up the insurance value, but they don't affect the value of the property as a living unit. Your house, bigger and much more modern, would be much less expensive to rebuild."

"Because our skirting boards are made of half-inch deal, three inches wide," grunted Green.

"Just so. But they don't detract from the value of your house as somewhere to live. So, even if your full rebuilding insurance is not as big as ours, the selling price may not be much different. And you have to remember that you've got a slice of ground that's worth thousands, where we have nothing in front and only a piece big enough to put up a playpen at the back."

"Go on," grunted Green.

"That's it."

"What is?" wailed Doris.

"Come through for supper," said Wanda, "and we'll discuss it at table." She got to her feet. "William, knowing how much you like prawns I've put some in a cold sauce to have with smoked mackerel for starters, and after that there's..." Her voice was lost to Masters as he ushered Doris in front of him through to the dining room.

"Jolly good grub," grunted Green some minutes later. "Those shrimps were a nice touch, sweetie."

"Prawns," corrected his wife.

"Whatever. I'm all of a do-dah over this house business so I can't tell t'other from which."

"I know how you must both be feeling," said Wanda, "because I know my own feelings about it. But we must answer the question Doris asked."

"Which was, if memory serves me," said Green, "brief to the point of nonobjectivity. She asked, 'What is?'"

"I only wanted to clear things up a bit," said Doris.

30

"None of us can go firm," said Wanda. "First, George and I have to decide whether what we have been offered will be right for us. And that means all the usual things like situation, style, size and condition as well as price. Only if all those suit us shall we want to sell this house for certain. As William guessed, should that happen, we should want you to have first refusal. And that is all we do want."

"At the moment, you mean?"

"We have made the offer simply because of what you have both always said about this house. And, believe me, we were a bit embarrassed, even so. We do not want to force your hand in any way, and George and I wouldn't hold you to your answer if you were to say yes straightaway. We should want you to take a good long time to think about it. But should you feel like flirting with the idea, then you would need to have your house valued for selling to see how it compares with our asking price. Then, if as George and I suspect, the two are about the same, we could reach agreement."

"I'm sure that wouldn't be fair," expostulated Doris. "There may be thousands of pounds of difference in the prices."

"Which could be either way," said Masters, rising to fetch the bottle of Madiran which was to accompany the main course.

"Rubbish," said Green. "And you know it."

"Let's not argue too much, William," said Wanda, "because all this, if not hypothetical, is completely unfixed-up at the moment." She held out her hand for his plate. "Would you like cauliflower to go with that beef?"

"And a couple more roasties, please. Doris served me short."

Wanda went on talking as she filled his plate. "And that brings us back to the do-as-you-would-be-done-by bit. If, as we suspect, we are being offered a great bargain by one set of our friends, why shouldn't we do another set a like service?" She handed back his plate and smiled at him. "And to tell you an even more im-

31

portant reason for our suggestion," she said conspiratorially, "we wouldn't like the idea of this house going to somebody who wouldn't treat it properly. If it were yours, you would care for it as much as we have done."

Green grunted heavily. "Yes, well," he humphed. "As you say, we'll have to think things over and get a sale price for our property."

"Which we'll arrange tomorrow," said Doris briskly. She turned to her husband. "If it is even remotely possible that I can have this house I am going, to use your own words, to grab it with both hands. And I know that saying of yours about opportunity knocking only once. Opportunity knocks only once at a man's door in a nightgown is how you usually put it. Now you can alter it, because this time it's knocked at my door gift-wrapped in boxer shorts and I'm all set to invite it in."

Green rubbed his nose reflectively with a pudgy forefinger. "Just because George here wants to offload a heap of useless bricks and mortar without paying a house-agent to do it, there's no reason why we should rush out and sell our nice 'tween-the-wars semi to help him do it."

"Oh, shut up," said his wife scornfully before turning to Wanda. "You can see he's as excited as a schoolboy at the idea because he's started to make schoolboy jokes." She put her hand out to her hostess. "When he gets a bit older we'll be able to have Michael to stay with us, now and again, won't we?"

"I certainly hope so," said Masters.

"You see, he'll know the house, won't he?"

Wanda smiled. "I suspect it will be hard to keep him away from you and his Mr. William."

"Hah," said Green, mightily pleased by this. "Now tell us where you are thinking of going."

"Not far from Tunbridge Wells, Bill. Less than an hour on the train into the centre of town, and the reverse, of course, for you and Doris. Frequent visits from you both will still be the order of the day, I hope."

"Not 'arf. And vice versa."

"Tell us about your house," said Doris eagerly. "What's it like?"

"It stands alone, but it's not isolated," said Wanda. "It's called Housmans, and . . ."

"I know," interrupted Green. "It's an oast-house, isn't it?"

"Yes, it is as a matter of fact. How did you guess?"

"The name. Housmans."

"How could that tell you what it is, Bill?" asked Masters.

"Hops," grunted Green. "Oast-houses."

"Very lucid and explanatory."

"Why hops, William?"

Green pushed his plate away and sat back. Then he quoted: "'Say, for what were hop-yards meant, Or why was Burton built on Trent?'"

"Go on," urged Wanda.

"Housman, *A Shropshire Lad*," replied Green.

Wanda sat back and smiled. "I see," she said slowly. "How very nice, and how very clever of you, William, to discover the connection for us. I had been wondering about it."

2

The guests at Hugh Carlyle's birthday party on the Saturday night were a mixed bag.

There were close friends from a distance. Mere acquaintances from nearby. Business colleagues and business clients. A leavening of young people, and finally a sprinkling of all manner of stage folk. It seemed the only fish that had been invited to swim into the net but had declined, because of the DCS's night duty stint at the Yard, were Wanda and George Masters.

As Mrs. Hookham had foretold, the weather was beautiful, so the Carlyles' plan to hold the party round the pool was put into effect. The already immaculate lawn had been retrimmed and the fairy-lights strung round the fences and hedges which protected the pool on all three sides away from the house. Hugh's room had been tidied and cleared of papers so that the desk could be used as the drinks table, while food was to be laid out on tables already in position at each end of the pool.

Carlyle's daughter, Rosemary, had travelled down from her vacation cottage near Cambridge and had brought with her a male postgraduate student—Tom Chesterton—to help, as Hugh put it, in providing a circulating nub for the younger guests.

By half past seven, most had arrived. The sun, though westering, still shone gloriously and it was more than warm enough for the women to wear sleeveless summer dresses without recourse to the cardigans most had brought with them as an insurance against the possible chill of late evening.

Somewhere in the background gentle music played softly, and the guests were gathering in groups to gossip.

"They'll stand around like this for a bit," said Hugh to his wife. "Just until the natural reserve is overcome and then even the most committed anchorite will start circulating."

"Probably coming outside was a mistake," replied Margot.

"Why on earth should it be?"

"There's too much space out here, and the pool separates side from side and end from end. If this number was all in one room they'd be rubbing shoulders and be obliged to make contact with each other."

"Nonsense, Mags. As soon as the booze gets to work and the young get warmed up there'll be plenty of movement. Look over there, for instance. There's James doing his stuff and involving Knight, while their wives are somewhere else, presumably."

James was James Murray, a near neighbour. Knight was Arthur Knight, a relatively new business acquaintance of Carlyle's. This was the first occasion on which the two men had ever met, but some chemistry in the make-up of both had drawn them together in such a way that they felt free to discuss their host.

"I'd never met him until about three months ago," said Knight. "I'd heard of him, of course. Very few in the engineering world have not heard of him. That's why I approached him when the need arose. We needed a rather tricky prototype to be built, incorporating the building with some testing for final design modifications which we felt sure would be necessary. He took it on, and now I'm pretty closely involved with him, at any rate for the time being. He's a hell of a businessman, wouldn't you say?"

"I know nothing about his business life," confessed Murray, "other than the fact that he must be fairly successful. He's obviously well-britched and has been for as long as I've known him."

"How long's that?"

"About twenty years, I suppose. Anyway, since they came here when he and Margot were first married."

"He's cagey about business, is he? I only ask because I like to know the people I deal with. We like to think our new designs are in good hands."

"Hugh doesn't say much about his work. No reason why he should, really. We're all very friendly round here and most of our neighbours have come along tonight, for instance. But we're all in different fields, so there's no common business interest to discuss. I suppose, really and truly, the only thing that all his neighbours discuss in common, concerning Hugh, that is, is his disablement and the marvellous way he has adapted his life-style from that of a very live wire to that of a semi-invalid. He's shown great strength of character over that."

Knight nodded his understanding.

"Mark you," went on Murray, "though he's reticent about his business affairs, Hugh will jaw the hind leg off a donkey talking about his stage interests. But that's his hobby. My missus and I play bridge. We talk about that incessantly if we can get anybody to listen, but I never mention commodity prices outside the office."

"Very wise, old boy," said Knight. "I'm that way inclined myself. I'm very conscious of the risk of industrial espionage though I've never actually suffered myself."

"In our case, that is in the City as a whole, it is insider dealing that is the spectre at the moment. But you gave me the impression that you know people in your own field who have suffered from industrial espionage."

"Heavens, yes! Several people I know have had ideas pinched from under their noses."

"Not, I hope, by Hugh Carlyle."

"There's never been a breath of scandal in that area as far as I know, otherwise I wouldn't have asked him to collaborate with me on our present scheme."

"I'm glad to hear it. Carlyle has always had the reputation, deservedly, of being the straightest of men. And that's not just my opinion. Everybody round here who knows him has said at some time or another how ironic it is that the most straightforward, generous and good-humoured man they know should be struck down by a crippling disease."

"Adding that it is typical of life, I expect?"

"Without a doubt."

Murray held out his hand for Knight's glass. "Would you like another of those?"

Knight drained the last few drops. "Yes, please."

Murray was back quite quickly. "This industrial espionage you mentioned. It interests me. What sort of thing goes on? Breaking into offices to pinch specifications?"

"Nothing quite so crude, usually." Knight raised his glass. "Cheers."

"No breaking in to steal research results, you say?"

"Planting a spy is more likely. You train up a girl to know what to look for and get her taken on as a confidential secretary in a rival's office. It's amazing how much can be learned that way. Or, alternatively, suborn somebody already working there."

"Just like international intelligence departments, in fact."

"Just like that. And it is a specialist field. The secretaries I mentioned really are highly trained secretaries with other qualifications to equip them to walk into almost any job."

"Not all the qualifications being academic, I suppose."

"Quite right. It's amazing how much more efficient a filing system seems when operated by somebody with a face and figure that are worthy of more than a passing interest."

"I can imagine."

"Mark you, I think most small businessmen lose out through lack of capital. Nobody has to be planted or suborned."

"How's that?"

"Well, let's try to think of a hypothetical case as an

illustration. Say you invented what? A revolutionary new washing powder?"

"Something every housewife would buy?"

"Exactly that. So although you are only a small man, you can envisage making a great killing, because the sales of your product will be continual, continuous and nationwide."

"A good prospect, in fact."

"Quite. So you set out to produce it. You can manage to do this in a comparatively small way to begin with by remortgaging your house and getting a few thousands from the bank. After you've started, you begin to realise that production is easy. It is promoting and marketing the stuff that takes the millions. Your potential customers won't ask for your product in the shops if they are not told about it, so you have to have a TV campaign and journal advertising, to say nothing of having to pay designers and printers for attractive packaging and so forth. So what do you do?"

"Tell me."

"You think you can just afford a pilot scheme. The usual thing—for obvious reasons—is to confine it to one television area. Yorkshire, say. So you go ahead, and you are successful. So successful, in fact, that with your limited manufacturing resources you have difficulty in meeting demand in that area.

"Now you are in a cleft stick. Do you invest your profit in more plant to increase supplies, or do you spend it on more promotion to sell your product elsewhere in the country?"

Murray grimaced. "I'll hazard a guess. I'd try to do two things at once. First, borrow more money from the bank for installing plant. That money should be available in view of my recent success. I'd do that on the basis that it is pointless to increase demand before you can meet it. Meanwhile, I would use the profit to maintain the increase in demand."

"Logical."

"But wrong?"

"Not necessarily. However, installing plant can be a lengthy business. Machines have to be built and factory space provided for them."

"A matter of weeks, surely?"

"Perhaps, if you're lucky. But weeks are vital, and during those weeks all manner of things not only can but will happen. Your success won't have gone unnoticed, remember. This could spark off some dirty tricks, of course, and others which are called just good business."

"Dirty ones first."

"Just an example. The new machines you wish to install and which you were told were available on Monday are suddenly declared to be not available on Wednesday. Somebody rings up to tell you that you were misinformed on Monday by an understrapper who didn't know the situation."

"I get it. Somebody who doesn't want you to have this specialised plant has either brought pressure to bear on the manufacturer or has bought them for spot cash, paying over the odds for immediate possession."

"Something like that. It works if there is only one manufacturer of that sort of machine and if the dog-in-the-manger is already a big customer. But, as I said, that's only an example. Supplies of ingredients could be unexpectedly delayed or the material for your cartons be in artificially short supply. Any part of your operation could be sabotaged."

"And the good-business tricks?"

"Other washing powder manufacturers will have noted within days that their sales have slumped in the Yorkshire TV area, and they won't have been slow in discovering the reason."

"My revolutionary new product?"

"Quite."

"Apart from resorting to the tricks already mentioned to stop me in my tracks, what are they going to do? Try to buy me out?"

"No fear. You've got a successful competitor to their

range, so you would drive a hard bargain. Why pay you when, by buying a packet of your product and analysing it..."

"I'd be protected by the patent laws, surely?"

"True. But the patent law only protects you from people who want to make an exact copy of your product. A similar product, one with very minor changes from yours, would be allowed. An alternative to one ingredient, perhaps. Maybe even something as unimportant as colour, perfume, bulk excipient or what-have-you."

"And the big boys are then in business on their own account?"

"They have the millions needed for promoting nationwide, the marketing set-ups to put their products into every shop in the land and, finally, to make offers to undercut you."

"Five pee off a packet?"

"Maybe. Or, preferably, bonus offers to the shopkeepers of the twelve-for-the-price-of-ten variety to encourage them to stock it. Whatever happens, in no time at all you are out of business. You've produced a successful new product and yet you'll be lucky to get out of it still wearing your shirt."

Murray grimaced.

"A hypothetical case," reiterated Knight. "Just to illustrate what I mean. Any woman who has trouble with her nylons will tell you similar stories about chaps who have invented tights that won't ladder being driven to the wall by the big names in industry."

"I've heard them," admitted Murray. "That's another facet. Preventing a product reaching the market rather than taking one over to sell."

"And you've heard of Japan, too, I suppose. How they used to rename some spot in their country so that they could stamp 'Made in Sheffield' on their pirated products?"

"Lighters," said Murray, "were a bit of a scandal at one time, I seem to remember." He grinned. "But you have specifically absolved our host from all involvement in such chicanery?"

"Most certainly. I was merely suggesting why he—and I—don't discuss our business affairs outside our offices."

"Well, as I said to begin with, I don't really know what he does, except that I once heard that his company does specialist engineering."

"And markets it," said Knight. "He sells abroad quite a lot."

"Would it be indiscreet to ask where you come in?"

"A little, perhaps. I'd thought up something I couldn't manage. I was advised to approach Hugh."

"For what? Financial help?"

"Not quite. Expertise and facilities would be nearer the mark. When one is only expecting to produce and sell relatively few of some item it may be pointless—or even impossible—to install the plant necessary to do the job. If somebody with the necessary machines is willing to let you muck in . . ."

"At a price?"

"A fair price."

"He has to be assured of a return, presumably?"

"Or be knowledgeable enough to accept a risk."

"Ah! I see. He will then co-operate for the common good."

"Quite. It's not an unheard-of practice, but not all that general."

"Hugh risks money on stage productions. It seems to be his way of life."

"It's not all that dangerous if you know your business. I'm satisfied that Carlyle does. Then the risks for all concerned are minimised."

"I'm sure. Ah! There's my wife. Come along and meet her."

"Daddy an engineer?" Rosemary Carlyle smiled at Maurice Fowler, the middle-aged cameo actor who was reputed never to be out of work because virtually every

41

show in every medium needed a father or uncle, rogue or saint for which parts his particular versatility seemed to be ideally suited. "You could say that, I suppose, though he is not qualified as one, except perhaps by decades of experience."

"I set great store by experience, my dear."

"But you are a trained actor, Mr. Fowler. Drama school and all that, aren't you?"

"Of course. And I had a long apprenticeship in spear-carrying after that. Come to think of it...," the well-known features creased into a cherubic smile. "Come to think of it, I'm still spear-carrying. This week I appeared as a lawyer, to read a will. Nothing more was required of me. Last week I was the mayor of a small town. Before that...let me see...ah, yes! I was a patient in a hospital scene leading the panic when there was a fire in the ward. And so I go on, my dear. Thank heaven for television repeats."

"But I've seen you in the theatre when you weren't carrying a spear. I enjoyed your performance in *The Squash Court*. That was a big role and it ran for a long time."

"You've no idea how much an old actor loves to hear a pretty young girl praise his work. But you said your father isn't an engineer, although I've always understood he owns an engineering company. We actors are very nosey about our Angels, you know, and your father is a sort of member of one of the higher orders of heavenly beings."

"Daddy is a physics man. Applied physics, actually. That's halfway to being some sort of engineer, I suppose, as it includes a lot of mechanics and maths and stuff like that. And he also has a degree in business studies. He's supposed to be pretty hot on modern methods of running a concern."

"Just what we need in our business," conceded Fowler. "Very few of us know how to cope with that side of things. Ah! Isn't that Carla Sanders in the doorway?"

Rosemary turned to look towards the open French

window. "Yes, I think it is. I don't know her, but I heard she was coming."

"What's she doing here?"

"I beg your pardon?"

"She's in *Round the Barley*. It only opened on Thursday. She can't have...I mean, your father wouldn't have suggested that the understudy...not so soon."

"She shouldn't be here," agreed Rosemary, "but she injured a leg and ankle on Thursday night after the show. You must have heard about it."

"No, not a word."

"Well, she fell down a flight of iron stairs, or some such thing."

"She would," muttered Fowler. "Shallow little piece of goods." He seemed to recollect that Rosemary was still listening. "I beg your pardon, Miss Carlyle. I shouldn't have said that."

Rosemary laughed. "Please don't worry about that, Mr. Fowler. My mother and father were saying much the same thing earlier today."

"Were they? I imagine they thought she should have appeared in her play, even with a game leg. The real trouper does."

"I haven't seen the show, but I believe there are a number of important scenes which depend very much upon the girl's physical prowess and her nimbleness of foot to avoid importunate males."

"Ah! That's why she was cast, is it?"

"Apparently the gymnastics have been very carefully arranged and even more carefully rehearsed. Daddy was saying it would look stupid for an amorous young male not to be able to grab a girl so patently lame, whereas, if the various bits are done exactly as rehearsed, it looks quite natural for him to end up falling over a tea trolley or with his head cracking a bedpost."

"I see. So there's a great chance for the understudy, eh? That would not please Sanders in the least. I suppose the invitation to this party was by way of recompense for her injury, was it?"

"Something of the sort. Now, if you'll excuse me, Mr. Fowler, I must go and greet her." Rosemary grimaced. "The duties of a hostess, you know."

Fowler smiled. "Of course, my dear. That is, if you are not too late. She seems to have latched very firmly onto that young man."

"Tom! Good heavens, I must fly. I don't want her getting her hooks into him."

"If he's your boyfriend, watch him, my dear. Sanders eats nice young males like that for breakfast."

Tom Chesterton said to Rosemary: "I thought you said that the McRolfe bloke wouldn't be here?"

"Daddy said he wasn't coming."

"Until Daddy told him you'd be here, I expect. When he heard that, whatever excuse was going to keep him away suddenly disappeared and he found himself free to come."

"Now you are being stupid."

"Am I? He hangs about you like a truffle-hound snorting round the roots."

"So what?"

"What do you mean, so what?"

"First off, I can't help it if the man fancies me. After all, you say you do, so that puts the two of you on a par. Second, I rather like having men thinking I'm attractive. I'd be a pretty poor specimen if I didn't like it, and an even worse one if it didn't happen."

"I see."

"No, you don't. You want to monopolise me. Fair enough. But I'm still a free agent and I can talk to any man I want who wants to talk to me."

"Or who wants to be boss of an engineering firm."

"And what's that supposed to mean?"

"Do I have to spell it out?"

"I think you'd better."

"It's very obvious that McRolfe would like to step into your father's shoes, and the best way he can see of bringing it about is to marry his daughter."

44

Rosemary's nose was in the air. "Thank you very much for the compliment. And what do *you* want to marry me for?"

Chesterton grinned. "Your sweet self. I'd be a hopeless engineer."

"And a hopeless anything else," replied Rosemary heatedly. "So now, if you've finished, I'd like to go and speak to my parents' guests."

"McRolfe, you mean?"

"I shall make a point of speaking to him."

"In that case, my beloved, I shall return to the spot from whence you dragged me, protestingly, a few minutes ago."

"Back to Carla Sanders, you mean?"

"Who else round here has such obvious allure for the rejected male?"

Rosemary turned without a word in reply and hurried off among the guests. As she did so, a voice behind Chesterton caused him to swing round.

"Having a spot of bother, Mr. Chesterton?" The voice was Anglicised, but the faint "air" instead of "er" in the middle of Chesterton betrayed a Scots background to the keen ear.

"Nothing of any importance," growled Tom, annoyed that his tiff should have been overheard and, even worse, commented on by this thin, beaky, middle-aged man whom he had only met briefly once before when visiting the Carlyle office with Rosemary.

"I heard you mention McRolfe."

"What about it?"

"Mr. Carlyle has a high opinion of the laddie. He's one of his senior managers. An up-and-coming young man."

"I know who McRolfe is."

"Then you'll know he's a design man."

"Yes."

"And why do you think a designer should be so highly thought of in a specialist engineering firm like Carlyle's?"

"I haven't the faintest idea. I am not an engineer myself and know very little about the Carlyle business."

"But you'd not be averse"—he pronounced it *avairse*—"to learning a little more about it, perhaps?"

"You are obviously intent on telling me whether I want to hear it or not, Mr. Carpenter."

Carpenter laid his hand on Tom's arm and said quietly: " McRolfe is using his position at Carlyle's to further his own ends."

"That is quite an accusation, Mr. Carpenter."

"Maybe aye and maybe hoohaye."

"I don't know what you mean by that, but if you have definite knowledge of professional misconduct by McRolfe, shouldn't you be telling it to Mr. Carlyle rather than me?"

Carpenter stood with his head on one side for a moment. "I just thought the hint might be of use to you in seeing that the lassie doesn't end up in McRolfe's arms."

"Thank you very much. From all of which I take it you have no proof against McRolfe to present to Mr. Carlyle. In other words you're making the whole thing up."

Carpenter shrugged. "I like to help young lasses and lads..."

"Oh, cut it out. What are you really after, Mr. Carpenter? Could it be that you hope I will pass on to Mr. Carlyle what you have just told me? For some purpose of your own?"

Carpenter shrugged and stared at Tom for a moment, the scraggy neck and hooked nose giving him a buzzardlike air. Then he shook his head. "I've tried telling Carlyle."

"But he wouldn't listen, is that it?"

"Aye. He wouldn't listen."

"In other words he was loyal to a member of his staff about whom there was some unspecified accusation with no proof to back it up."

Carpenter shrugged. "Take it any way you like, laddie.

But when I first met you with Hugh Carlyle's daughter I thought you were a fine pair. I'd not like McRolfe to come between you."

"That's very nice of you. And now, Mr. Carpenter, if you would excuse me, I think I'd like to join my friends."

"Andrew."

"Rosemary."

"How are you, Andrew?" Rosemary was finding it slightly difficult to be natural with this young man. She still had Tom's words in mind and, deep down, felt there was some justification for them. At twenty-nine, McRolfe had reached a senior and responsible position in the Carlyle company. Her father, she knew, had the highest regard for his ability as a design engineer and it was this fact that had helped the man to rise so quickly. But underneath there was an ambition which had played an equal part in taking McRolfe so high so quickly. Smooth-haired, long-faced, with rimless spectacles, he looked more of the academic than the practical man of the design board and test bench. But he was practical enough, as Rosemary knew. He had made a set at her. So much she guessed. But she wasn't so sure about any underlying affection in his moves. Tom had noticed the man's manoeuvres. Had read them as the first moves to becoming a member of the Carlyle family, with the firm within his sight if not yet his grasp. The question was, had Tom read the motives correctly?

"Well enough, Rosemary, thank you. How are you?"

It was heavy going. Rosemary wished now she hadn't been quite so high-handed with Tom.

"I'm fine, thank you. It is nice to see you, especially as Daddy said you wouldn't be here."

"I had a previous engagement which I felt I couldn't break and then, to my delight, the little meeting I was to have attended was put off. So I was able to phone your mother to ask if I could be reinstated on the guest list."

"I see. Are you going to have a drink?"

"Well, now, let me see. Perhaps a hock and seltzer. A little white wine topped up with carbonated spring water if such a thing is possible."

"Perhaps it would be better if you were to help yourself, then you would get it right. And you might like to leave your jacket indoors if you are too hot. It will be quite safe in there."

"I think perhaps I will keep it on."

"Just as you like, of course, but you do seem to be weighed down by it and the evening is gloriously warm."

"Of course. Maybe I will later."

"Good. Off you go then, and I'll see if there is anybody else without a drink."

"I shall see you again, I hope?"

"I shall be about," said Rosemary. "Circulating, you know."

"Joanna," said Margot to one of her close friends, "how nice of you to come."

"Couldn't resist it, Mags. Apart from seeing you and Hugh, Robert and I just had to be here to see all these actor types. We get the same treat every year on Hugh's birthday and we regard it as an annual outing."

"Your mother is a little better, is she?"

"Much better, thank you. Sitting up and taking nourishment."

"I had expected that Robert would be looking after her tonight."

"Not on your life. As I said, he's here, like me, to look at all the stage people, though I'm positive he's more interested in the so-called decorative ones than people like dear old Maurice Fowler."

"He'll be in luck then. Carla Sanders is here."

"That'll suit Robert. He's a great leg man."

"In that case, he could be disappointed. She's got a leg injury and is wearing a trouser suit to cover the bandages."

"Something serious, I hope?"

"Actually, it is. By that I mean she's missing her new

48

show because, besides spraining the ankle, she has gashed the lower part of the leg."

"Opened it up?"

"Quite a bit, and for somebody whose legs—among other things—are her fortune, it could be nasty. Scars on one of one's best features are not exactly desirable in her particular meat market."

Joanna laughed. "We're being catty, Mags."

"Are we? Look at her now. Four males round her."

"Anybody would think she was in season."

"By all accounts she always is."

"No comment. Ah! Here's Hugh."

"Joanna, my pet!" Carlyle reached upwards from his wheelchair to hold her as she kissed him. "Lovely to see you. I've had a word with Robert and told him where the special bottle of malt is hidden."

"How are you, Hugh?"

"Thriving, old love. Thriving. Margot is cross with me. Thinks I'm doing too much, but I'm fine."

"You look a bit tired."

"Old age, my dear. Wrinkles round the eyes and all that. I'll have to have a bit of cosmetic surgery to restore me to my former beauty and then grow a beard to hide the scars."

"You can joke, Hugh, but just you take it easy."

"I've promised to." He took his wife's hand. "Mags and I are going on a cruise so that I can laze in the sun and have salt-water baths. Isn't that so, my poppet?"

Margot smiled. "If we ever get round to it."

"Get round to it, my sweet? I've already made a tentative booking. Kept our options open, of course, so that you could choose exactly which particular trip you'd like to take. Three or four to choose from. Atlantic Islands, Med, West Indies and so on. In September, I thought."

"I didn't know you'd got that far, darling. You didn't tell me."

"I was proposing to. Tomorrow, after all this is over. Just the subject for a comfy Sunday morning chat. We'll make the decision then."

Margot shrugged prettily. "Men!" she said in mock despair to Joanna. "Now, I'd better see what's happening about food. These monsters will soon start growling for something more than caviare canapes."

As she left them, Robert Culp came up. "Can I freshen your glass, Hugh? You've been carrying that stranded slice of lemon about ever since I got here."

"I'll stall for a bit, thanks, Robert. I'm fairly careful with the old alc these days. And with liquid volume in general, too. It's not so easy for me to visit the loo as it is for the likes of you."

"Talking of loos," said Robert, "did I tell you that verse I saw written up in one the other day? When I was over on the Suffolk coast?"

"Not graffiti," groaned Joanna.

"No. Properly scribed above a lifeboat-shaped collecting box. How did it go now? Ah, yes! 'Spend a penny, then relax. Forget about the Income Tax. But spare a thought and pennies, please, For those in peril on the seas.' I liked it, that's why I stayed put until I'd got it off by heart."

"Neat," said Carlyle. "I hope you showed your appreciation of the artistry of the work."

"Not really, but I put a couple of pound coins in for the RNLI."

"Good. There's no better cause. Ah! Food is beginning to appear. That'll keep the troops quiet for a bit."

"Darling! How lovely to see you. And what a lovely party!"

Mary Hamilton stooped to peck Hugh Carlyle's cheek. They'd known each other for many years. The actress was effusive and madly overdressed with a fox fur round her shoulders on an evening such as this. But, thought Hugh, she was incredibly well-preserved if one didn't look too closely. She was Margot's age: had been around when he and Margot had first met. She was still playing youngish parts and getting away with it. She knew her craft, but even she should have realised that by now she should have been moving up the age scale and have altered her entry in *Spotlight* accordingly.

"Glad to see you here, Mary."

"But I'm not in your new play, Hugh. You left me out."

"I didn't cast it."

"Don't tell me you had no say. He who pays the piper calls the tune."

"A popular misconception, particularly in the world of theatre."

"I know for a fact, Hugh, that you are always consulted when you back a show."

"A courtesy only, my dear. But in any case, there was really no part for you in *Round The Barley*—except the glamorous granny, and you wouldn't have accepted that, would you now?"

"Grandmother?"

"To a grown-up, nubile daughter."

"Oh! Sanders!"

"Quite. Two generations up from her. It would have been a big leap for you to cross that particular age gap."

"I see what you mean, darling. But don't forget me next time."

"Even if it's a granny?"

"Beast, darling."

"Society hostess?"

"That's more my style now, I suppose. I've just turned down a farmer's wife. They wanted me to wear gumboots and milk a cow. Me!"

"You should have taken it, Mary. It would have shown people what you are made of."

"I shall ignore that remark, Hugh, and go to say hello to Margot."

"Do that. She's about."

As Mary Hamilton left him, the coloured lights came on. Somebody was eager, he thought. The sun was still shining even though it was low in the sky. He supposed the caterers thought the lights would enhance their food or make a more romantic ambience in which to eat it.

"Pretty, aren't they?" said Knight, stopping beside the wheelchair. "Can I get you some food, Hugh?"

"No, thank you, old boy. Help yourself, though."

"You're sure?"

"Positive."

"Another drink then?"

"Not just now, Arthur. I don't get rid of booze as easily as you others. And I must find James Murray. I've not had a word with him yet."

Knight raised his hand in farewell and made for one of the tables.

As Carlyle manoeuvred his chair to round the end of the pool Margot appeared at his side. "What have you been saying to Mary Hamilton, darling? She's seething."

"Nothing I've said to her could cause that."

"She says you told her it was time she stopped playing glamour parts and . . ."

"And what, Mags?"

"Well, I think she said something about milking cows."

"Rubbish, old girl. I advised her to take a part that had been offered to her. A farmer's wife. The script calls for a cow to be milked. As like as not they'd have shot the scene with a stand-in."

"She does go on," agreed Margot. "She's one of those who get the profession a bad name. Always talking about herself and her work."

"Go and calm her down," suggested Hugh. "I'm going to look for James."

"You'll find him at the deep end," replied his wife. "Slim Piper is entertaining a few of them with a bit of sleight of hand."

"Really? I'll join them. He's good, you know. Slim. He's always fascinated me. I'm a sucker for the three-card trick. It's a pity he went legit."

"There are no halls for him to work now. He's better off playing his bit parts."

"I suppose so."

Carlyle steered his chair in a wide loop across the close-cropped turf behind the food tables. He passed almost under the foliage of the taller flowering shrubs and small trees which carried the cable for the coloured lights and which sheltered the pool on the side away from the house. Then he jinked back towards the water at the deep end where Slim Piper was sitting on the steps of the diving board entertaining a small group of guests. Among them were James Murray and Maisie Firth, his physiotherapist.

"You're not tiring yourself, are you, Mr. Carlyle?" asked Maisie as he came up.

"No, my dear. And let me say you are looking lovely."

"In the fading light, you mean?" Maisie Firth was an athletic young woman, tall and strongly built, with the features of a handsome youth. Carlyle had said she would make an admirable principal boy in pantomime, had she had any acting training. He had no doubts about her superb legs and figure. He'd seen quite a lot of them when, in the early days, she had gone into the pool with him to teach him his exercises.

"The sun is going," agreed Carlyle, "but we're not in complete darkness yet, my dear, and I repeat, you look good enough to eat."

"Thank you, kind sir."

"Now, what's old Slim up to?"

"Find the thimble. He must have come prepared to give a show. He's used a pack of cards, three little coloured balls, coins and various other bits and pieces. He was carrying them all in his pockets, except for the cups which he got from a table."

They watched in silence as Slim entertained the young folk closest to him, drawing them into the act, bamboozling them, getting them guessing—always wrongly—and never moving his hands more than a foot or two away from their faces, as if to challenge them to see how he did this intimate legerdemain.

"Is he a friend of yours, Hugh?" asked Murray, and then added hurriedly, "That's a damn silly question when he's here at your party."

"Not a friend exactly, James. I've known him for a few years and admired his skill for many more."

"He baffled everybody very nicely with his three thimble trick. Ah! The show appears to be over."

"That's it, folks," announced Piper. "If I go on any longer you'll be saying it was the darkness that deceived the eye, not the hands."

The little crowd clapped as Piper stood up. He gave them the bow of the old pro and then came to join Carlyle and Murray.

"Evening, Mr. Carlyle. I've been paying for my party, you see."

"Come off it, Slim. You can't help yourself. You do that sort of thing at the drop of a hat—even for an audience of one. I'm not sure I haven't seen you performing for an attentive old Labrador dog, and I've certainly seen you doing your act backstage for a couple of cleaners."

"Got to keep my hand in. You never know when it could be useful. Sooner, rather than later, I might have to take up entertaining at kids' parties."

"Things aren't as bad as that, surely?"

"I'm resting, Mr. Carlyle."

"At your age, Slim, you need the occasional rest."

"All I've got on the books at the moment is a fortnight's stand-in at a summer show, starting a week next Monday. I'm relieving a bloke who's been called into hospital then for some minor operation and doesn't want to lose his place in the queue, waiting-lists being what they are."

"I'm sorry to hear it, Slim. As soon as you get away to the seaside, offers will start pouring in. You'll see."

"All for the same time. I know. Life's like that. Start rehearsing one thing and they want you for a commercial you can't accept."

"Slim, this is James Murray, a neighbour of mine. He admired your little show."

"Anything to do with anything that would interest me?" asked Slim, shaking hands.

"Hardly," said Murray with a laugh. "I'm in the City. Though come to think of it, there are a few I meet there who could give you a run for your money."

"The trouble is," replied Slim, "I haven't got any money to be given a run for. Oh, well, never mind."

"Go and get yourself another drink, Slim. You've earned it."

"I haven't eaten yet. Better get a bit of sponge cake inside me to soak up what I have had already before taking more on board. Nice to have met you, Mr. Murray."

Piper moved away.

"Your party is hotting up, Hugh," said Murray. "The young are getting jolly."

"Jolly? I'd call it boisterous. But it isn't out of hand yet. Nor will it be. The kids of today have a bad reputation but I've always found them pretty sensible and reliable."

"That's my experience, too. But that glamour girl, Carla Sanders, seems to be the centre of some frivolity. I see Rosemary's boyfriend is in constant attendance on her, with a few more like him."

"Lads of his age will always be attracted, for a short time at least, to somebody like her who's always willing to bare her ample bosom in TV plays. I'd think there was something wrong with them if they weren't interested. But I imagine Rosemary will be spitting rust at the sight of Tom fluttering round the candle flame. And not only my lass. All those young men arrived with female partners. There'll be a bit of sour talk later."

Murray laughed. "T'was ever thus."

"Nevertheless, James, if you'll excuse me, I think I'll make my way round there and gently break it up before too many hearts are broken."

"Politic," agreed Murray. "See you later."

This time Carlyle's progress was not so easy. There was less room at the deep end of the pool and the throng of guests seemed to be thicker in that area as though, now that night was falling, they were seeking the confines of the pool's surround. A tall wooden fence covered with trained plants of various kinds provided the wind break here, and although there was no wind, but merely the warmth of a summer night, the two long garden tables with cushioned chairs, umbrellas and overhead lights seemed to draw the older guests into an amicable huddle.

The side of the pool nearer the house was bathed in the overspill of light from the French window. This luminance highlighted the ramp, deserted as though left for his exclusive use. On each side of the concrete runway, however, where he and Margot had breakfasted and its twin area on the other side of the slope, was an animated group of the not-so-old. That nearer to him was the knot of young men grouped round Carla Sanders, talking to her, laughing, joking and indulging in mild horseplay. As he approached them he saw his daughter intercept Tom Chesterton who was going towards this group, carrying a plate of food. Both seemed unaware of his presence.

"Who is that for? As if I didn't know," said Rosemary.

"It's for Carla. She's got a bad leg, you know, and can't get round to the tables."

"So you offered to get it for her."

"You know me. The perfect little gent."

"The perfect example of a blithering ass, you mean. Look at you! All of you. All gawping at her and acting the giddy goat whenever she moves a false eyelash."

"It's not the movement of her eyelashes that's so magnetic."

"I know, it's her false . . ."

"Nothing false about them, Roz. Take my word for it. She's taken her jacket off and she isn't wearing a bra."

"You make me sick, Tom Chesterton. And as for her, I'd like to push her into the pool."

"Do that, Roz, and it would be quite a sight. If that blouse got wet we'd really get an eyeful."

Slightly amused, Carlyle watched his daughter swing round and march away from Chesterton. He decided to follow her to say a few soothing words before joining the group round Carla Sanders.

It was a difficult manoeuvre. He had to pass between the end of the ramp and the edge of the pool, the way that was only just wide enough to take the chair and which the builders had insisted on leaving free for him.

By the time he got through to the other side, Rosemary had disappeared. He spoke to one or two people as he made his way slowly, trying to spot her among the groups. But she had gone. He was just acknowledging a greeting from a business colleague and his wife when all the coloured lights went out.

"Fuse blown," said somebody.

"Main fuse?"

"Depends where the coloured lights are plugged in. No, the room's still lit, I can see there's light elsewhere in the house."

Fortunately there was still a remnant of twilight to delineate the ramp and the pool, but the spaces at the ends of the pool seemed to be in total darkness. Carlyle, powerless to rush to repair the damage, did however notice that young Chesterton and another youth were being ushered indoors by Margot. It was obvious that she had sought their help to examine the fuse box. There should be no difficulty. All the ring mains were named, as indeed were the light circuits.

After a couple of minutes or so, the lights came on again. Margot had obviously pointed out to the young men the spare fuses Hugh always kept ready wired for such emergencies. The restoration of the light seemed to be a signal for the chatter to increase again after the comparative silence induced by its absence.

A youngish couple, near neighbours, pushed their way through to Carlyle.

"We've come to say goodnight, Hugh," said the girl

prettily. "And to thank you for a lovely party, of course. We have really enjoyed ourselves, haven't we, Tim?"

"Too true," said her husband. "Lapped up every minute of it."

"Then why go so soon? You're the first to desert us, you know."

"Baby sitter," said the girl. "We promised not to be too late. She's mid-European and a bit nervous of being out after curfew."

"In that case..." Carlyle put up his arms and drew the girl's face down for a kiss. "Thank you for coming. And don't forget I told you to come for a dip in the pool whenever you like, Sara. Bring the baby. You can dangle him in, too. I understand that the very young like it."

"We shall love to do that, thank you," said Sara Bracken.

"Promise?"

"I'll make sure we do come, very soon."

"That's the ticket."

Carlyle was soon involved with others of his guests. The more elderly, mellowed by food, drink, sweet music, soft lights and the warm evening air, were chatting quietly to him and among themselves. The stage people had foregathered elsewhere for a bit of nostalgia and the younger guests were still split into two groups, one on each side of the ramp, with Carla Sanders still holding court on one side. Carlyle noticed that she was, as he put it to James Murray, getting nicely stewed, an impression borne out by her increasingly extravagant gestures and frequent intimate droopings onto nearby male shoulders.

One or two other guests came up to take their leave, but for the most part people seemed to want to linger. Mrs. H. and a couple of helpers were moving around unobtrusively collecting dirty crockery and carrying it past the shallow end of the pool, down the side of the house to the kitchen door. Mrs. H., herself, was collecting empty glasses and dirty plates from near the ramp where they had been scattered by the youngsters who had made no attempt to return them to the tables as had most of the older people. She had a trayful of glass, crockery and debris as she made to pass the end of the ramp. As she drew close to the water's edge there was, for some reason, a sudden upheaval among those surrounding Carla Sanders. The tray, with its pile of plates, glasses, cutlery and food debris was knocked from Mrs. Hookham's hands by a sudden push in the back made by a body falling backwards into her. The whole load shot into the pool, closely followed by a human body.

Mrs. H. stood where she was, mouth open and hands still held as if carrying the tray. Her scream and the other noise had silenced the chatter round the pool and all eyes were focussed on the water as Carla Sanders surfaced, spluttering and pushing back the once carefully coiffured locks before making a pathetic stroke or two to reach the side of the pool. Two or three young men were kneeling there, hands outstretched, to haul her onto dry land.

Tom Chesterton had stood back once he was assured his assistance was not needed for the rescue. As Carla Sanders stood up on the edge of the pool, he heard a voice in his ear: "You get your wish. How does she grab you now, in spite of her big boobs? Mascara streaky, hair lank, half a meringue on one shoulder and a strip of lettuce on the other? *Très chic*, wouldn't you say?"

Tom had the grace to whisper back: "But what a spot for a glacé cherry! The one about to slide down into the Valley of the Kings, I mean."

"It's not glacé, it's maraschino," replied Rosemary, and was about to add some further apposite remark when Margot appeared to lead Carla Sanders away. As she did so, she said to her daughter: "Bring her jacket and come and get her some dry clothes."

"None of mine will go anywhere near her," whispered Rosemary to Chesterton.

"Oh, I dunno."

"Cheeky beast."

"I was referring to that big, sloppy, roll-neck sweater of yours. The one that drapes you like an oversize bell-tent."

"Good idea. That'll iron out even her bumps."

She sped after her mother and the bedraggled Carla. Maisie Firth came up to Hugh's chair. "Don't you dare go into that pool until it has been cleaned out, Mr. Carlyle. There could be broken glass in the bottom, so no early morning dip for you tomorrow."

"Not to worry, Maisie. I'll ask Mrs. H. to get her old man onto it first thing in the morning. He won't like doing an extra fill on a Sunday, particularly with a scrub out as well, but she'll see he does it, never fear."

"It wasn't her fault that trayful went into the water. I saw what happened. It was knocked out of her hand."

"I know that, Maisie, I saw it, too. So I shan't suggest that her husband does the job just to clear up any mess Mrs. H. may have made. But what I didn't really see was how the fracas actually boiled up to its finale."

"It was getting a bit boisterous long before that."

"Maybe, maybe, but I got an impression."

"What sort of an impression?"

"That the final explosion, if I can call it such, was not an accident. It wasn't natural. It seemed contrived, if you get my meaning."

"Stage-managed?"

"That's how it appeared to me."

"But just an impression, you say?"

"I was very near. I was actually going to join that group to try to calm things down a bit, so I had my eye on them."

"So you saw who started the scrimmage."

"That's my point, Maisie. I was aware somebody gave the initial nudge, but I'm damned if I know who it was. That's why I say it was a deliberate move, stage-managed to use your own word."

"But who would want to push Carla Sanders into the water? Not one of those boys, surely."

"Oh, I don't know," said James Murray, who had been

standing listening to the conversation. "Getting that blouse wet produced quite a show—a thought that could have occurred to more than one of those young men."

Maisie shook her head. "No. They knew that by ducking her they would be bringing to an abrupt end the interlude they were all enjoying so much. If you ask me, I'd say it was the jealous girlfriend of one of those young men who would want to drown Carla Sanders."

"That's a thought," said Murray. "Had that idea occurred to you, Hugh?"

"I must confess it hadn't," replied Carlyle. "And I don't think I saw a girl, other than Sanders, in that particular group."

3

Carla Sanders died in the early hours of the following Tuesday morning, little more than forty-eight hours after her unintended dip in Carlyle's swimming pool.

She died in her own bed, the one she shared with her live-in lover, Howard Collier. The fact that she died in her own home was an indication of the surprise felt by her doctor. Had he had the slightest inkling that this notable nonentity among his patients was in any danger of losing her life, he would have had her taken to— probably—a private hospital for treatment.

Not only was he surprised, he was unhappy. No medical man who is called to an otherwise healthy patient, suffering from the relatively minor troubles of a sprained ankle and less-than-serious leg abrasions, expects his patient to die some four days after the causative accident. Hence the surprise. The unhappiness and worry stemmed from the fact that not only had he been unable to make a firm diagnosis of any disease liable to carry her off during her last few days of life, he was equally unable to do so after being called in to find her dead. This meant he was unable to make an unambiguous statement as to the cause of death, as the law requires before a death certificate can be issued.

Dr. Denyer was in no doubt as to the course he should pursue. The death had to be notified to the Coroner. He, himself, was not legally bound to pass the information direct. He could have left it to the Registrar to do this duty, but most doctors, in cases where death is due to unknown causes, prefer to do their Common Law duty—as being a person "about a body"—and to notify the Coroner of the circumstances which they know are likely to require the holding of an inquest.

The Coroner, like many of those in the London area where Carla Sanders lived, was doubly qualified in medicine and law. He listened to what Denyer had to say, asked a few pertinent questions and decided, there and then, to enquire into the cause and circumstances of the death. He, accordingly, accompanied Denyer to the scene of the death, viewed the body in the bed, and then had his officer take a statement from Denyer while he, himself, rang the Professor of Pathology whom he and Scotland Yard often called upon in cases of suspicious death, and asked the eminent man to be so kind as to perform a full postmortem examination.

The body was, as a result, delivered to the Professor, who reported to the Coroner two days later that though the cause of death could well be natural, it was of so uncommon a nature as to be rated as highly obscure and, therefore, merited investigation. He added that in his opinion the circumstances in which Carla Sanders had contracted the disease should be discovered as a matter of high priority lest others should be at risk from the same source and because the strain was so virulent. In Carla Sanders' case the attack had been fulminating and encephalitic. So much so, in fact, that the Professor gave it as his opinion that there was a likelihood of the disease having been induced in the girl with criminal intent. He finished by saying that even if this were not so, the danger to public health demanded a full-scale enquiry.

The Coroner read the Professor's report and had no hesitation in calling for a police report much fuller than could be provided by his own Officer. He decided, therefore, and also in view of the fact that Carla Sanders was a well-known actress whose early death had already attracted a great deal of publicity, merely to open the inquest and then adjourn until the main police report should be ready.

He had no desire to rouse public fears concerning obscure but fatal diseases, so he restricted the opening to determining who Carla Sanders was, identification, when and where she died, and to accepting from the Professor the cause of death as uraemia brought on by an acute infection. Reporters consulted their medical dictionaries and found that uraemia was totally unglamorous, being a condition which results from the failure of the renal function, and, therefore, not newsworthy. The retention in the blood of urinary constituents due to failure of the kidneys to excrete them and the constitutional failure resulting from this breakdown was considered slightly distasteful, particularly in connection with one so glossy and ornamental as the late but curvaceous Miss Sanders.

Such was the state of play when Detective Chief Superintendent George Masters was summoned by the AC (Crime) and thereupon required to make the enquiry the Coroner had demanded.

"It's right up your alley, George," said Anderson. "This pin-up girl caught this damned disease somehow, and I don't reckon discovering how is our pigeon. But the Coroner, egged on by the pathologist, reckons there could have been foul play, and that *is* our business. Though I can't for the life of me see how we're going to go about tracking down somebody who fed a virulent bug to a gadabout like Carla Sanders. But, the Coroner has to be satisfied one way or the other so, in view of the medical connotations, you're the one to see it off. Don't be too long about it, there's a good chap."

Masters grinned. "Unless I find the pathologist to be right, sir. Pathologists have a happy knack of being right."

"Of course they're right. Sometimes, at least. So do what you have to do, George. It's just that we could do without obscure infections to wrestle with."

"Even if they are instruments of crime, sir?"

"Get out, George. There's a file with bags of long-winded medical stuff to read. I couldn't make head nor tail of it. But you'll have to, and I wish you joy." As Masters rose to go, Anderson said: "Give my regards to Wanda."

"With pleasure, sir, but as you and Mrs. Anderson are dining with us this evening, you'll be able to give them in person almost as soon as I will."

Anderson looked surprised. "Tonight? My missus didn't remind me." He consulted his desk diary. "Sorry, George, I thought it was tomorrow."

"That was yesterday, sir."

"What? Oh, yes. Got some of that upstage Langenbach chilled, I hope?"

"We're never without it."

"Good. See you this evening, then."

Though he was now sailing under the slightly false colours of SSCO which was, on paper at least, a civilian appointment, Green was still regarded as a Detective Chief Inspector and was treated and addressed as such by all except the members of Masters' team who, while respecting his experience, expertise and age, were, nevertheless, on more intimate terms with him than the difference in ranks might normally demand.

Green, with Detective Sergeants Berger and Irene Tippen—Tip to her friends—was waiting for Masters on his return from the AC's office. Green, as Masters' number two, had always been accustomed to giving a warning order to the other members of the firm whenever Masters was called in by Anderson, because this indicated more often than not that a case had come up which could involve them all.

"Who, what, where, how?" began Green as Masters entered the office. "The mayor of Ashby-cum-Fenby? Ashby-de-la-Zouch? Ashby Folville? Ashby St. Ledgers?"

"We know you're a map buff," said Berger, "but there's no need to parade the fact that you know the Ordnance Survey Index off by heart."

"Just showing interest, lad."

"Showing off, you mean."

"Is it out of town, Chief?" asked Tip. "If so, I'd better ring through and ask for the car to be filled up."

"If you've been reading your papers this last few days, you'd know that the star of the new show, *Round the Barley*, appeared for one night only and has now died."

"The Sanders floozie?" asked Green. "What's there to investigate about her? I know she's snuffed it, of course. You couldn't help seeing it in the papers, but it said she died naturally of some attack of the staggers."

"Staggers?" queried Tip.

"Disease that knocks off cows," supplied Green, airily. "And for the information of Sarn't Berger, to stagger also means to arrange in such a way that some parts stick out further than others, and if you've ever seen that lass stripped for action you'd know what that can mean in the flesh. She'd have made a good ship's figurehead, breasting the waves an' all that."

"You're running on a bit, aren't you?" asked Berger. "What's your beef about? We don't even know what the job is yet."

"Forget it," commanded Masters, sitting down at his desk and opening the file. He looked up. "Despite anything that may have been reported in whatever papers you read, Carla Sanders died of a really vicious attack of Weil's disease."

"Viles?" asked Green. "Never heard of it."

"Weil's. WEILS," spelled Masters. "Or to give it the scientific name, leptospirosis. Fulminating and encephalitic leptospirosis."

"Fulminating meaning quick as lightning, Chief?" asked Tip.

"More or less, and encephalitic means that it caused inflammation of the brain, as viral infections sometimes do. Encephalitis may occur as a complication of the more common infectious diseases but not all that often, perhaps. I think, for instance, that it only crops up in one out of a thousand cases of measles, so that will give you some idea of its prevalence.

"Prevalence being important?" asked Green.

"I think it has a bearing on why we have been given the case. Rarity perhaps rather than prevelance."

"I see. How do you catch this what's-his-name? Leptospirosis?"

Masters looked at him and said without any trace of humour: "From the urine of infected rats."

Green's face set in a disbelieving mask.

"Talking of urine, you're not taking the mickey, are you, George?"

"No. I'm not. It's the truth, unpleasant as it may sound. And I'm not going into full details or we'll really complicate things too much for our own understanding, but I'll just tell you that leptospirae are a group, or genus, of spiral microorganisms normally found in rodents, in which they cause no harm. When transmitted to man by these animals, however, they give rise to very serious illnesses."

"It's the plague all over again," said Tip. "That came from rats."

"Bubonic, though, that time," Berger reminded her.

"I know that. It was just that the similarity struck me."

"Quite right, too," approved Masters. "We've been asked to investigate the death just in case there could be the chance of a major outbreak."

Green scratched one ear. "That sounds as if we've been given the job of finding the infected rat that did it."

"In a nutshell, yes. And before you ask why anybody should tip onto our plates what sounds like a completely insoluble problem, I'll tell you the two reasons given to me. Both were supplied by the pathologist.

"First, he believes the attack was so vicious that the poison could have been deliberately fed to Carla Sanders or, second, that there is some source of infection of so virulent and fatal a nature that in the interest of public health it should be tracked down. And that is roughly the point Tip made and why I commended her for it.

"But to continue. As Weil's is not a notifiable disease—don't ask me why—the health authorities are in no way bound to investigate, though they would obviously be called in to clear it up should we discover a plague spot."

Tip asked: "With all the marvellous drugs at their disposal, couldn't the doctors have saved her?"

"That is a reasonable question and one to which I have no answer," confessed Masters. "I shall have to read it up and consult the medics."

"So where do we start?" asked Green.

"First things first, I think, Bill. Investigate her recent comings and goings and—in case there are criminal connotations—try to pick up hints as to means, method, opportunity and motive for killing her. I know one thing, though."

"What's that?"

"When Wanda and I saw her on stage about a week ago, at the first night of *Round the Barley*, she was very much alive and kicking."

"You saw her?" demanded Green, as though accusing Masters of holding back information.

"Wanda had two tickets given to her to see the opening night. That was the only performance Carla Sanders appeared in. Wanda heard next day that she had fallen down a flight of steps between the stage and her dressing room and damaged an ankle badly enough to keep her out of the show for a few nights."

"When you say Wanda heard about it, where did she get that titbit from?"

"From a friend she spoke to on the phone the next day."

"I see. Just checking," grinned Green. "I'd not like to hear of Wanda consorting with any of these leptospirosis types. We want to steer her clear of anything like that."

Masters laughed. "She'll be touched by your concern, Bill."

Green grunted and held his hand out for one of Berger's cigarettes.

"Motive will be important, Chief," said Berger, putting his cigarette packet back in his pocket and ignoring Green's outstretched hand. "They're a matey lot on the surface, these theatrical types, calling each other darling all the time. But passions run high, don't they, in that set? Envy of somebody else getting a coveted role, jealousy at somebody else's success, anger at being up-staged or whatever?"

"So we are led to believe," murmured Masters.

"That's our starting point settled then, is it?" grunted Green, sarcastically.

"It could be," said Tip, "and don't get all grumpy just because Sergeant Berger didn't give you a cigarette. You've got plenty of your own. I bought you a new packet this morning."

"Did you, petal? Ah! So you did. They are here in my pocket. I'd forgotten."

"Liar," retorted Berger.

"Watch it, lad."

Berger ignored him and turned to Masters, who was reading the file. "The Victory Theatre is pretty old, isn't it, Chief?"

Masters looked up. "I imagine so. It gives me the impression of being late Victorian, probably Edwardian. What's your point?"

"Old buildings—like old theatres, I mean, Chief—are bound to have rats running about. Under the stage and up in all that clobber above the stage."

"The flies?"

"If that's the name, yes, Chief. There's all manner of food for them. Stagehands taking in sandwiches, actresses with boxes of chocolates in the dressing rooms, doormen brewing up in their bothies, and so on. Couldn't she have picked something up at the Victory while she was rehearsing this new play? Say she'd eaten a chocolate or a biscuit that she didn't notice had been nibbled. Couldn't that have given her this Weil's thing?"

Masters sat back. "You may well have a point there,

Sergeant. I think you should do something about it."

"Right, Chief. Tip and I will look into it."

"Go hunting for rats?" Tip shivered.

"We'll ask at the theatre if anybody has ever seen rats there, and we'll get the theatre hands to set traps. Any rats we catch we give to forensic and ask them to tell us whether they are leptospirosis carriers."

"And if they are?"

Berger shrugged. "We warn everybody and get them to delouse the joint over next weekend. End of case."

"It would certainly be the simplest solution," agreed Masters, "and we shouldn't overlook it. So I'd like you and Tip to undertake that chore straightaway."

"Now, Chief?"

"I think so. It is Friday morning, so somebody at the theatre should be able to set traps today and, if they catch a rat, we could arrange for it to go to forensic for testing tomorrow. Tests would not take long, as the laboratory people would know what they were looking for and could go for it without any preliminaries. That would leave time for a battue against any further rats from after the show tomorrow night until curtain up on Monday."

Green shook his head gloomily. "It sounds simple," he grunted, "but I'm damned sure it won't be."

"We've got to try it," urged Tip.

"Of course, flower. But rats are funny things. Remember what Conan Doyle said."

"We're on to Sherlock Holmes now, are we?" asked Berger scathingly.

Green ignored him. "About the giant rat of Sumatra. He said it was a story for which the world is not yet prepared, and I'm just not prepared to believe that the pigmy rats of the Victory caused this page three girl to kick the bucket. I ask you! Can you see Carla Sanders eating a chocolate that's been half-nibbled away by a rat or any other agency?"

"It wouldn't have to be nibbled away," said Masters

quietly. "If Carla Sanders was in the habit of leaving a box of chocolates open on her dressing room table, so that she could just lift one out while she was putting on her make-up, she could have been asking for trouble, not from a rat who gnawed one of the goodies, but from an infected one that just ran over them."

"You mean the bugs could have been on its paws, Chief?" asked Tip.

"There is that possibility," admitted Masters. "But I was envisaging another possibility. Rats crouch and run, crouch and run."

"Got the picture," grunted Green. "They crouch to sniff the air and then gallop on."

Masters nodded. "I've already told you these micro-organisms come from rats' urine. Well, rats don't use toilet paper. When they urinate it's a thousand to one that some of the fur on their undercarriages is splashed or dampened."

Tip said, quite chirpily, "I see what you're getting at, Chief. If one had a wee and then a second or two later ran onto an open box of chocolates, crouched for a moment and then dashed on its way, one or two of the chocolates could have been infected."

"Quite right. And it wouldn't have wetted the chocolates so as to make them obviously ruined. All it would have transferred to them would be lethal microorganisms which, as the name implies, are totally invisible to the human eye."

"I knew it," said Green disgustedly. "A real choice investigation we've got on our hands." He looked across at Tip. "I hope you never leave the lids off your boxes of chocolates."

Tip shivered. "I certainly shan't in future. Not after this conversation."

"You do get boxes now and again, then, do you, petal? From admirers, like?"

Tip blushed and looked across at Berger. "Now and again," she murmured.

Masters sat up and closed the file. "Right. That's as

far as we'll go at the moment. Sergeant Berger, if you'll take Tip and get your own investigation under way at the Victory, the DCI and I will do a bit of book research."

Berger rose.

"Don't lay too much store by what you are going to do," warned Masters. "Remember that a few minutes ago you were supplying us with a list of possible motives for somebody who wanted to get rid of Carla Sanders."

Berger nodded. "And I shall remember the DCI's scepticism, Chief. His nose is telling him it wasn't a four-legged rat that killed La Sanders, and though I hate to say this, I've got quite a respect for his nose. It's the only part of his anatomy . . ."

"Out!" growled Green, not displeased by the compliment paid to his investigative perspicacity, and unwilling to let the moment be spoiled by some less than complimentary reference to his body. "Out. And get back here in time to do some real work this afternoon."

They met again in Masters' office at two o'clock. Berger and Tip reported that the stage-door keeper at the Victory had sworn there was no such thing as a rat on the premises but the theatre manager had intervened to say that whether there was or not the staff would co-operate fully with the Yard and traps would be bought and set immediately. As soon as a rat was caught—if it was caught—Berger would be informed. Berger had advised the manager to call the local Town Hall for advice as to how to bait the traps and where best to site them.

"If they play their cards right," grunted Green, "the local rodent-operative will come and do the job for them."

"The manager was hoping for that," said Tip. "But it was clear to me that he doesn't share the doorkeeper's belief that there are no rats backstage, and he's also in a blue funk at the idea of any other actors suffering the same fate as Carla Sanders. He's obviously got a popular show on his hands and he doesn't fancy the stars of the piece getting knocked off like flies."

Masters nodded. "He could have lots of trouble. The actors might refuse to play, and were it to get out that infected rats are scampering about the place the audiences would begin to thin appreciably."

"We kept it as quiet and low-key as possible, Chief," said Berger.

"I'm sure you did. Now to other matters. Miss Sanders was unmarried, but shared a flat with a Mr. Howard Collier, also an actor, and her current boyfriend of the last eighteen months or so."

"Current?" asked Green. "She'd had others before him?"

"We shall have to enquire into that, Bill, in case a former partner could have been feeling sufficiently rejected by her as to wish her harm."

"That's highly likely," said Tip bitterly. "These tarty pieces like playing the field without a thought for the sensitivities of others. I can imagine some former lover feeling jealous if he was kicked out just because she was getting ahead in the profession."

"It's unlike you to be so bitter, Tip."

"Women like that give the rest of us a bad name, Chief. And set a bad example to ordinary girls who, without such encouragement, might settle down to happy stable relationships. But you don't want me to give you the full spiel, do you?"

"No, thank you. Just the normal woman's point of view. We appreciate that."

Green winked at Tip and Masters consulted the file before saying: "Sanders and Collier lived at Flat 19, Hammer Head Court."

"I know where that is," said Berger. "Very nice, but not too upmarket."

"In that case," said Masters, "you can take us there."

As Berger had said, the flat was in a pleasant enough modern block, set on a corner, at an angle across its own plot, so that the triangle of ground in front of it

73

made a sizeable lawn and shrub garden which could be entered from both streets. The carriageway led under the centre of the block to lock-up garages behind. A door on each side of this entrance led to the two halves of the block. Flat 19 was on the left as Berger drove in.

The door was opened by a man in his thirties, wearing a broad-striped, multicoloured dressing gown apparently over his naked body. Bare feet, unshaven chin, unkempt hair and less-than-fully-functioning eyes suggested he had come from his bed to answer the ring.

"Mr. Howard Collier?" Masters asked the question though he recognised the face despite its appearance.

"Yes. Who are you?" The tones were those of many a television ad voice-over.

Masters introduced himself and his colleagues and requested entry. Collier let them in willingly, asking their business as he did so. When he moved aside to let them pass, Masters was pleased to glimpse that the actor was actually wearing boxer shorts under the gown.

"I am here to ask a few questions concerning Miss Sanders' death."

The man ran a long-fingered hand through his hair. "The police are interested in Carla? Why?"

"If you are putting the percolator on, chum," said Green, "make sure there'll be enough in it for five."

Collier stared at him for a moment or two. "That sounds as if you're anticipating a long session."

"Could be."

"In that case come through to the kitchen." Collier padded through ahead of them. "I'll use the Cafetière," he said. "It's supposed to hold enough for eight."

"Would you like me to do it for you, Mr. Collier?" asked Tip.

The actor declined the offer and as he filled the electric kettle he invited them to sit on the breakfast bar stools.

Masters watched him getting mugs from one of the wall cupboards and grinding coffee beans in an electric mill. "You seem to be very adept in the kitchen, Mr. Collier."

"And you seem to be very adept at not telling me why you are interested in Carla's death, Chief Superintendent."

"I'm not trying to avoid doing so," Masters assured him. "Mr. Green suggested coffee merely to allow you time to accustom yourself to our presence and, if you'll forgive me, your eyes to the daylight."

"Fine. Now that that bit of blarney is over, let's have it. The reason why you're here."

While Collier continued to busy himself, Masters said: "Miss Sanders was, according to the doctor who attended her eight or nine days ago, that is on the opening night of her new play, a perfectly fit and healthy young woman. He did not, of course, do any medical tests in her dressing room, but he did take her temperature and pulse and examine her limbs for damage other than abrasions on one leg and a twisted ankle."

Collier had turned to face him. As he leaned against the work-top, he said: "She was totally fit. She had to be. Her part in *Round the Barley* was as much physical as anything else. Movement the whole time."

Masters nodded. "I was lucky enough to see that first night and admired Miss Sanders' movement and timing very much."

"Then you don't need me to point out that five or six weeks rehearsing that show was a gruelling time, yet Carla came through it without a sign of fatigue."

"Quite. And the observations made by the doctor who attended her that night were borne out the next morning by her own doctor whom she had been advised to visit, I believe. My information is that as Miss Sanders was so anxious to get back to the stage, her own GP examined her thoroughly."

"And gave her a completely clean bill of health except for the damage to her leg. I know. I was with her. Took her there and stayed throughout. Heard everything that was said."

Masters nodded his understanding of this and waited while Collier put four heaped tablespoons of coffee into the heated container and added the boiling water. As Collier then stirred the brew and inserted the filter plunger just into the top of the container, he continued: "The pathologist who carried out the postmortem thinks it more than a little strange and highly frightening that a young woman who is superbly fit and healthy on Friday morning should be dead of a galloping infection by the early hours of the following Tuesday morning."

"So do I."

"Find it disturbing? Speaking generally, I mean. Not as the man who has just lost his ... er ... partner?"

Collier stared at him for a moment, perplexed by the question. Then he said, slowly, "Let me see if I've got this straight. You are asking me if, apart from this bug killing Carla, I am not scared stiff on my own account?"

"Not quite. I meant are you disturbed in general by the sudden occurrence of the disease and the possibility of it being at large to damage other people?"

"I haven't thought about it." Collier turned to the coffee pot and pushed down the plunger. "It never struck me," he declared vehemently, "to consider it in that light."

"Understandable," grunted Green. "In the circumstances. The loss of your girlfriend would be your main concern."

"Only concern," amended Collier, handing him a mug of coffee. "We were ...." The sentence petered out.

"What were you?" asked Masters quietly.

"I was going to say mates, and then felt it to be somehow inappropriate." Again the actor ran his hand through his tousled hair. "What I mean is, Carla and I got on together." He handed Masters a mug of coffee.

"Well-suited in every respect?"

"That's about the size of it. And consequently there were no storm clouds on the horizon. I know a lot of

76

people thought she was just a body without a lot up top..."

"But?"

Collier handed out the rest of the coffee before continuing. "She had quite a lot of sense, actually. The trouble is, or was, that in our profession you have to be fly, competition being what it is."

"Except for the favoured few, perhaps?"

"The real top liners rise on their undenied ability. The rest of us are also-rans, in comparison. Others better than some, of course. Some who can't act for toffee get a meal ticket for life in a soap opera, playing some meagre, gimmicky little part..." He spread his hands, theatrically. "But that's the luck of the draw. Carla knew the problems and she devoted all her nous to furthering a career which she knew was based on nothing much more than a smashing figure. So she turned all her intellect to cunning, if you like to call it that. She acted a part offstage as well as on. Always the same part, playing the role people expected of her. But, as I say, she did it deliberately, or at least she did in the beginning. After that it became second nature to her."

"But you saw through it to the real woman beneath the playacting, did you chum?" asked Green.

"I think I did."

"So what did you do about it? Or did you string along with the idea?"

"I had just about got her to let down while at home here: to be herself with me and to take an interest in living a normal life when she had to go and catch the bloody bug that killed her." Collier was controlling any emotion he may have felt, but even so he turned his face away. For a moment or two Masters left him to gaze sightlessly out of the kitchen window.

"Have your coffee, Mr. Collier," he said gently, at last.

Collier turned back to face them. "Sorry for the display. God! Fancy letting myself go in front of four cops!"

"Don't worry about that. Two of us have wives we

wouldn't want to lose, too, you know, and I don't think the other pair are totally insensitive either."

"Still! Oh, hell! What were you saying? Asking me if I didn't think her death so strange as to merit investigation. Was that it?"

"More or less. You did think it strange, didn't you? Surely the thought must have struck you that Miss Sanders' rapid death was out of the ordinary?"

Collier frowned. "As I said, I haven't deliberately thought about it in that light, but now you mention it, I must admit to having a feeling there was something not right."

"The illness, you mean?"

"Yes. One can accept that people, young and old, do get illnesses. Severe ones at times. Even fatal ones, and the fact causes sorrow, of course, but not disquiet, if that's the right word. At the back of my mind there's been a niggle."

Masters waited to see if Collier was going to continue along this line of thought. As the actor didn't do so, he said: "There's been the same niggle at the back of the mind of officialdom, too. That is why we are here. To resolve that niggle, if we can."

Collier shrugged. "How can you do that? There's nothing concrete to go on as far as I know. I'll tell you all I can, of course."

"Thank you. Can we discuss the events of the last few days of Miss Sanders' life?"

"What do you want to know?"

"Everything."

"Go ahead. There's nothing you shouldn't hear about."

"Excellent. When did you last see Carla Sanders when she was really and totally fully fit? We'll start from there."

"Fine. The answer to the question doesn't need thinking about. The last time I saw Carla fully fit was a week ago yesterday. Last Thursday week, the day of the night when she opened in her new play which you tell me you saw."

Masters nodded. "What happened—or didn't happen—during that day? Before the evening show, I mean?"

"I was trying to keep her cool. That was the biggest job. But I suppose you can imagine what it's like during the day before a big opening. Nerves, excitement, fear, nausea and every other emotional and physical nasty one can experience mixed up with a hell of a lot of to-ing and fro-ing when you should be resting.

"Carla had to go to the theatre in the morning. Some last-minute alterations to a dress or a scene to change slightly. I don't know, because I don't think she said, and in any case she was chattering on about so many things I could very well not have picked it out from all the other gabble that was going on. Then from the theatre she went for a hairdo which took hours. Then back here for a late lunch, but she wouldn't eat anything. She'd had no breakfast either. No solids, that is. You can imagine how it was."

"I know very little about the theatre but, as you say, I've always believed that the day of the opening night is something actors don't look forward to if they haven't got an iron nerve."

"They are few and far between, believe me. But I did get Carla to agree to rest for an hour or two late in the afternoon. Then I got her up and insisted on her having an omelette with me. I had to go off to the theatre, too, remember."

"I suppose you did. I had forgotten that. What are you appearing in?"

"*Mirror Writing* at the Leader. It's a thriller."

"I remember reading about it. You play a detective, I believe?"

Collier had the grace to grin. "After meeting you I'd say 'play' was the right word. You don't seem to be going about your business in anything like the way I portray Seneschal—he's my part, Seneschal. But to get on with what we were talking about. I like to get to the theatre by soon after six and take my time over getting ready. And I need a light meal before I go, because there's no dinner or supper for the likes of us before eleven at the earliest."

"Miss Sanders ate the omelette?"

"Wolfed it down, actually. I had to tell her to go easy or she'd give herself indigestion. And after it she had some cream crackers and cheese and a cup of black coffee."

"It would appear there was nothing wrong with her appetite despite her eating nothing earlier in the day."

"Nerves," said Collier.

"You are quite satisfied she was completely well at that time, then?"

"Completely. We went off together to our respective theatres. I dropped her at the Victory. She was a bit quiet in the cab, where earlier on she'd been chattering nonstop, but I put that down entirely to nerves."

"Entirely? I ask because I want to be absolutely sure."

"She was perfectly fit. The performance she gave proves it. You must know. You saw that her role called for no end of movement on stage, and it called for a lot of good timing in all the business."

"I certainly saw no signs of anything but superb fitness and timing. But I didn't read the notices last Friday. Were they good?"

"Couldn't have been better. Of course, it's a commercial piece rather than great drama, but the indications are that it will run."

"Even without Miss Sanders?"

"Oh yes. As I tried to convey to you earlier, basically Carla had no illusions about herself. She knew that, given the chance, there would be scores of girls in London who could equal her for face, figure, movement and so on. Now one of them has that chance and, from what I hear, is making the most of it."

"Could I have her name, please, Mr. Collier," asked Tip, playing her role of Masters' immediate assistant and making sure she had a note of all names mentioned.

"Her name? Whatever for?"

"The record, sir."

Collier stared at her, and then said, "Look here, I know you lot are taking a few soundings to see if there's anything fishy about Carla's death, but I don't like the idea of you wanting to know about the girl who took over."

"Why not, sir? Only her name. But if you feel there is some reason why you shouldn't supply it, I can get it from the billboards or by ringing the box office."

Collier scowled. "You know damn' well what I mean. If it turns out there was some monkey business you'll start looking at the girl who has benefited by Carla's absence from the cast."

"Most certainly we will," agreed Tip. "And at you, of course, as the only member of her most immediate family, if you don't mind my calling your set-up here a family. And at others, too. Former boyfriends, for instance."

"All right, all right." He turned to Masters. "Do you allow your junior officers to carry on like this?"

"Like what, Mr. Collier? Has Sergeant Tippen been anything less than frank with you? I would have said she had been perfectly open. Those she mentioned are people we shall have to consider, if we have to consider anybody. It is by no means certain that we shall decide there was any foul play or anything of that nature to be investigated, but we have always to be prepared for the worst, as Sergeant Tippen very kindly pointed out to you in a manner which I consider was perfectly frank and open."

"So frank and open as to be tantamount to an overt threat."

"Nonsense, lad," grunted Green. "Be your age. You don't imagine a team such as this is sent out to ask questions everytime anybody trips over a matchstick and knocks themselves out on a tram ticket, do you? There's concern about your girlie. Genuine concern, because the doctor can't sign her certificate, and the Coroner and pathologist are worried, too. And it's when people die unexpectedly and people like coroners and pathologists get concerned that we appear. Unexpected deaths are our job. To find out why they happen. And when we start asking questions, we do it as gently and honestly as possible, but we also do it comprehensively, because we always have to bear in mind that unexpected deaths can have all manner of causes from wasp stings to murder. And that is what Sergeant Tippen has been telling you. Straight out. No cover-ups. If there was monkey business, then everybody close to Miss Sanders will be looked at closely. But only if there was monkey business. So now, lad, what's the name of the understudy who's taken over?"

"Viola Young," replied Collier and then, after a short pause, he said to Tip, "I'm sorry. I shouldn't have taken offence as I did. I suppose I feel a bit edgy." He spread his arms. "Look at me. Only just out of bed, unwashed, unshaven. And it's mid-afternoon."

"What time did you go to bed, sir?" asked Tip.

"Five o'clock this morning," said Collier shame-facedly. "Somehow, after the show last night I couldn't face coming back here alone so I . . . I stayed out till dawn."

"Understandable," said Tip, maternally. "But you'll be all right from now on."

"I managed Tuesday and Wednesday nights, but last night, no. It was too much."

"Last night was the low point," said Tip, sapiently. "From now on it will get better. Of itself, I mean. And I even think that talking things over with Mr. Masters and the rest of us will help, you know."

Collier nodded.

"Tell us about Miss Sanders' accident. When she was leaving the stage, she fell didn't she?"

"Yes." Collier turned to drain the coffee pot into his cup before addressing Masters again. "I don't sup-

82

pose you've ever been backstage at the Victory? No?"

Masters shook his head.

"It's old-fashioned. The stage itself is big. So big that on the prompt side there's a hole cut in it, in the wings, to take the head of the stairway to the dressing rooms. It's an iron semi-helix, actually. Safe enough from the point of view of fire precautions, because it is just like a fire escape. Safe enough, too, I suppose, if you hang on to the bannister, but you can imagine the shape of each step."

"Triangular?"

"Exactly. And bloody difficult to negotiate at the best of times, but nigh-on impossible for somebody like Carla weighed down with flowers, wearing high heels and drunk with success after umpteen curtain calls. Anybody is liable to be a bit less than ultra-careful at such a time, turning round to chat excitedly to somebody instead of watching where they put their feet. Fortunately for Carla there was somebody in front of her who broke her fall, otherwise she could have done in her back."

There was a moment of silence while the four from the Yard all wondered whether Collier had realised what he had said. Carla Sanders was fortunate not to have strained her back! Masters and his team, each in his or her own way, was speculating whether, had she strained her back, she might not still be alive. Whether events might not have pursued a completely different course had she been confined to a bed of pain for a few days instead of doing whatever she had done since that opening night. They had yet to discover her movements over the critical days, but each knew that Masters would be relentless in tracing her activities during the relevant time.

At last Green spoke.

"Or killed herself," he said as a remark to follow on Collier's observation.

"Very possibly," said the actor who apparently had

not noticed the import of his own remark nor the silence which had followed it. "As it was, one foot slipped. She crocked the ankle and scraped the skin off her leg for a matter of eight or nine inches above the joint. And when I say scraped I don't mean she just marked and bruised the flesh. She stripped the skin off so that the whole area started to weep and there were several gashes that bled. Just like a severe case of gravel rash, it was."

"So there were open lesions," mused Masters.

"If that's the term for a bloody mess, yes. Of course, they got a doctor to her at the theatre, as you know. He told Carla she wouldn't be able to go on next night, Friday, and not before Monday at the earliest—and only then if she was lucky. I wasn't there when she fell but I'd arranged to rush round there from the Leader to join the party they were going to have. So I heard how Carla took it when she was told she'd be out of the show for at least over the weekend."

"She created a bit of a fuss, did she, lad?" asked Green. "Got the old hysteric temperament out to give it a bit of an airing?"

"What do you think? I told her to cool it and an old boy in a wheelchair who'd put up most of the money for the show steered himself into the dressing room to have a few words with her. I must say he was pretty good. He can't walk because of disseminated sclerosis or something like that, but he's a jolly sort of chap and without actually drawing the comparison between Carla and himself he gave her to understand that even with her injuries she was a damn' sight better off than he was. Anyway, he seemed to do the trick and capped it by telling Carla that if she couldn't appear on Saturday night she'd be free to go to his birthday party. She liked the idea, apparently."

"Why?"

"Because Hugh Carlyle—that's his name—is one of the bigger investors in our commercial theatre and so he's a good chap to know."

84

"And to keep in with, presumably?"

"You've got it. I'm doubtful whether our Angels, as we call them, have much say in casting, but as I said earlier, Carla wouldn't miss a trick like that even though she was lame."

Masters looked at his watch and stood up, much to the surprise of his three companions. "It is getting on for four o'clock, Mr. Collier, so I think we had better stop there so that you can have time to get ready for the theatre and have a meal. I should hate to be the cause of the curtain going up late."

Collier looked a little surprised. "Oh, lord, is it that time?"

"You have been so involved in telling us your story that you haven't been aware of time. I'm glad of that, because I think that it means talking about things has done you a bit of good. But we shall want the rest of the facts tomorrow. What time do you normally get up in the morning, Mr. Collier?"

"Normally? Oh, about nine. Yes, nine. I've just been skulking about these last few days."

"Understandable. We shall call on you at ten o'clock."

"I'll be ready."

"Just one thing I'd like to ask, which you might not know the answer to."

"What's that?"

"The name of whoever it was—actor or actress—who was following Miss Sanders down the staircase."

"I don't know," admitted Collier, "but I could probably find out for you."

"Please don't go about asking questions. I don't want a probably innocent person to think that we suspect them of causing Miss Sanders harm. It was just one of those things that Sergeant Tippen mentioned. A fact we should have just for the sake of being thorough."

"I see."

"Good. Until tomorrow, Mr. Collier."

*   *   *

"Why pull us out at that point?" asked Green as they got into the car. "It was just going to get interesting. And it's not like you to allow an appearance on stage to muck up an investigation."

"I would agree with that," replied Masters, "if I was sure we have a criminal investigation on our hands. If, however, we are merely making enquiries of a general nature I can see no reason for upsetting Collier's routine more than necessary. By the look of him he'll need a hell of a lot of washing and brushing up before he's fit to go to the Leader tonight, and you heard him say he likes a meal before he goes."

Green paused in the act of lighting a cigarette. "Now tell us the real reason," he grunted.

Tip turned in her seat. "What do you mean?" she asked. "The Chief has given us a perfectly valid reason for breaking off where he did. It was a natural place. The end of the business at the theatre. Tomorrow we can go on from there. Besides, as I understand it, and from his expertise with the coffee pot, I got the idea that Howard Collier prepared all the meals in that house, so he'll be cooking whatever it is he'll have to eat before he goes to the theatre. And even sausages take a few minutes to frizzle."

Green gazed at her for a moment or two before replying. "There's a lot of things that are not in the books that you'll have to learn in this job," he said kindly. "Particularly in this firm."

"I'm listening."

"Good, petal. First off, in your own mind you must question every single thing that happens and that includes what His Nibs does, Sarn't Berger does and what I do. Why? Because if we're doing the job right we have to have a reason for our actions. You'll find, as often as not, that you can think of several reasons for every move. Sometimes an ostensible reason and an alternative ulterior motive."

"With my own colleagues?"

"With everybody, flower. Now, tell me why you think

86

His Nibs broke off that interview when he did."

"He's given us the reason."

"What did you think his reason was before he gave you the easy one about Collier needing a shave and a meal?"

"Well . . . I don't think I thought about it."

"You just accepted what His Nibs said, but not until he said it. In other words, you didn't think for yourself."

Tip admitted the impeachment.

"If you had thought, and before hearing what His Nibs said, what would you have given as the reason for cutting short a fruitful interview?"

"I think I would have supposed that the Chief had heard something during the course of the interview which caused him to want to break it off to do a bit of checking somewhere else."

"Good answer, lassie. But would you have discarded your own opinion in the face of the facile excuse you've just heard?"

"It wasn't facile, it was valid."

"The fact still remains you'd have thought up an alternative."

"Yes, I see that."

"Why not stick to your guns?"

"I'm the junior sergeant around here, remember."

"And junior sergeants can't have opinions, even if they don't voice them? I thought His Nibs was teaching you to say what you thought at any time."

"So he is. If I'd heard something in the interview, as I said I thought the Chief did, I'd have mentioned it because I would have had a reason for questioning what you call his excuse. But I didn't latch on to anything to spark off any idea so I didn't suggest that what the Chief said was specious."

"All right, lassie. The other thing you've got to learn in this firm is a sort of mind reading. You've got to learn by His Nibs' attitude or tone of voice or whatever when he's trying to offer you a chunk of old cod's wallop in place of the real baked haddock. When you've learned that, and learned to think up your own alternatives to what he says, you can then call his bluff."

"Like you are doing now?"

"Yes. I reckon it was out of character to break off that interview just to give Collier time to fry a pound of sausages and have a quick shave and shower. And not only was it out of character, it sounded wrong as he said it. Facts you didn't pick up. So you didn't ask yourself why the interview was curtailed; when you had thought of a reason you discarded it for a less good one; and when the less good one was offered to you you didn't suss it was phoney. To add insult to all those injuries you then turned on me when I did spot the bogus excuse and the phoney manner and said so."

"But that is monstrous," flared Tip. She appealed to Masters. "Chief, I haven't got to question everything you do, have I?"

"A lot of the burden of what the DCI said is right. You must accept nothing blindly, whether it's from one of us, a witness or a suspect. Not that I am suggesting we would mislead you, but if you are going to keep abreast of affairs you must ask yourself these questions at all times. And please note I said ask yourself. You don't have to plague the rest of us with your doubts unless you really are out of your depth or think we are. There's no telling when a word from you could put us right. So there's another lesson to learn, which the DCI didn't mention, and that is to know when to put in your oar at times when we are not brainstorming. And by that I don't mean to save yourself embarrassment or to save you from feeling a nuisance, I mean for the good of the rest of us. If you've got a valid point, you must make it, whatever it is."

Tip looked crestfallen, so much so that Masters said: "Cheer up, Tip. You're doing famously. But you can't learn everything after being with us for only three cases. The DCI was right to give you this little lesson, because it was appropriate. He was right, you see, I had another reason for breaking off the interview. And that reason

88

makes you right, too. I did hear something of interest. The DCI's point is, you should have reached that conclusion right from the start even though a little later you decided to be kind enough to accept my reason."

"You mean I shouldn't have defended it when Mr. Green disbelieved it. I know. His experience against my inexperience. There's not much comparison, is there?"

Green laughed. "No, love, but you're prettier than I am."

Tip flushed. "What's that got to do with it?"

"Everything. And if you're going to tell me that God-given beauty—in whatever area—should be ignored just for the sake of some idealogical whim, then I'm ashamed of you. Ashamed and sorry. A tree, a mountain, a beautiful sky or a beautiful woman should all be appreciated and their presence revelled in, if that's the right word, and anybody who says otherwise is an immature clod."

"Hear, hear," said Berger from the driving seat.

"Oh, you!" Tip flounced to face front.

"You've joined a man's team, Tip," said Masters. "There may be equality of sexes, but the male and female worlds are still miles apart. You and we are getting along very well together, but just as we must make them for you, you must make allowances for us, and not try to make us forget all our old shibboleths."

Tip turned again impulsively. "I do make allowances for you, Chief..."

Her words were drowned in a peal of laughter from all three men. It reduced the tension in the atmosphere. Tip smiled and murmured: "You all know exactly what I mean."

"That's right, petal," said Green. "And now there's another lesson you've just been taught."

"Oh! What's that?"

"You've just been treated to a perfect performance in the ducking of inconvenient questions. Here we are at the Yard, and you'll notice His Nibs has managed to steer clear of giving us an answer to our question by the simple expedient of drowning everything in a foam of words."

"I had realised that," said Tip. "And I suspect an ulterior motive, as instructed."

"Good girl, what is it?"

"That he doesn't want us to know about it—yet."

4

"Okay, George, spill it," said Green as he followed Masters into the latter's office a few minutes later. "The kids have gone, so there's nobody here but us chickens."

"Close the door and take a seat, Bill."

Masters sat at his desk and started to rub a large flake of Warlock for his pipe. Green carefully extracted a cigarette from what appeared to be a battered packet. The cigarette was pristine. Masters always wondered how Green managed to have perfect cigarettes when his packets invariably looked as if they had been trodden on. He wondered if he should ask his assistant how the trick was done and then thought better of it.

Green waited until the pipe had been carefully packed, lit, tamped down again and then relit to get the level, even burn that Masters always aimed for. Green wondered how Masters managed it so well when other pipe smokers never seemed to achieve the same result without the expenditure of at least half a box of matches. He didn't bother to ask. Instead he said: "Something's bugging you, George."

"Just a little, at the moment."

"But liable to cause trouble later?"

"I hope not, because it's personal, Bill."

Green sat up in surprise. "Let me get this straight. You heard something in Howard Collier's flat this afternoon which affects you personally?"

"And perhaps you, too, Bill, in a way. That's why I broke off the interview when I did. I wanted time to think and to discuss it with you."

Green shook his head. "There was nothing said there that affects me. Why should there be?"

"Earlier today you learned that Wanda and I had been to the first night of *Round the Barley*."

"You said a friend of Wanda's had given her a couple of complimentaries."

"Right. The friend's name is Margot Carlyle."

Green pursed his lips and gave an inward whistle.

"The wife of the chap in the wheelchair who puts up the money for these shows?"

"The same. Hugh Carlyle."

Green grimaced. "So what? You know him. Or should I say your missus knows his missus? He couldn't have pushed Sanders downstairs and I don't suppose his wife did. I mean I don't suppose this Carlyle, being chair-bound, gets up to any funny business with blown-up actresses. Not to make his wife jealous."

Masters smiled. "From what I know of Carlyle, Carla Sanders would be the last woman he would leave his wife for. Margot is quite something."

"If she's Wanda's friend, I would expect her to be."

"Quite. They are very much of a type."

"So, what's the problem?"

"As yet, there isn't one. But you remember Collier saying Sanders had been invited to Carlyle's party on Saturday night."

"Again, so what?"

"Wanda and I were invited to that party, Bill. It was held at Carlyle's house. We didn't go because, as you know, I was Duty SO on Saturday night, and you and Doris very kindly kept Wanda company during the evening."

Green looked across the desk. "The party was at Carlyle's house, you say?"

Masters nodded.

"Is that significant? I mean, is it any different from holding a party in a hotel or a pub or a church hall, even?"

"It remains to be seen," replied Masters. "But the

written reports we've had say that Sanders was taken ill early on Sunday morning."

"Oh, lord! I was forgetting that." Green stubbed out his cigarette. "What you are saying is that there is the possibility that something happened on Saturday night that blew up on Sunday. But that's rubbish, George, and you know it. How could a girl like Sanders get bitten by a rat at a party in a house such as I imagine this bloke Carlyle owns? He's pretty wealthy, isn't he? With a posh house that's done up and dusted so much there wouldn't be a crumb for a rat to feed on."

"Quite right. A lovely home."

"Then the only way Sanders could have been got at by any rat that night was if she left the party and took to the nearby fields for a bit of nooky. A tumble in the hay which upset a rat nesting in it. That sort of thing."

"You could be right, but I can't imagine Sanders going in for hay-making. She's the sort that would commandeer the master bedroom for half an hour."

"And there'd be no rats in the master bedroom. Not four-legged ones, anyway," argued Green. "So whatever your fears are about Carlyle's party on Saturday night, they are absolutely groundless." Green took out another cigarette. "But that's not what is really worrying you, is it? It's the fact that you know Carlyle and his missus and if they are mixed up in this business, even if in name only, you're wondering whether you oughtn't to declare your interest to Edgar Anderson and have him give the job to somebody else."

Masters nodded. "That's exactly my point, Bill." He looked up. "You see, you haven't heard it all yet."

"No?"

"It is the Carlyles who have offered us Housmans at the very low price Wanda mentioned the other night when we first discussed the move with you and Doris."

Green frowned and sucked his partial denture noisily for a moment or two. Masters leaned back and waited for his colleague to speak.

"You're worried about that, are you? I can see why.

93

It could be said by some people to come into the bribery and corruption court. Getting a house at the right price from somebody you're investigating! It could be made to sound like a bit of a pay-off."

"What do I do about it, Bill?"

"The arrangement was made before this show, *Round the Barley*, started its run, wasn't it?"

"It was. Just a few days before. But there's nothing in writing yet. Just a verbal agreement subject to the results of our survey and my personal inspection. I haven't seen it yet. Wanda has, of course. She's been over it and is thrilled at the prospect of getting it."

"Knowing you, if Wanda likes and wants it, it's hers."

"Quite."

"Sight unseen?"

"Apart from doing my best to give her pleasure, I trust her judgement in most things, but particularly when it comes to houses. You'll remember her first cottage and what she had made of that. And then there's our present house. She was the one who could see the possibilities and turned it into what it has become."

"You don't have to say any more, chum. I've never come across a nicer pad."

"So you understand my problem, Bill?"

"Of course I do. It's mine as well, remember. You would do anything you could to stop Wanda being disappointed, but what about my missus? She's dreaming about taking over Wanda's Palace. And I don't want to disappoint her either. She was like a dog with two tails this morning because the surveyor was coming. By now he'll have told her what we can sell for, with a written confirmation to come in a few days' time. If we've been as lucky as we hope we have, she'll have done all her little sums and...oh, hell, George, there's no hint of corruption here."

"You know it, and I know it, Bill. But if some bit of paper had been dated and signed a week ago we'd have proof that there was no hint of bribery involved. As it is..." He spread his hands. "Strictly speaking, I should

94

present myself to Edgar Anderson now and put it all on his plate."

"Just a moment," said Green, leaning forward on the desk. "Let's suppose you were to go up to see the AC (Crime) this minute. What have you got that you can tell him?" Without waiting for a reply, the DCI went on: "Nothing, except the fact that you are negotiating to buy a house from a certain Mr. Carlyle who, because he backs theatre shows, knows Carla Sanders whose sudden death you are probing. All Edgar will say to that is, 'So what?' You then go on to say that on the Saturday night before she died, the Sanders bird attended one of Carlyle's parties. Invited there as a sort of recompense for being left out of the show on account of injury. What does Edgar say to that? His only reply will be to thank you for telling him and to order you to get on with the job he has given you to sort out. He'll say all this is irrelevant because the bird didn't die until Tuesday and although we've been called in to sniff around we don't even know if there was foul play involved." Green grinned. "I reckon our Edgar will think you've dredged it all up in the hope that you can skive out of the en-quiry—that he'll feel obliged to palm it over to somebody else to sort. You know Edgar. He always looks for the ulterior motive and he won't play ball."

"I'll admit it sounds a bit thin when summed up like that."

"And you know you're not accepting bribes or doing business with a convicted crook."

"Of course."

"Then, my advice to you, George, is to leave it for the moment. If we find Carlyle is more actively involved, then you may have to think again later."

"That's exactly what I'd like to do, Bill, but you know how things are. You say Edgar would kick me out of his office if I went to him now. I agree. He would. But if in two or three days time Carlyle begins to figure prominently in this business, Anderson would demand to know why I hadn't gone to him immediately his name cropped up."

"You can't win, George. But ask yourself this. Can you possibly see any way in which Carlyle or his missus can be involved in Carla Sanders' death?"

"No."

"Right. Leave it for now." Green got to his feet. "And don't you worry about the oast-house. You'll be telling the truth, if you have to say anything at all, by claiming that the negotiations were Wanda's business in the first place, and not yours."

"Thanks, Bill. Sorry to have burdened you with my tender conscience."

"Tender conscience, my foot. We all thought these house deals were going to be completely free of all the usual troubles that beset such transactions. Now a completely different can of worms has been opened and you were right to let me have a look at them squirming around before we clap the lid back on once and for all. Now, if you don't mind, I'll get off home. Doris will be bursting to tell me what the surveyor had to say."

"Of course. Thank you for listening and your advice, Bill, and I hope the news is to your liking when you get home."

Shortly after ten the next morning, Masters and his team again called at Collier's flat. This time the actor was prepared for the visit. He was up and about, shaved, and dressed in blue slacks with a fawn shirt and brown shoes of very orthodox pattern, well-polished and worn enough to suggest that they were his normal choice of footwear.

"Did you have a good night, Mr. Collier?"

"Thank you, yes, Mr. Masters. Talking to you four yesterday afternoon did something for me."

"Got it off your chest, lad," said Green, following Masters who was being shown into the sitting room of the flat. "Great relief to talk it over, you know. Bottling it up is never any good."

Collier grinned at him. "Any more old bromides?" he asked.

Green stared back. "Yes. Get it out of your system is another of them. You know the old saying."

"Which one?"

"Better an empty house than a bad tenant."

"I have heard that," agreed Collier, "but with a slightly different connotation."

"Aye, I dare say, but the sentiment still holds good." Green plonked himself in an armchair covered in material with broad green and yellow slashes in its make-up. "Mind if I sit here?"

"That's the cat's chair."

"Don't give me that. He'd have to be a chameleon to choose this nest of rest, otherwise it would make his nose bleed."

Collier laughed aloud and turned to invite the others to sit. He himself squatted on a camel saddle covered in a West African Kano cloth with purple and orange stripes. Tip had offered to sit on it to allow him the use of her chair, but he forbade the exchange. "Carla always made a man sit here if we were short of chairs for the full company," he said. "She reckoned no girl in an ordinary dress could be demure on this, and she admitted to being a spoilsport. At least as far as I was concerned."

"With other women, presumably?" queried Tip.

"Oh, lord, yes. When we were alone she never minded what sort of an eyeful I got. And yet, and yet . . ."

"Yes?"

"I was only going to say there was quite a lot of the prude in her make-up, which I don't suppose any of you will believe after having seen some of her displays."

"I'll accept that, Mr. Collier," replied Tip. "Not everything one has to do is necessarily to one's liking."

Masters interrupted. "I am grateful for these sidelights on Miss Sanders' character, but could we consider them later if needs be? I don't want to stop you reminiscing, Mr. Collier, but I would like to get on with the somewhat different history of the last few days in Miss Sanders' life. Yesterday afternoon we got as far as hearing how Mr. Hugh Carlyle went to the dressing room, calmed her down and then invited Miss Sanders to a party on the following Saturday evening."

"That's right. And I think I mentioned that Carlyle was a good chap to know from Carla's point of view."

"And to keep in with?"

"You've got it. As I said earlier, Carla wouldn't miss a trick like that, even though she was lame."

"Good. What happened next?"

"I brought her here in a taxi and helped her to bed."

"There was no question of staying for the party?"

"Not a hope in hell. Not that it was even suggested. I wouldn't have agreed whatever she'd said. I got her here and put her straight to bed. She was quite heavily bandaged, of course, but the doctor had given her a painkiller and I think that helped her to sleep. I gave her a cup of Horlick's, too, though she said she wanted brandy. But I thought that on top of an analgesic I'd better not let her have any booze."

"Quite right, chum," murmured Green. "Drink and drugs don't mix."

"You say she slept well?" asked Masters.

"Very well. I kept awake till she dropped off and she didn't disturb me at all during the night."

"You were with her?"

"I could see no reason for not sharing the bed as usual."

"I agree. Though she was asleep your presence would be a comfort to her, no doubt. Then came the morning. Yes?"

"She was still in some pain, but fit enough to take the coffee and toast I gave her in bed. After that I got her up without doing anything to the wound or the dressings and then drove her to see her own doctor. He examined the damage, redressed it and gave her a prescription which he said was a muscle relaxant for the sprain and a mild painkiller, too."

"Tablets?"

"Yes."

"Are they still here, or did the doctor take them?"

"They're beside the bed. Everybody who came looked at them and said they could have had nothing at all to do with her fever."

"Nevertheless we should like to have them."

"Just for the record?"

"Yes."

"Help yourself. Anyhow, Carla rested all Friday, reading and watching the box. One or two people rang up and she was able to speak to them—I'd put the phone by her side. Before I left for the theatre that night a lot of the stiffness had gone and she could move about enough to get out of her chair and get to the table without much difficulty. And go to the loo, of course."

"She ate her meals?"

"Oh, yes. I knocked her up some light stuff, you know. Cheese on toast for lunch. Smoked salmon salad for early supper before I left her."

"Not bad," murmured Green.

"When I got back," continued Collier, "she was in bed, but she told me she'd been to the bathroom to top and tail herself, as she put it. She didn't get into the tub because of the bandages."

"Which was wise."

"I think so. By Saturday morning she was almost back to normal. There was still a lot of bruising round the ankle, but the swelling was down and most of the pain gone. The deep scratches had begun to heal, too, but I reckoned they were still severe enough to need a dressing to keep them clean, so I put a clean bandage on."

"They'd scabbed over, had they?" asked Green.

"Actually, no. Not like when you fell down and cut a knee as a kid. They used to crust over, I remember, but Carla's remained red, and deep, even, but they were dry and clean and I suppose well on the mend by then."

"Knitting," agreed Green, solemnly.

"I beg your pardon?"

"What? Oh, cuts like that are either stitched by the doctor or they knit of their own accord."

"I see. Sorry I was all...I mean, I didn't know the phrase."

"Miss Sanders was fit—in herself, I mean—on Saturday morning?" asked Masters. "I know you said the swelling had gone down and the lesions were healing, but what about, say, headache, nausea, pain in the stomach or anything not to do directly with the injury?"

"Absolutely fit. The pain had almost gone, although she was, of course, very conscious of the ankle."

"More so than anybody else would have been?"

"At a guess I would say it was psychological. What Carla wanted was to be free of the bandage. She left me in no doubt about that, but I insisted it should be covered. By as light a bandage as I could manage. However, no matter how small, the presence of a dressing to a girl like her was an affront. She'd got marvellous legs, you know, and I reckon that she felt that an injury and its dressing were...well, you know..."

"I think I understand," said Masters. "It would affect her as if some raving beauty like the Venus de Milo had grown a wart on the end of her nose."

"You've got it. It offended the pride she took in her person. Like I said, psychological. She got a bit petty with me. She wanted to leave the bandage off on Saturday, but I wasn't having any." He heaved himself to his feet. "This is usually the time I have coffee. I've prepared everything against your coming. Would you mind if...?"

"Go ahead, lad," said Green. "I'm pretty clammed myself."

"It will be plastic coffee this time, no waiting for it to brew," said Collier as he went through the door.

Tip looked across at Masters. "I bet she gave him a time of it, Chief."

"When he insisted on the dressing, you mean?"

"Yes. An uncooperative patient of any sort is a nuisance as anybody will tell you, but a temperamental girl

100

like her, when her pride was hurt more than her body, could have been pretty petulant. And I reckon she was. I imagine Collier had his hands full on Saturday morning, even though he's making very little of it."

"Are you suggesting I should question him a little more closely about the bit you imagine he glossed over?"

"I raised the point, Chief, just in case it had escaped you and there was, in fact, a blazing row here on Saturday."

"Ah! That had not occurred to me, I must admit."

"But it's valid," grunted Green.

"Of course."

"A row which dragged on all day and spilled over into Sunday, perhaps," said Green.

"Then what?" demanded Berger.

"One thing at a time, lad," counselled Green. "Let's move forward cautiously."

"But something could have happened between them that resulted in..."

"Careful," said Tip quietly and got to her feet to go to the door. She opened it just as Collier, who was carrying a tray, was about to tap it with his foot to ask for admission. He thanked Tip and set the tray down on the sofa table.

"Help yourselves to biscuits," he said. "I've only got ginger-nuts left. Carla didn't care for them, but I've always kept a stock in because somewhere I once read they are the most sustaining of nibbles if you're hiking or climbing, and sometimes stage rehearsals and the like are akin to scaling the Matterhorn."

Green helped himself to a couple. "Nice and crisp," he said, breaking one noisily in his teeth.

Masters was keen to get back to business.

"You said you insisted on Miss Sanders wearing her bandage on Saturday. Can we go on from there, please?"

"Can we all call her Carla, do you think? It is so much easier, and friendlier than the Miss Sanders bit."

"If that is what you would like."

"Yes, please. But to get back to the script... the quack

had laid down the law about the bandage, so I wasn't acting on my own opinion. He'd said that if Carla wanted to be back on stage by Monday she had to wear a bandage, not only to protect the wound but to support the injured ankle and to restrict the foot movement. He'd even taught me how to put it on—doing figure-of-eight turns round the instep and up the ankle."

"Basic first-aid bandaging," said Berger. "We have to do it in recruit training."

"I suppose so, but I was never a Boy Scout."

"So you did the bandaging on Saturday morning?" asked Masters.

"Yes. She wouldn't let me fasten it with a safety pin. Had to use a lump of sticky tape. She wanted to wear tights, you see, and she thought she'd better have white ones to camouflage the bandage. I suggested slacks but the perverse little madam insisted on tights."

Masters caught a quick glance directed at him from Tip as they heard this and the accompanying hint of frustration in Collier's tone. Meanwhile, the actor had taken up his cup of coffee and was taking a sip or two. As he put the cup down again, he continued: "Of course, all the white tights she had were laddered, so we had to go out shopping for more. She got a couple of pairs so that she'd have a new pair for the party that night."

"Excuse me, Mr. Collier," interrupted Tip. "Were you quite happy at the thought of Carla going out to the party on Saturday evening?"

"Not in the least."

"So you suggested she shouldn't go?"

"No. I think I explained to you that Carla regarded this particular invitation as a bit of a must, but I did say to her that I would have been happier if the venue had been a little nearer home. I had to lay on the friendly neighbourhood mini-cab driver to take her."

"And to bring her back, presumably."

"I wanted to arrange for him to go back for her at a stated time, not too late, say eleven o'clock, but she wouldn't have that. She said she was certain to be able to get a lift back into town. Which she was, of course."

"Thank you."

He turned back to Masters. "The trouble over the tights was worth it. By the time she got them on and selected the right gear and shoes you'd have had to look hard to see she was bandaged. But of course it wouldn't do. You've probably guessed Carla was so proud of her legs that she didn't like wearing slacks. But she reckoned with the bandage on, after all the tarradiddle over the tights, that she was still less than perfection. So in the end, after all, she wore a trouser suit for the damned party."

"What had you to say to that, lad?" asked Green.

Collier shrugged. "After living with Carla for eighteen months or so, I'd got used to little changes of mind like that. So I said nothing. It kept her so busy for most of the day that she seemed to forget the injury, as such. It was the unsightliness we were concentrating on. But she ate up at lunchtime and she had a bit of something with me before I went to the theatre. She was being picked up at seven, because Carlyle's house is about an hour away by car.

"I rushed back from the theatre so that I should be here when she got back or if she wanted picking up somewhere. But to my amazement the lights were on when I got here and I found her in bed. And I must say that was a surprise. I hadn't expected her to come home so early."

"Why had she done so?" asked Masters. "Was she ill?"

Collier grimaced and picked up his cup again. He took a gulp of the, by now, half-cold coffee. "No." He put the cup down and looked across at Masters. "She fell into the swimming pool. I must confess to you that sometimes—particularly at parties—Carla used to take a bit on board. That's one reason why I wouldn't let her drive herself to Carlyle's house—besides the busted ankle, of course. So I suppose she had a few drinks and

103

got the staggers as well as having a groggy ankle. Anyhow, she went in. They fished her out, gave her some dry clothes and some Samaritan drove her home."

"Is that all you know about the incident?"

"That's it. As I said, she was in bed when I got home. There she was, well before midnight, all tucked up, hair dried, the lot."

"Did you speak to her?"

"Yes. She told me about going into the pool, and there was a large plastic bag with her wet clothes in it sitting in the middle of the bedroom floor."

"Did she explain how she came to be in the water?"

"Not exactly, but I could gather what happened. Five or six of them in a group beside the pool. All fairly well tanked up, I imagine, holding glasses and laughing, probably moving a bit unsteadily. One of them was bound to go in, I'd have thought. It just happened to be Carla."

"She didn't claim she was pushed?"

"She made no deliberate accusation. I imagine in a group like that there was bound to be a nudge."

"Arms round each others' necks, I suppose," grunted Green, "and staggering about. Probably got too near the edge and in she went."

"I think that must have been it," agreed Collier.

Masters asked quietly: "Was Carla coherent when she spoke to you?"

"Completely. No sign of alcoholic haze. I imagine the ducking had sobered her up quite a bit, and then there was the drive home, of course, to complete the process."

"That sounds reasonable enough, but was she—apart from being completely sober—in apparent good health?"

"As far as I could tell she was. Mark you, I wasn't looking for anything wrong. What I mean is, I asked about the ankle. She said she had kept the bandage on, even though it had got a bit tight when it got wet, because she hadn't wanted all the bother of redoing it. That's if she'd been in a fit state to do it for herself."

"She should have had it off," grunted Green. "When the bandage tightened it would have been bad for her circulation."

"I told her that, but she said it loosened again when it dried, so I didn't take it off at that hour of the night to put a new dressing on. Carla wouldn't have let me anyway. She was nicely snuggled down after the events of the evening and she'd not have taken kindly to being disturbed for that."

"I know the feeling," said Berger to Collier. "We sometimes get hoicked out of bed like that in the force, and I can't think of much worse. I know it always annoys me."

Masters asked, "If Carla was perfectly all right at midnight on Saturday, when did she first complain of feeling ill?"

"On Sunday morning at about, oh, I suppose eight o'clock, when I got up to make coffee. She said she thought she'd got flu."

"So what action did you take?"

"At first? I gave her a cup of hot lemon and a couple of paracetamol tablets. I didn't think it could be flu."

"Why not?"

"The weather was gorgeous, and flu doesn't seem to fit in with heat waves, somehow. I guessed at a cold brought on by falling into the swimming pool. I've heard of summer colds. They're quite common, I believe. But not summer flu."

"I think you made a reasonable assumption," said Masters. "And took the right action in giving her a hot drink and a couple of paracetamol. There's very little else you could have done at that stage."

"When did she dry her hair?" asked Green. "At the party when she changed into dry clothes? Or did she wait until she got home?"

"I asked her that. She said she had borrowed a hair drier from Mrs. Carlyle, but I reckoned she hadn't dried her hair all that well. Carla had a lot of very fine hair which took a devil of a lot of drying, and in her state,

105

having had a drink or two and then a ducking, to say nothing of her injury, I thought she hadn't done it too well and had travelled home with it half damp."

"You said all this to her?" asked Masters.

"While she had her hot lemon stuff. But she wouldn't agree." Collier looked round at the four attentive faces of his audience. "She insisted it was flu because she felt rotten in herself. She said that didn't happen with a cold. Feeble, was how she said she was feeling. I thought, to be honest, she was feeling glum because she'd made a bit of a fool of herself at Carlyle's party and as a result had developed a cold which might keep her out of her show for even longer than the damaged leg, and that she was, consequently, dramatising a bit."

"How soon did you change your mind, Mr. Collier?"

"Quite soon. Carla refused all food, so after spending ten minutes or so trying to persuade her to have something I went into the kitchen to get myself a bit of breakfast and to brew the coffee I'd intended to make but had substituted for her hot lemon. I thought she might like a cup of coffee, but I didn't want to rush her, so I sat in the kitchen for . . . oh, about half an hour, I suppose, looking through the Sunday paper. There was a write-up of her show in it, so I took it through, with the coffee, for her to read, and that was when I saw that she really and truly wasn't well. She was very flushed and her forehead was sweaty."

"Was that when you first called the doctor?"

"Yes. It wasn't much after half past nine when I rang. The quack was a bit put out, but I insisted he should come. He arrived about ten o'clock."

"And what was his diagnosis?"

"Flu. A heavy bout. He gave me a lot of instructions for looking after Carla and a prescription for one of those soluble analgesics."

"Then he left?"

"He had a word or two with me in here. Just to say that he reckoned the attack would be short-lived and I wasn't to worry about the sweating because flu is accompanied by marked sweating as well as headache, muscle pains, weakness and shivering. I remembered them as he reeled them off."

"Like learning a part, perhaps," suggested Tip.

Collier smiled at her and then turned back to Masters. "I accepted what he said, of course, and it accounted for Carla saying she felt feeble. But I did ask him about her show because I knew Carla would be busting a gut to get back."

"Did he give you a probable time for her return?"

"Not exactly. What he did say was that I hadn't to let her worry about *Barley* because she wouldn't be able to start work until her temperature had got back to normal for a couple of days and all weakness and dizziness had gone. He even suggested that the attack could be a blessing in disguise as it would give her ankle and leg time to heal completely before she took over her part again."

"You said the doctor gave you a prescription. Did you take it to some Sunday-opening chemist yourself?"

"No. I felt I ought to stay with Carla. I toyed with the idea of getting a nurse in, but you don't engage a nurse for flu, do you?"

Masters shook his head. "They would probably refuse to come for so trifling a reason as a common-or-garden febrile disease such as flu."

"Thanks," said Collier, feelingly. "I'm bloody glad to hear you say that because I've been wondering whether, if I had had a trained nurse here, she might have spotted something in Carla's condition . . . something that might have saved her."

"Forget it, son," growled Green, gruffly. "The medics didn't, and you were here most of the time."

"That's how I saw it." Collier ran his hand through his hair. "I knew I could be with her until I set out for the theatre on Monday night, and I reckoned that by that time she would be over the worst and if she wasn't I'd get one of our friends in to sit with her."

"Quite right," said Masters. "The doctor had told you

the attack would be short-lived and, after all, scores of thousands of people every year contract flu and get over it quite safely. But you were about to tell us how you got the prescription made up."

"You're interested in that prescription," said Collier shrewdly.

"Naturally. I'm trying to discover the reason why Miss Sanders developed the illness that killed her. Anything she took must be of interest to me."

"I suppose so," said Collier, wearily. "It was a simple matter, really. A few days earlier we'd asked two friends of ours, Rex and Annette Dent, in for a prelunch drink."

"On the Sunday?"

"When else?"

"Actors?"

"Yes. At a bit of a loose end at the moment, though. I rang Annette and explained the position to her. She immediately jumped to the conclusion that I wanted to put them off, but that was the last thing I wanted. I asked her if they could come round earlier than arranged so that they could collect the prescription from here, take it to the nearest chemist that was open and then bring the medicine back before we had our drinks."

"Mrs. Dent agreed?"

"Like a shot. She's a nice person. They both are. They were round here in no time, and Rex had even rung a police station to find out the nearest chemist that was open. They had to wait until eleven for it to open up, but they were first in the queue and they were back here very quickly, so I gave Carla her first dose before half-past."

"How was she then?"

"Not good. She was shivering and complaining of a headache. She also said her legs and thighs—I suppose she meant the muscles—were painful." Collier again ran his hand through his hair and looked round at them all as if completely bewildered. "It was exactly what the quack had told me to expect," he said wildly. "So I didn't worry. I was concerned about her, of course, but

I thought everything was just taking its natural course and going exactly according to plan. Annette Dent thought so, too, and she's the sort of woman who has nursed people through flu. She said Carla's condition was just like a heavy dose of flu would be."

Green looked across at Tip. "If you can find your way about the kitchen, love, make us another brew of coffee, there's a good lass. We could all use one."

As Tip collected the already used cups before going to the kitchen, Masters again addressed Collier. "You had been told by the doctor that Miss Sanders had influenza and a married woman who, as you said, had encountered flu on previous occasions and so was likely to recognise the symptoms, also supported the diagnosis. Why should you have believed otherwise? What could you have done?"

Collier spread his hands. It was the first really theatrical gesture he had made, and though it came as a surprise from a man who had shown himself to be down-to-earth in every way, it was nevertheless a convincing sign of resignation.

Masters continued. "When I asked what could you have done, I really meant what *more* could you have done, because I am presuming you sent for the doctor again?"

Collier nodded miserably. "Annette, Rex and I had our drinks. It wasn't exactly a rowdy party, with Carla lying ill next door, but we had a couple apiece and nattered a lot. I suppose it was getting on for one o'clock when we heard the noise from the bedroom. Annette jumped to her feet and said, 'Carla's being sick.' It was a retching noise we'd heard, but we weren't prepared for what we saw when we rushed into the bedroom."

"What did you see?"

"Carla had vomited, but her face and the bed cover were . . . well, not covered in blood, exactly, but heavily spattered."

"You mean," said Green, "that the lass had been coughing up blood?"

109

Collier shook his head. "That was my first thought, but it turned out to be a heavy nosebleed."

"Nosebleed?" echoed Green in surprise. "What had she been doing? Blowing it too hard? Or had she fetched herself a fourpenny one, somehow?"

"There was no sign that she'd hit herself, and she hadn't got a cold. Not enough to warrant hard blowing, anyhow. But I was pretty scared. The quack hadn't said she would vomit, let alone start to bleed, so I decided he'd got to come and see her again. While Annette cleaned Carla up, I got on to Denyer. I thought I might well be in for a bit of a battle with him, but when he heard about the vomiting and nosebleeding he whipped round here pretty smartish."

"What was his attitude when he did arrive?" asked Masters quietly.

Collier considered this question for a moment or two without answering. As his reply did not seem to be immediately forthcoming, Masters added: "You said he answered your call very quickly. That suggests that what you said to him caused him some concern. Would you say that concern was for himself, or for Miss Sanders?"

"I don't understand your question."

"Something you said on the phone caused him to react promptly instead of—as you say you had expected—his telling you that you were worrying too much and that a second visit from him, so soon after the first, was not necessary."

Collier nodded to show he had understood so far.

"Do you think Dr. Denyer hurried round here because he was concerned about Miss Sanders' condition, or because the signs and symptoms you described to him caused him to think that her illness was more severe than he had first imagined and that he felt there was a distinct possibility that his diagnosis of flu was incorrect? In other words, did he hurry round here to correct his own mistake?"

Collier scratched one ear, thoughtfully. "You expect

110

me to be able to separate out his emotions?"

"It would be helpful if you could try."

"Christmas bloody night! You don't want much, do you? Have you any idea of the state I was in at that time?"

"I can imagine your state, Mr. Collier. And I believe that at such a time a person like yourself would be very aware of what went on around you. You are a man trained—if I can put it this way—to be aware of and react to nuances and even to create impressions by slight inflections of the voice, small gestures, registration of emotions... the art of good acting, in fact. How did you react to Dr. Denyer's vocal inflections and so forth when he paid his second visit?"

"He was different, certainly," said Collier. "But whether I can put my finger on it... look, he did his stuff. He was a bit het up, but he was thoughtful, kindly and... oh, yes!"

"What?"

"I remember now. He said he wanted to take a blood sample."

"And did he?"

"Yes."

"Didn't you think that taking a blood sample was unusual in a bout of flu?"

"He explained it."

"Can you remember what he said?"

"I think so. More or less. He said that the local hospitals and all the doctors round about were cooperating because they were interested in the... is there a word epidemiology?"

Masters nodded.

"They were interested in the epidemiology of flu in the district. Were studying it, in fact. To get the true information he wanted to take a blood sample so that the lab could categorise the particular virus."

"But he hadn't taken a sample when he first diagnosed flu?"

"Now you come to mention it, he hadn't, and that

111

sounds bloody funny to me. He had a long spiel about flu in summer not being unknown, but that severe cases were so comparatively rare that if he took the blood for testing it would be valuable and he might even get some useful hints on the best medication for Carla."

Tip had come into the room with a tray of cups of coffee. She handed the first to Collier. As Masters accepted his, he said: "Thank you, Mr. Collier. We now know how and why a sample of Miss Sanders' blood found its way to the path lab. Did the doctor change the treatment at that time?"

"He gave her an injection of penicillin."

"Did he say why?"

"I seem to remember he murmured something about it being some sort of safety measure in case there should be meningitis."

"And that was everything?"

Collier nodded and sipped his coffee. Masters looked across at Green, inviting his colleague to put any questions he might have, but Green shrugged to indicate there was nothing he wished to ask.

Masters frowned in thought for a moment or two.

"Did the doctor come again on the Sunday?"

"At about eight o'clock in the evening as near as I can remember. Yes. That would be it. Annette Dent had offered to stay to help look after Carla overnight. She'd made the offer after we'd had a cup of tea about half-past four." He thought for a moment or two. "Yes. That was it. Annette had spent the afternoon putting the dirty bed linen through the washing machine and generally tidying up Carla's wet clothes from the night before. It was teatime before she finished. When we sat down she said she and Rex would stay the night. So, after tea, she went to make up the spare room bed for herself and Rex. I was to kip on the sofa in here. Annette sent Rex back to their flat to collect washing gear and night-clothes and so on, while I got a meal together. Rex had got back and we were just about to eat, at eight as near as dammit, when Denyer came to see Carla. I reckon

112

he was a bit concerned about her, still. At any rate he gave her another big jab of penicillin. After he had gone, we left Carla, who seemed to be quite settled."

"You didn't give her food."

"No. She was too snoozy to rouse for something I knew she wouldn't want. And all remained quiet while we had supper. After that we talked a bit. There was no sound from Carla, but Annette and I looked in several times. It was about midnight when she began to get a bit restless. I heard her from here and went in. Annette must have been listening out for her, because she joined me. We stayed with Carla, just watching her, except that Annette sponged her face from time to time. At about half past two there was a flurry..."

"Flurry?" queried Masters.

"Carla got more restless and started to moan. A sort of general movement of distress, if you like."

"I understand. Please go on."

"I said I would call Denyer, and Annette agreed with me."

"Immediately you noticed the change?"

"No...o. I think we thought it was just a phase which would pass. Probably quite quickly. But when it didn't stop, after about a quarter of an hour, I suppose, I got on to Denyer. He took no more than twenty minutes to get here, but during that time Carla went quiet. Completely quiet, and by the time Denyer got here she was dead."

"You and Mrs. Dent knew that? Recognised she was dead before Denyer arrived?"

"Yes. I'd never seen death before. Certainly I'd never been present when it happened." He looked round in bewilderment. "It seemed so trivial, somehow. A girl as lovely and...well, full of life, as Carla, going out so almost unnoticed that I couldn't believe it. I didn't expect her to die, but had I done so I'd at least have expected some significant sign."

"It's not always like it is in your plays, lad," grunted Green. "And even if the trumpets sound on the other

113

side, it doesn't mean there's a fanfare laid on on this side."

Collier sat slumped on his camel saddle. "I know that now," he said quietly.

"What was Denyer's reaction?" asked Masters.

Collier looked up. "I got the impression he wasn't all that surprised, but he made a bit of a fuss. Saying he couldn't write a death certificate and how he must warn the Coroner. He told Annette and me that we shouldn't touch anything. So we turned out the light, locked the door and came in here. Denyer went on his way, Rex gave us a stiff whisky, then he and Annette went back to their bedroom. I stayed here. We were all pretty dazed."

"The Coroner actually came here, I understand."

"Pretty early. About half past eight, I think, then an ambulance came for Carla and a policeman—Coroner's Officer, would it be?—came and looked round. He didn't say anything except that there'd be an inquest."

Masters sat silent for a moment or two and then got to his feet. "Thank you, Mr. Collier. I think we should leave it there for today."

"You mean you'll be coming back? I can't think of anything else I can tell you."

"We shall return only if there are any specific points we should like to clear up with you. We shall talk to Mr. and Mrs. Dent, of course, so if you would give Sergeant Tippen their address..."

"Checking up on me, are you?"

"Certainly. Or rather, confirming their part in this sad business."

Collier, standing small beside Masters, smiled despairingly. "It's all going to last a long time, isn't it?"

"I hope we shall clear it up as quickly as possible, but I know what you mean. At the moment it is a wearying experience for you, and I've no doubt the memories will linger for some time." Masters moved towards the door.

"Before you go, Chief Superintendent..."

"Yes, Mr. Collier?"

"Do you really believe somebody killed Carla? Actually set out to kill her and succeeded, I mean?"

Green grunted: "I wondered when you were going to ask that, chum."

"I've held off because it seems too ridiculous even to think about. I still believe what I thought before you came to see me. That she caught some damned bug in the same way as anybody catches bugs. The trouble is that this one did for her because the quack didn't recognise it for what it was."

"You could well be right, lad."

"But don't blame the doctor too much," counselled Masters. "He'd probably never encountered the disease before, and the symptoms masked its true nature."

"In fact, sir," said Tip, "it is because the illness is so rare and, in this case, so virulent that we are investigating Carla's death. And I think you and your friends did all you could for her and acted splendidly."

"Acted?"

"Behaved, if you like. What I mean is, you should have no feeling of guilt about her death."

"You were a bit premature, weren't you, petal?" asked Green, as Berger drove them towards the Yard. "Telling that chap he need have no guilty feelings about that bit of capurtle's death?"

Tip turned in the front seat to look at him. "I thought that was a tactically correct thing for me to say."

"Oh yeah? Go on, love, expand."

"As you keep on telling me I should, I thought."

"Good. What?"

"That we don't want to give Collier the idea Carla Sanders was murdered when we have no proof that she was. That, after telling him we would question him very closely, there was no good reason for letting him suppose we suspected him of criminal behaviour. That it was the humane thing to tell him not to feel guilty lest he had overlooked anything he could have done to save her life."

115

"Ah!"

"What's the significance of that grunt?"

"It wasn't a grunt, it was an exclamation with a splash after it."

"I know," said Berger. "I felt it on the back of my neck."

Green ignored him. "There's one big question young Collier is asking himself, sugar."

"What's that?"

"Whether he should have stopped his lady-love going to the party on the Saturday night."

Tip was indignant. "How could he have possibly done that? Carla Sanders was a person in her own right and free to come and go as she pleased. She wanted to go to the party and she went."

"That's jumping to conclusions, love."

"It's what?"

"Hasn't it occurred to you, honeybun, that Sanders might not have wanted to go, especially as the party was so far away? That she might have been feeling groggy and wanted to cry off?"

"But that's preposterous. She was a free agent and if she'd wanted to cry off she would have done."

Green grinned. "Even in the face of her Mr. Collier dinning it into her that she couldn't afford not to go? That she must on no account disappoint the important Mr. Carlyle? That her career depended on her staying in the public eye, particularly the eye of a chap who had grown so important in the business of backing plays that he could make a career by keeping an actor in mind, or break it by neglect?"

Tip stared at him for a moment. "You mean you disbelieve Collier's account?"

"Not disbelieve, petal. But we have to look for possible different interpretations. You said Sanders would go to the party of her own free will. All I'm saying is that, if she was havering, a few well-chosen words of encouragement from her bedmate could have swayed the balance. And as it seems fairly clear that Saturday evening was the crucial time in this little guessing game we must ask ourselves whether the young lady jumped at going to the party or was pushed into going there."

"I see your point," agreed Tip. "I never seem to get things right, do I?"

Green shrugged. "None of us does that, love. If *you* did, the rest of us would be redundant by now. In fact, I'd say you were doing pretty well."

"I think so, too," said Masters. "You are still a little short on scepticism, Tip. The DCI has given you another good lesson. What do you think the corollary to it is?"

"To be sceptical of what he's just said, Chief."

"Go on."

"If Carla Sanders was persuaded to go to the party, even though she may not have been all that keen, was it Collier who persuaded her? Couldn't it have been somebody else? A new boyfriend she'd got her eye on? Not necessarily one to replace Howard Collier, but one to have a bit of extra fun with. Was it Carlyle who rang her, unbeknown to Collier, and gave her a story about real troupers always appearing, so he'd expect her to be there no matter what? Or a woman perhaps? One who was jealous for some reason? For having a man pinched from her, or a coveted role, perhaps?"

Masters smiled. "You'll do, Tip. Keep it up and the DCI won't be able to try to teach you anything."

"That'll be the day," said Berger, turning the big Rover in at the Yard gates.

"Nearly one o'clock," said Masters as they all followed him into his office. "I think we'll call a halt until Monday morning."

Berger was astounded. "In the middle of a case, Chief? A free weekend? Or half a weekend at any rate. Not that I'm complaining, but I've never known you let up before."

"We haven't a case," growled Green. "We're investigating to see if there is one. And you won't get the weekend off. You'll have to go to that theatre to ask about the rats in their flies or wherever it is they keep them."

Tip exploded with mirth. Berger turned to Masters. "The questions at the theatre will not take long, Chief. Do you want me to ring you with the answers?"

"Just a moment." Masters picked up the phone and pressed the single button that would put him through direct to his own home. Wanda answered. There followed a conversation which the other three tried not to listen to by starting an inconsequential conversation among themselves. Even had they not done so they would have heard little except a few laconic replies from Masters. When he put the handset down he turned to them.

"We'll stop now, as I said. Berger, you can ring me at home this afternoon if you think it's necessary. But not tomorrow." He turned to Green. "Wanda has earmarked tomorrow for taking me down into Kent, Bill. If the weather is like this she proposes to picnic near a spot called Housmans."

"Housmans?" said Berger. "I've never heard of it. Is it some little village, Chief?"

"Just a picnic spot, lad," grunted Green.

"The point is, Bill, Wanda wondered whether you and Doris would like to join us. If so, would you like her to pack a sandwich or would Doris provide?"

"If young Michael's going to be there..."

"Which he will be, of course."

"Then wild horses wouldn't stop Doris joining you, and if Doris is there, I'll have to be, I suppose."

"Good. I'll come and pick you up at ten, unless..." He looked round at the two sergeants. "Unless you two would like to join us?"

"I don't know, Chief," began Berger.

Tip looked from face to face until her gaze finally rested on Green. "Would one of your lessons suggest the advisability or otherwise of accepting such an invitation?"

"The advisability," said Green with a straight face.

"Close to Housmans, the Chief said."

"That's right."

"And Housmans is a picnic spot."

"Yes."

"Not Mr. Hugh Carlyle's residence by any chance?"

"No."

"But in the vicinity of it."

"Very adjacent as the cricket commentators say, but don't take that as gospel because I don't know where Carlyle lives, but knowing His Nibs and his devious mind, a trip to Kent at this juncture must be relevant, particularly when he worms his way round to inviting the three of us to join him."

"Good thinking, that man," said Berger. He looked across at Tip. "What do you reckon? Beer and sandwiches at Housmans tomorrow?"

Tip nodded. "Mrs. Masters gets some lovely ideas. Let's take advantage of her kind offer, then you and I can pick up the DCI and Mrs. Green and join the Chief at his house."

"Sarcasm doesn't suit you, sugar," said Green. "I'll be ready from half past nine onwards."

5

After the sergeants had left them, Green asked: "How much are we going to tell those two, George?"

"Everything, Bill. I don't want them playing guessing games and coming to the wrong conclusions. Besides, I trust them. My belief is that they'd support the two of us through thick and thin."

"You don't think it will come to that, do you?"

"At the moment, I don't. We'll see what tomorrow gives us, if anything, and then we can decide whether I should go to Anderson on Monday."

"That's what I'd have advised," said Green, getting to his feet. "Now I think I'll be off, George. Doris always cooks sausages for Saturday lunch and I feel I could do a lot of damage to four or five of them."

"We'll see you tomorrow then, Bill. Love to Doris. Tell her I'd like her to travel in our car with Wanda and Michael. We others will use the Yard car so that we can brief the sergeants as we go."

"Good idea. See you, George."

So it was with things arranged in this way that the two cars left the little house behind the Westminster Hospital in the comparatively light traffic of Sunday morning. Wanda led the way in the Jaguar as she was the only one who knew exactly where Housmans was.

Tip was driving the Rover. Almost as soon as they were clear of the narrow little road in which the Masters' lived, the DCS began his briefing, and with a little help from Green, put the two sergeants fully in the picture.

"I can see what you are worried about, Chief," said

Berger, who had listened attentively to every word. "Whiffs of scandal and all that, but there are several things I think you ought to remember. Apart from the fact that there is no hint of corruption, that is."

"Let's have it then, lad," grunted Green, who, though never happy when travelling in a motor car, nevertheless found this pleasant Sunday morning run on roads free of lorries less unsettling than usual.

"First, as the Chief said, we don't know that we have a crime on our hands. Second, as far as we know there is no known criminal involved or even anybody in whom the Yard is or has been interested. Third, the Chief has completed no deal over this new house, and is unlikely to before anything that is going to break does so. Fourth, and I think this is as important as any of the others, the Chief has told us three about his negotiations. How can you be accused of corruption if you have given every last detail of your business to three police officers of the rank and standing of Scotland Yard detectives? We don't benefit in any way, so we can't be said to be a party to any jiggery pokery. That means nobody, not even the AC (Crime), can accuse the Chief of . . . well, whatever it is you two think he might try to clobber him for."

"Good arguments, all of them, lad," said Green. "In return for that compliment you can give me one of your fags." As Berger turned to offer the packet, Green continued: "I particularly like that bit about giving every detail of the transaction to three people of CID rank and standing. It sounded good."

"Because it was right," said Tip.

"You keep your attention on the road, lass, and keep your piping treble for more pertinent remarks than that," retorted Green.

"Very good, sir," replied Tip, sweetly, staring straight ahead. "As my small pipe best fits my little note, perhaps I shouldn't say what I have in mind."

"Now what are you on about?" demanded Berger.

"I was merely going to remark that the Chief should let me do the report today. If I were to type it all out

121

and date it with today's date and sign it and put it in the file there would be proof that our concern was recognised and discussed before anything untoward could happen."

"Better still," said Green, "date it as of last Friday, which was when His Nibs first broached the subject, and I'll sign it as my report for the file."

"Very good, sir."

"And cut out all that sort of rubbish," growled Green, "or I'll prove the point that a little WPS best fits a little shrine."

"Chief," wailed Berger, "what are these two on about?"

"Surely you know," replied Masters. "A little meat best fits a little belly."

"I didn't," confessed Berger, "but one thing I am sure of, and that is that what you've just said doesn't apply to the DCI."

"How come, lad?"

"With your appetite it would have to be a gargantuan meal."

"For that, son, you can buy me my first drink."

"We're going on a picnic, remember, not a pub crawl."

Masters intervened. "Keep a sharp lookout along here, Tip. The road winds and I think my wife will be pulling up any time now."

"Nearly there, are we?" asked Green.

"Very close. What do you think of the area?"

"Couldn't be beaten anywhere," said Green, "though, come to think of it, you could say that about so many places in this country that you're spoilt for choice when you try to select a lovely spot to live."

"The Jag's pulling in a couple of hundred yards ahead," said Berger quietly to Tip.

"The gate to Housmans," said Wanda as the Rover drew in and they all descended. "There's the house, William. What do you think of it?"

"At first glance," said Green with a grin, "I'd say it had a funny-shaped roof."

Wanda turned to her husband. "Darling? What do you think of it? This is your first sight."

Masters smiled. "I'm delighted. Can we go in?"

"Of course. Into the garden only at the moment, because I have to fetch the key from Margot. You can run your car in and look round the outside for a while. I shall only be gone about twenty minutes."

As Wanda was about to drive off, Masters said to her: "Would you ask Hugh and Margot if I could have a word with them after lunch?"

"When we take the key back?"

"That would suit me very well."

"You want to talk about buying the house?"

"If we decide on it definitely, yes. But just mention that I have some other business in mind, too."

"What about?"

"Sorry, I was forgetting I hadn't told you. The powers-that-be are a little worried about where Carla Sanders picked up the bug that killed her. We've been asked to help trace the source. As she was at Hugh's party on the Saturday before she died I want to ask if she went frolicking in any barns or hayricks."

"That's highly likely, I'd have said. Right, darling. There's coffee in the Thermos flasks. Help yourselves."

"Thank you."

Green, waiting a few paces away during this conversation, came up to Masters as the Jag drew away. "My missus is in raptures, George. Asking all manner of questions about the house. I know nothing about them, so can you enlighten her?"

Masters smiled. "As you might guess, Bill, as soon as the idea that we might move to Housmans was mooted, Wanda went out to the library and she even bought a book on oast-houses. I've been through it, so I know just about enough to give you an idiot's guide."

"Salient points only?"

"Some of them, at least. I'll spout while we have coffee, if you like."

The car had been drawn into the drive and they were

all congregated about it as Doris and Tip prepared the coffee and a beaker of diluted orange juice for Michael.

"Just one technical word before we go any further," started Masters, as he accepted his coffee. "Plenum. The heart of an oast-house is the plenum chamber."

"Plenum?" queried Tip. "Something to do with full, Chief?"

"Derived from that. I had to look it up myself. A plenum chamber in this sense is actually a cavity or roomfull of matter or material through which air can be forced."

"Ah!" said Berger. "Hot air through piles of hops to dry them out."

"In a nutshell, yes. That is the only *raison d'être* of an oast-house."

"Three-storied buildings just for that?" asked Doris. "Surely there was more to it than that."

"A little, but not much. Most people, I suppose, imagine oast-houses with roundels, that is, the round tower at one end with the conical roof and a cowl on top."

"I must say that is what I was expecting to see, George. But you've got a square one," said Doris.

"I know. It seems a pity in some respects, because the round kilns look so very picturesque, but Wanda tells me that as an oast-householder I should be pleased because the rectangular ones are stronger. They have quoins at the corners for strength whereas you can't have strengthened corners in a circle."

"Good thinking," grunted Green.

"Anyhow," continued Masters, "on the ground floor of the kiln were the hearths for the fires. Literally, just hearths with all manner of simple brick constructions above them, perforated at the top to direct the hot air upwards into the plenum chamber. It was kept in there by walls sloping from the top of the kilns out to the side wall. So they got an enormous funnel of hot air, and across the top of it they had the floor of the drying chamber, only it wasn't a true floor. Just well-spaced slats to let the air through. On these slats they used to lay a covering like a blanket—an open-weave cloth, at any rate—and onto this cloth they tumbled a good thick layer of fresh hops for drying. The hot air rose through the hops and carried the moisture off up the conical roof and out through the cowl."

"The cowl moved, I suppose?"

"Yes. About a third of it was open to allow the reek to escape."

"It was a nasty smell, was it?" asked Doris.

"I'll bet," said her husband. "If you've ever been near a genuine brewery, like they used to be in the old days, the pong of hops was pretty foul at that stage in the process when they were doing whatever it is they did with hops."

"Reek is the proper term," said Masters. "I suppose it started as the name for the smell of drying hops and then passed into the language to describe any similar odour. I know Wanda says my jackets reek of smoke." He set down his cup on the grass. "The cowl was on a long central spindle and could be turned by hand until the opening was downwind so that the fumes weren't driven back in. But the later ones had flyboards—like weather vanes—that automatically kept the cowl opening away from the wind."

"That thing with the cut-out of a horse on it up there?" asked Doris, pointing upwards.

"That's right. The Horse of Kent."

"I'd like a round one," said Michael, handing his drinking mug back to Doris. "Thank you. No more," he said.

"A round what, darling?"

"House with a horse on top."

"Sorry, old son," said his father. "If we have this house we'll have to have the square tower."

"Why?"

"Because that is how it is built."

"Oh! I saw a round one in the motor car."

"Yes. You passed lots like that on the way here."

"Why can't we have one of those?"

"Because other people are living in them."

Michael seemed to accept this and turned to Green. "Mr. William," he said, "do you like round ones?"

"I do, son, but you can't always have the one you like best."

"Why not?"

"Because," said Green, breaking into a ditty with a reasonably well known tune, and thus recognisable even when he was singing it:

> "There's round 'uns and square 'uns,
> There's square 'uns and round 'uns,
> But you can't put your muck in our dust tin,
> Our dust tins's full."

"Bill," exclaimed Doris, scandalised. "The things you teach that child. You should be ashamed of yourself. I'm horrified."

"Besides," said Berger, trying to keep the mirth out of his voice, "why teach the boy that rubbish is put in tins when everybody knows it's bins."

"Not in this case," replied Green airily. "Have you ever seen a square dustbin?"

"No, but..."

"There you are, then. One has to be strictly accurate and factual with the young."

"Exactly," said Masters drily, looking towards the gate as he did so. "Ah, here's Wanda with the key."

"Now the dog will be able to see the rabbit," said Green, heaving himself to his feet.

"Where is the rabbit, Mr. William?"

"Sorry, son, there isn't one. I was just hoping there was. It looks like rabbity country, you see. The sort where they like to live and..."

"Hush," said Tip, urgently, and took Michael by the arm. "Across there, look. On that sort of little grass path." She pointed his arm in the right direction.

"I'll be damned," said Green quietly.

The rabbit lolloped unconcernedly away.

"There *was* a rabbit, Mr. William," said Michael accusingly.

"Come along, everybody," said Wanda, handing a bunch of keys to Masters. "Opening-up time."

The door was of heavy vertical planks, painted white, with large wrought-iron T-hinges, the curlicues of which reached almost across its width.

"This leads into the barn part," said Tip.

"We can see that, love. The whole place is like a barn shoved end on to a church tower with a comic roof. I wonder if they've got any bells in there."

"Barn?" demanded his wife. "Church tower?"

"Well, you must admit, love, those windows look a bit ecclesiastical."

"They are lovely," said Doris, "with stone surrounds and shutters everywhere."

"Bogus," snorted Green, "else why aren't they closed over the glass?"

Wanda, who had led the way in, turned to speak to them all. "I'm not going to give you a lecture, but this hall was originally part of the stowage space for the big bags of dried and pressed hops. To the left is the kiln room. The hearths have been removed, of course, but the floor is still of brick. That will be our sitting room. To your right is the space where the great hop press operated. That will be the dining room. That's basically all the ground floor except for kitchen and pantry and things like that behind here."

"She means loos," whispered Green to his wife.

Wanda continued, "When you go up the stairs at the back of the hall you'll see there is a funny sort of arrangement of floors and doors. That's because the barn side of the house has three floors, where the kiln has only two, though the latter is the higher. So, on your right, and first, you will find two bedrooms and a bathroom built in what was once the area for cooling the dried hops and the top of the great press. To your left and half a floor up, as it were, is another bedroom which occupies what was the drying floor. There's been a ceiling put in there halfway up the cone. Then, another half floor up on the barn side you will find three smaller bedrooms, and they are in the space where the green hops were taken in by the hoist you'll still see sticking out above the window—which used to be a loading door—at that end." She looked round. "That's everything I think I need to say for you to understand the layout."

"Thanks, love," said Green. "I think we've got the picture."

"I don't think I have," wailed Doris.

"I'll draw it for you," said her husband. "Have you got an old envelope in your bag?"

As the others went off to explore, Green drew a rough outline sketch for his wife. "It's a simple, early production line, love. Henry Ford didn't invent it. Blokes who worked in places like this did. Look. The bags of newly picked hops were brought by horse and cart to the end of the barn where the gantry is. They were hauled up onto the top floor and pulled towards the kiln. There they were tumbled through the top door onto the blanket they were to be dried on. The fires were lit down below. The hops dried out. The blanket they were on was rolled up and pulled out by the lower door onto the middle floor to cool. From that heap, on the same floor, they were put into the press shaft which ran down to the bottom floor where more big bags were hooked on. The cool hops were pressed into the bag which was waiting for them. When full, the bags were stored just about here where we're standing. Got it?"

"I think so."

"You will as we go round. Keep the drawing and I'll explain each bit."

"It's in tidy nick, George," said Green as they sat down to the picnic lunch. "Inside walling good, floors sound, windows not rotted or anything like that."

"I thought the stairs weren't very straightforward,"

said Doris. "Not for Michael. All little turns and half steps."

"Not half steps, love. Half risers."

"Well, yes, but you know what I mean. They're not regular."

"That's part of the charm," said Wanda.

"Oh, I know that, and I think it's lovely. I was just thinking of the little ones."

"I think a judicious use of stairway gates will cut out any danger on that score," said Masters.

"Didn't you tell us the ground floor room in the kiln was brick, Chief?" asked Tip.

"So I did. I thought it was. Now Wanda tells me the brick floor is still there, covered by about an inch of pitch and then floored on top of that, so it should be dry and warm."

"Especially with that nice big fireplace they've put in. And I like the way the chimney has been hidden. And the ceiling in..."

The conversation went on and on until finally Masters said: "It's time we went to see Carlyle."

"All four of us, Chief?"

"Yes, please. I don't want to make too big a thing of this officially, but equally I don't want to give the impression that I'm only there for a cosy little chat and don't mean business."

"Understood, Chief," said Berger. "We wear our helmets but leave our truncheons behind."

"Quite."

As they got into the Yard car, Wanda said, "We others will see you in about an hour. I'll bring the key back then."

"Fair enough, sweetheart."

"Then we can all drive home and have tea together. I've made one of my special Chantilly cakes for William."

"Not one with all green and red bits in and bags of nuts?" asked Green.

"Yes."

"Let's get this interview over, George. My mouth's already watering."

"Pig," said his wife.

"And herringbone noggins to you, too."

"What did he mean by that?" demanded Doris as the car drew away.

"Noggins are the areas of brickwork between the oak posts in the building. Perhaps you noticed they were laid in a herringbone fashion," explained Wanda.

"Hugh, let me introduce my immediate colleagues. DCI Bill Green and Detective Sergeants Berger and Irene Tippen."

"How d'you do," said Carlyle. "As you can see, it's a bit difficult for me to rise to meet you." He turned to the girl who had shown the quartet into the sitting room. "Thank you, Freda. Would you tell Mrs. Carlyle we'd like tea for five in about an hour?"

"Yes, sir. She's out working in the garden."

"Splendid." As the girl left, Carlyle waved them to seats. "Now, George, what's all this about? I understand it is sort of semiofficial."

"I'd like you to regard it that way, Hugh, but the investigation we are on is totally official."

"Something to do with Carla Sanders, Margot tells me."

"Her death, certainly."

"I was extremely sorry to hear about that. She was here, you know, at the party you couldn't come to, only a few days before she died. But I hadn't heard that there was any foul play suspected. Connected with her death, I mean. The newspapers suggested it was some galloping disease she contracted."

"It was, Hugh. But the nature of the disease and its virulence suggested to the pathologists that it had been cultured."

"For felonious purposes?"

Masters nodded. "Probably."

"And then fed to Sanders?" Carlyle guffawed. "Nonsense, old boy. I just don't believe it."

"In that case, sir," said Tip, "could you suggest how and where she might have picked up such a very dangerous bug?"

"Which bug was it?" asked Carlyle.

"*Icterohaemorrhagiae,*" replied Tip, pronouncing the name of the sero group with great care, as though she had been practising it, syllable by syllable, in front of her dressing table mirror.

Carlyle laughed again. "How do you spell that mouthful?"

"If you would really like to know, sir, I could print it out for you."

"I'll bet you could. But no, thank you. The pronunciation was enough for me." He became serious. "When did she get this disease, George?"

"That is what we are trying to establish."

"But can't the quacks tell you?"

"Not precisely. You see, Hugh, when it starts to manifest itself in the human body, it masquerades as flu and, in some cases, I believe, as even less severe illnesses than that."

"Meaning that diagnosis is difficult?"

"Very difficult. And as the average practitioner is unlikely ever to meet the disease, when he's called to a patient exhibiting all the signs of flu he treats it as flu."

"Until it is too late, I suppose."

"In the virulent cases, yes. By the time Miss Sanders' doctor had begun to realise he was faced with something other than summer flu, and had taken a blood sample for the path lab to test, it was too late. The blood went off to the hospital, but path labs don't usually operate on Sunday afternoons, and when they are testing, they quite rightly take their tests in order—both those from inside the hospital and those from outside. Normally, any delay this causes doesn't matter so much that it becomes a case of life or death, but on the very, very rare occasions when something like this crops up, the system can fail the community."

"It oughtn't to," said Carlyle.

"It doesn't if the doctor presenting the blood for testing can be sure enough of himself and his diagnosis to take it into the lab himself and express his opinions and fears as to what it might be. But crying wolf over some fairly esoteric bug can't be to their liking, especially as, if they do guess correctly, it means they know enough about the disease to realise that in moderate cases the febrile stage lasts for about five days. So there would be no need for indecent haste in an already busy path lab. In Sanders' case this was cut to something less than forty-eight hours and—to quote the postmortem report—features of tubular necrosis appeared immediately thereafter."

"I can see why the GP was fooled. He treated for flu and then this second stage struck when he wasn't expecting it. Am I right?"

"Quite right, Hugh. We want to stop it happening again."

"But why you and not the DHSS?"

"The DHSS will cope with it when found."

"I see. They're not quite as good at running things to earth as you people?"

"Roughly right," grunted Green. "We also want to know there was nothing fishy about the way the girl got this Weil's disease."

"You mean why only she got it while nobody else in the country has been reported to have had it?"

"Seeing it's what might be called an epidemic disease, yes. Not that it is passed on like colds, flu, measles and the like, but bugs such as this one can't be isolated completely."

"I get your drift. They live and move and have their being, as the saying has it. So there must be at least a colony of them somewhere and, having at times heard how such things can multiply, there could well be millions of the little blighters sculling around somewhere at this moment."

Masters nodded. "Quite right. We are trying to locate

that particular somewhere."

Carlyle rested his hands on the arms of his wheel-chair. "But why come to me, George? If the plague spot were here, wouldn't we all have croaked by now? Seeing the species is so virulent?"

"You are probably right, Hugh. I hope you are, but we have to trace back over every minute of Sanders' time during the last few days of her life. As you know, she fell and damaged her leg in the theatre on the opening night of *Round the Barley*. That was the Thursday. She was inspected by a doctor at the theatre and, except for the abrasion, was given a completely clean bill of health. We are assuming that the doctor found no rise in temperature or any other indications that Sanders had flu or anything like it. I think the style and facility of her acting that night bears out our assumption that she was totally fit at that time. To support that belief there is not only the assertion of her flatmate, Howard Collier, that she was completely well at the time, but also the word of her own doctor, who gave her a thorough medical inspection on the Friday morning and found nothing wrong."

"So that's your starting point, is it? Friday morning?"

"Not quite. The two sergeants have been taking an interest in the theatre itself, lest she could have contracted something backstage on the opening night. They have been looking for all sorts of wildlife there, and although they've run rats and mice and such like to earth, so far they have all been found free of the feral leptospirae we are looking for."

"It's from animals that the bug is caught?"

Masters grimaced. "It thrives among the smaller mammals, I believe."

"But no luck at the theatre, you say."

"None whatsoever, but that was only one of the lines of investigation. I was never too sanguine about it, because if the leptospirae were rampant at the Victory some other person could be expected to have fallen foul of it by now. But as I've said, we are looking at everything. And that includes everywhere she's been since the time when she was declared fit by two doctors who examined her after her fall."

"So that's why you are here. She came to the party on the Saturday night."

"That's it. We'd like to know what went on, who was here and so on."

Carlyle laughed. "She and some of the other young-sters were getting a bit boisterous."

"Drink?" asked Green, sapiently.

"I should say that was the main cause, but you know what youngsters are like, sometimes. They can get merry on strong doses of their own company. Booze is only the catalyst. And when young men of twenty or not much more have a raver like Carla Sanders in their midst they are liable to go a bit goggle-eyed without the help of drink. When they have had one or two they start showing off. You know the score. They begin to talk too much and too loud and indulge in a little horseplay. Nothing serious. They poke fun at each other, lean on each others' shoulders in mock seriousness or despair, pull shirttails out and so on."

"Nothing more than that went on?" asked Masters.

"I watched it," growled Carlyle. "I was shunting my-self around in this tank pretty well all the time." He grinned. "As a host should," he added.

"But the Sanders girl went into the water as a result of these relatively mild high jinks?"

"Yes."

"But it is difficult to see why, if the boisterous element was not more rowdy than you say it was."

"I assure you, George, that girl's descent into the pool came as a big surprise not only to me, but to everyone present."

"Which suggests," growled Green, "that she was helped into the water."

"Helped, perhaps, but inadvertently in my opinion."

"She was on the edge of the pool?"

"On the surround, certainly. At its narrowest part. The

134

ramp for my chair goes down just there—from the French window of the room in which the drink was laid out. The young congregated just there, I presume, in order to be in close touch with the bar."

"Strategically placed?"

"That's about the size of it. And when Sanders arrived, Margot brought her out through that room, naturally, and introduced her to the first young people available. That was the gang near the ramp. They monopolised her, and as far as I know she never left them. The young chaps danced attendance on her, but I think the other girls soon wandered away in the face of the mammary competition."

"I get the scene," said Green. "A big twin endowment policy, a thin blouse and no bra."

"That about sums it up. It was a warm night, after all."

"I'll bet!"

Masters intervened. "Was it still daylight when she went in?"

"No, after dark. But we had fairy-lights round the pool and the spill of light from the bar room made the area where the incident took place as light as day. But it's funny you should mention lights. Earlier on the fairy-lights went out, and I never did discover why. Not that I asked, because I forgot all about it after they were put right, but I know I was surprised, because nothing else in the house was on that circuit."

"The fuse in the plug top, sir," said Berger. "Probably had a three amp instead of a thirteen in it."

"I suppose that was it," agreed Carlyle. "Anyhow, Tom Chesterton, a young man who came with my daughter to the party, fixed it in no time at all. I suppose that's why I forgot about it."

"And it was not during that period that Miss Sanders took to the water?"

"No, no. Her bath was much later. As I recall it, one of the women who does for us, Mrs. Hookham, was collecting dirty crockery and glasses. It was after supper you see."

"Hang on," grunted Green. "Supper was a moveable feast, was it? Smally eats round the pool? That sort of thing?"

"Exactly. There were two long tables laid out for the food—one at each end of the pool. But there were the usual bits of garden furniture about—tables, benches and chairs—and people just used them for depositing their empties instead of returning them to the tables. Freda, the girl you saw when you came in, is Mrs. H.'s assistant. She was washing up while Mrs. H. collected the debris. It was when Mrs. H. was trying to get past the group with Sanders in it . . ."

"The narrow bit?"

"Yes. She'd got a big, heavily laden tray and I think she must have thought it would be best to bring her load in up the ramp rather than go round the side of the house to the door of the kitchen quarters."

"That seems logical. To take the shorter way with a heavy load."

"Margot and I have great respect and affection for Mrs. H., and we know it's reciprocated. But she's a far from cultured woman, if I can put it that way."

"Meaning?"

"She wouldn't dream of asking those kids to get out of her way. She might demand it or alternatively elbow her way through without a word. A large heavily laden tray is quite a battering ram."

"You mean you think she pushed Sanders in?"

"No. But I think she nudged somebody pretty heavily, and the natural reaction to a good hefty shove is a stumble forward or a sudden turn to face the attack. Whatever happens, it becomes a dangerous manoeuvre in the circumstances we are talking about. A narrow path by a pool, a group of merry young people, an injudicious push with a tray, they all add up to disaster. At any rate, Sanders went in, probably because the sprained ankle made her unsure on her pins and the balance of her body was disturbed." He laughed aloud. "Sorry about that, but it just slipped in as, indeed, did the load on Mrs. H.'s tray. Whatever the movement in that group was, it decanted not only Carla Sanders in the pool, but quite a large number of mucky plates, glasses and so on."

"Close to Miss Sanders?" asked Tip quietly. "Did any of it hit her, sir? To break and cut her, I mean."

"No. She came out unharmed except for the odd strip of lettuce and glacé cherries dotted about her anatomy."

"Then what, Hugh?" asked Masters.

"Margot took charge. She whistled Sanders upstairs, shoved her under a shower, presented her with a hair drier, and then asked Rosemary to supply some dry clothes. The only thing Rosemary had which would fit Sanders' upperworks was what I believe is called a Sloppy Joe sweater. But she was clothed somehow and sent off home with a plastic bag full of wet togs."

At that moment the door of the sitting room opened and Margot came in. She was still dressed in her gardening outfit of rather washed-out blue slacks, a white open-necked shirt and linen sun hat. She had obviously kicked her shoes off at the back door, because she came in in her sock feet. As the men got to their feet she said: "Hello, George. Is this your famous team? I've been looking forward to meeting them."

As they sat down again, she with them, Margot said: "Freda will be bringing in the trolley in a moment, but please don't let me interrupt your discussion."

"I'd just told them how you togged out Carla Sanders, Mags. After her involuntary bath."

Masters asked, "How did Miss Sanders get home?"

"I sent her with two young people who were at the party. The boy drove, because he is a teetotaller and so had taken nothing stronger than orange juice. The girlie who went along—I'd thought it best to provide the young man with company for the drive back..."

"And protection on the way up," interjected Hugh with a laugh. "Even after a cold bath Sanders would

137

have been capable of mischief with a defenceless young man. Even a teetotaller."

Margot smiled. "There was a little of that sort of reasoning behind my arrangements. I was sorry for having to send the young couple off, but I must say they made excellent time. They were back here before the last of the youngsters and a couple of Hugh's heavier whisky-drinking friends had gone home."

Freda brought the tea trolley in and Margot began to pour, helped by Tip who handed round. Masters was anxious that teatime should not become a break. He said to Carlyle: "Apart from the results of the unintended dip, I take it that Sanders was completely well when she left here."

"Ask Margot. I said goodnight to her, but other than that had no part in the affair."

"She was perfectly well," said Margot from across the room. "Distinctly miffed at having to make so undignified an exit, of course, but otherwise completely fit as far as I could make out. I offered to rebandage her leg for her because I thought a wet dressing could be uncomfortable, but she refused to let me do it, and I didn't pursue the offer because I thought that the wet bandage on the ankle would not be too bad a thing. Cold compresses are good treatment, I believe."

Masters nodded. "And the rest of the household, since then? You've all been in good health?"

"Perfectly fit," said Carlyle. "There were six of us in the house at the time. Margot and myself; Rosemary and her friend, Tom Chesterton; and Mrs. H. and Freda. Freda sleeps in, Mrs. H. lives down in the village with her old man, but she's been in every day since then, hasn't she, Mags?"

Margot sat down. "I think so. Yes, she's been perfectly fit. Her husband was off-colour one day, I think she said, but nothing serious enough to keep her at home to look after him." She looked round. "More tea, anybody?"

After that the talk became general for a few more

minutes and then Wanda arrived with Michael and Doris. While the Carlyles and the Masters discussed Housmans and a firm commitment to buy was given by Masters, Green and the two sergeants wandered out into the garden to look at the pool. Doris took Michael into the main part of the garden. After a few minutes Masters came out to join his colleagues, explaining that Margot and Wanda were discussing local curtain-making firms.

"Just one thing, George," said Green. "Do I understand Carlyle bathes here every day?"

"Without fail if the weather permits. Otherwise he has an exercise bath indoors."

"That Saturday night was warm enough for the party to be held out here."

"Yes."

"So was the Sunday warm, too?"

"It was a beautiful day," said Tip. "I remember it well. Sergeant Berger and I went to Rye, and that's not far from here."

"Thanks, lass. So what happened about Carlyle's bath that morning?"

"How do you mean?" asked Berger.

"Did he go in with half a ton of broken glass in the bottom and gobs of cream floating on the top? To say nothing of strands of mustard and cress and the stringy ends of sucked asparagus?"

"I see what you mean," said Berger.

"Thanks, Bill," said Masters quietly. He turned to Berger. "You and Tip go round to the kitchen and ask the maid, Freda, what happened about the pool on the Sunday. Hide it in among inconsequential chatter."

"And help with the washing up," added Green. "We'll wait here."

By the time the two sergeants returned, Hugh, Margot and Wanda had joined them. Doris and Michael were still in the main part of the garden looking at the fish in the ornamental pool. Berger gave Masters a lift of the eyebrows, but said nothing. Tip, however, turned to Margot and said: "Freda has been showing us your kitchen, Mrs. Carlyle. I hope you don't mind, but it is so marvellous."

"Of course I don't mind, Sergeant."

"It was the units that intrigued me. So perfect."

"They were tailor-made. Hugh has his own craftsmen, you see."

"Ah! I thought they didn't come from a DIY shop."

Carlyle, who had heard this, laughed aloud. "That's exactly where they did come from, old girl. My place is a sort of DIY shop, but we actually do it, not just sell the materials."

When they were once more in the cars and heading for London, Masters said, "I interpreted your glance, Sergeant Berger, and Tip's follow-up conversation about kitchen units, as meaning you had discovered something significant during your conversation with Freda. What was it?"

Tip was driving. Berger turned round in his seat to report. "The pool is cleaned out pretty regularly by Mrs. Hookham's husband. Evidently Carlyle's physiotherapist is very insistent on frequent changes because they can't put chemicals in the water to keep it clean."

"On account of the old boy's illness?" asked Green.

"That's the reason. They have to be pretty careful with his limbs, apparently. Anyhow, Mr. H. cleaned and re-filled the pool on Friday and then on Saturday night his missus went home and told him he had to do it again on Sunday morning and he had to make sure the bottom was swept clear of all broken glass and everything well scrubbed out."

"I'll bet he was pleased," said Green. "He'd have to be up early to do it. Those pools take a long time to fill."

"According to Freda he cleaned it out and turned on the water and then went in for his dinner. He kipped in a deck chair until time came for him to turn off, then he went off. A few days later his missus came in and said he'd got a mild attack of flu which he was building up into the biggest catastrophe of the century and blaming it onto the fact that he'd had to work on Sunday."

"That's the lot?"

"That's all there was, Chief. Freda says he probably slopped some of the water into his wellies when he got down into the pool. Evidently his wife is always telling him to work in his bare feet but he won't do it though he's always grumbling about the mucky footprints his boots make on the wet tiles."

"He was wise to wear boots that time," said Green. "Seeing there was broken glass about."

"Does all that help, Chief?"

"I think so. Now, I know we all had a cup of tea at the Carlyle's, but I noticed nobody ate anything, so let's get home and tackle that Chantilly cake that's waiting for us."

"Hear, hear," grunted Green.

6

The Greens were staying on for supper. So it was after the sergeants had gone off in the Yard car that Wanda said to her husband: "Darling, there was something Margot wanted to mention to you and William, but didn't want to do it in front of Hugh."

"So she told you while the pair of you were discussing the best place to buy curtains?"

Wanda smiled. "We really did talk about shops."

"I'll bet," grunted Green.

Doris asked: "Was it something about the house?"

"No. I think that's all settled now except for whether or not you want this cottage."

"Oh, we want it," said Doris.

"Have to wait until tomorrow for the final answer," said Green.

"You'll have to advertise your house, won't you, William?"

"Private sale, you mean? Evidently not. My solicitor says you've only to mention it to somebody in the city these days and you've got immediate takers. So we'll see what happens. But he says he's already put out feelers and has had a nibble or two. But tomorrow we shall have the full surveyor's report for insurance. He's told us roughly, of course, but once we have it on paper we'll be more sure of our ground and Harkness can go ahead and sell if he can get what the surveyor says it's worth."

"Cash sale?"

"These bankers in the city can borrow at low rates

from their employers, so if it does go that way there should be very little delay."

"Oh, I am pleased," said Wanda. "But please don't rush and do something silly on our account. We don't mind waiting a few weeks, do we, George?"

"As long as we can get into Housmans by the autumn, there is no hurry. I've arranged that with Hugh. Talking of which, what was it Margot wanted to say out of her husband's hearing?"

Wanda looked serious.

"Hugh has been getting anonymous letters."

"Threatening ones?"

"Threatening and abusive."

"How many?"

"Five or six so far, Margot thinks."

"Tell us the story, love," counselled Green.

"It's quite simple, really."

"It always is."

"The room with the French window and ramp is basically Hugh's office at home. Margot goes in to tidy up and so on, though she has nothing to do with the business. Hugh leaves letters on the desk sometimes if he opens them in the morning and then goes off before he has time to deal with them. Margot just straightens them up on the blotter and weeds out any junk stuff offering double-glazing and so on. A few weeks ago she saw one printed by hand. It looked odd, so she read it."

"Threatening and abusive, I think you said."

"Yes. Sometime later she tackled Hugh about it because by then two more had arrived. Hugh didn't show them to her, but she had made sure she was downstairs to take in the post each morning and she'd recognised the printing on the envelopes."

"Did she say what Hugh's reaction was?"

"According to her he just laughed, like he always does these days." She turned to Doris. "It's one of the usual signs of his illness, you know."

"Laughing is?"

"Happy, carefree temper, yes."

143

"How very odd."

"Never mind all that," snarled Green. "What about the letters?"

"Hugh just told Margot they were from some crank and that they would stop eventually."

"Did she get to know who they were from?"

"She said she asked Hugh and he swore he didn't know. She believed him because she says he tells her the truth. They have complete trust in each other."

"But he didn't tell her about the letters. She had to find out for herself," expostulated Doris.

"I don't think you are quite right about that, Doris," said Masters. "I imagine Hugh didn't tell Margot about the first ones because he didn't want to worry her, but he didn't go to any great lengths to conceal the matter from her. After all, he left the letter open on his desk for her to find."

"True enough," said Green. "And what happened to the letters—as if I didn't know?"

"You are quite right, William. Hugh destroyed them and he refused to yield to Margot's plea to tell the police."

"A pity, that," said Masters.

"Why?"asked Doris. "They couldn't have anything to do with Carla Sanders' death, could they?"

"As to that, I can't say. I must admit I can see no clear connection at the moment, or even an unclear one if it comes to that, but I'd still have liked to have seen the letters."

Wanda smiled at him. "Margot played a small trick on Hugh. As he wouldn't keep them to show the police, she didn't show him the last one that came. It was about a fortnight ago, and since then there have been no more, so she is beginning to think Hugh is right, and that they have stopped coming."

"What was the point of not showing him?" asked Doris.

"She kept it to show to George."

Masters sat up. "She did? Good for Margot. When can I see it?"

"Now," said Wanda, opening her bag. "She gave it to me for you." She handed the very ordinary white envelope across to her husband.

"Unopened?"

"Yes. Margot says she's read that the police prefer threatening letters not to be handled too much."

"Quite right," breathed Green. "Here, George, give it to me and I'll perform, if I can borrow the dining table and a knife."

Masters handed the letter across and they all followed Green to the table where, with the help of the cutlery there, he split open the envelope, carefully extracted the single, folded sheet of paper and held it down with two dessert spoons.

"All yours," he said. "But don't touch, anybody, and I'll want a pair of eyebrow tweezers and then a large envelope for taking it away in."

They all bent over it to read:

> YOU ARE ALREADY LOADED YOU RUTH
> LESS BASTARD A WASH OUT
> WITH YOUR CRIMINAL SET UP FOR
> MAKING DISHONEST MONEY FROM OTH
> ER PEOPLES INVENTIONS WHY DO
> YOU WANT MORE YOU WILL PAY
> FOR IT SOONER THAN YOU THINK
> YOU GREEDY SOD YOU

"Not a bit of the world's outstanding writing, perhaps," said Green, "but at least it gives us a clue to the author. Some disgruntled inventor is accusing Carlyle of pinching his idea and making a mint out of it."

"So much is obvious," agreed Masters. "The question is, is the accusation true?"

"George!" Wanda sounded outraged.

"Don't be upset, darling. I'm not calling Hugh a crook. But he's an inventor, or probably more precisely, an improver of inventions. Inventions are ideas, and all ideas spring from whatever is put into the mind by what a person hears and sees. Those who have the ability to look ahead to a possible need, or to collate information into a new or even different, but useful, form are called inventors."

"I don't see what you mean, George," said Doris.

Masters looked across at her and smiled. "Look at it this way, Doris. A man produces a very useful article for you to use in your kitchen. A mixer, say, in which are combined among other things a hinge, an electric switch, two whisks and so on. The man has invented the mixer for you, but he hasn't invented the hinge, or the electric switch, or the beaters, or probably anything else in the mixer."

"I see what you mean, now."

"Good. Now say Carlyle has produced a piece of earthmoving equipment which has some very good feet for clamping it to the ground. Unique feet, combining corkscrew-shaped teeth for biting into soil. Where has the idea for the feet come from?"

"Somebody else's idea?"

"Probably not directly. The idea probably comes from the fact that he has seen ordinary feet slipping at times. So he sees a need to dig the feet in. What digs in? A corkscrew. Carlyle didn't invent the corkscrew, he is simply making use of somebody else's idea. Fair enough. But say somebody had come to the same conclusions as Carlyle, not about an earth mover, but about the feet, for a patent form of scaffolding tower. Feet with corkscrews combined in them. Carlyle had seen the scaffold tower. Indeed, it had been submitted to him, and though it was a good implement, it was too heavy, clumsy and expensive for the ordinary local builder to invest in. So it failed to become a commercial success. Two or three years later Carlyle launches his new earth mover embodying the idea of corkscrew-held feet. Rich Mr. Carlyle makes more money, poor Mr. Inventor makes none, even though part of his brainchild is being used." He turned to his wife. "So you see, darling, it is possible that Hugh has lifted an idea from somebody else. And why not? Is humanity to be forever deprived of cork-screw-held feet just because the originator failed to put them to good use?"

Wanda smiled at him. "I understand what you mean. I'm sorry I sounded so outraged."

"So where have we got to?" demanded Green, lifting his empty glass from the dining room table as an indication that he would like another gin and tonic. "Carlyle has been getting rude letters accusing him of utilising or pinching some other chap's idea. But the letters have now stopped. No demands have been made, though there is a hint of a threat at the end." He looked across at Masters. "It looks as though it's just one of those things, George, and if Carlyle himself doesn't want to involve us I don't see what we can or should do about it."

"Quite right. If any police are involved it should be the local force down in Kent. Not us at all."

"So you are going to hand this letter over to them, are you?" asked Wanda.

"Not on your life, girlie," said Green. "Carlyle doesn't want to involve the cops, so we have no right to pass the letter on."

"You want me to give it back to Margot?"

Green grinned at her and shook his head. "I'll hang on to it, love."

"But you and George have just been saying that it's a trivial business and of no interest to you."

"On paper, sweetheart. But you know us. Or George, rather. He'll hang on to this just in case."

"In case what?"

"Dunno, love. Just in case. And for that reason I shall put the letter away very carefully and have it tested for prints tomorrow. So, if you'll get me a big envelope while I get another drink, we can put this table to its proper use."

"What do you mean?" demanded Doris.

"If I'm not mistaken I can smell liver, bacon, onions..."

"Greedy guts. In a moment you'll be quoting something about how good liver is for you so you'll eat twice as much as anybody else."

"Well, let me see now."

"Chesterton on bacon," said Wanda. "Talking about the Englishman. 'Unless you give him bacon, You must not give him beans.' Those are the only two lines I know."

"Good enough," applauded Green. "Onions?"

"'Recipe for a Salad,'" suggested Masters. "'Let onion atoms lurk within the bowl, And, scarce-suspected, animate the whole.'"

"I like it," admitted Green, "except the scarce-suspected bit. I like 'em in noticeable proportions."

"Sorry, can't help, though I suspect Chaucer could."

Green turned to his wife. "'Is life worth living?'" he asked.

"Now what are you on about?"

"'He suspects it is, in a great measure, a question of the Liver.'"

"You made that up," she said scornfully.

"No, I didn't, and you didn't spot the mistake."

"What mistake was that?" asked Wanda.

"That Liver had a capital L. It means the one who lives, not the delicious dish I can now smell and which I propose to do ample justice to."

At half past nine the next morning Masters called Green into his office at the Yard. For more than a quarter of an hour the men discussed a problem Masters had been mulling over ever since the Greens had left him the previous evening.

"So," finished Masters, "I am going to see Edgar Anderson, ostensibly to report progress, but really to make sure I've put up an umbrella for myself. He will learn of any possible involvement I could have in this case through my dealings with Carlyle. My guess is he will disregard them once he knows the score."

"He can't do anything else," agreed Green.

148

"So, Bill, will you and Berger go off to see Mrs. Carlyle? You can say you've tested the letter and lifted a print which is unknown to us, but we'd like to keep the document just in case the print does get into our files. After that, I want you to ask her for the complete guest list for Hugh Carlyle's birthday party and, some-how, get to know from her if any of them are Scots or have lived in Scotland for some time and, if so, where."

"Can do," grunted Green. "It's another lovely day for a run in the country."

After Green had left him, Masters called for Tip.

"I want you to go to the library of the Royal Society of Medicine. You have to get a ticket from Admin. This is what you ask for, and go armed with enough cash to pay for photocopies if you're successful." He pushed across his desk a sheet of paper with several two- or three-line notes on it. He explained these to her in detail and finished by telling her not to be afraid to ask the library staff for help. The more assistance she got from them the quicker the job would be done and the more comprehensive the information.

Then he went to see Anderson.

"I don't see what the hell you are wittering on about, George," said the AC (Crime) when Masters had fin-ished his report. "You are buying a house from a friend—an eminent businessman without a blemish on his record—into whose swimming pool a nubile blonde fell a few days before she died of some obscure disease. Nobody can suggest that you are involved in any skull-duggery because, as I see it, Carlyle is as clean as a whistle and too much of an invalid to be an active villain anyway." He looked straight at Masters. "Or are you going to tell me I'm wrong?"

"You could be, sir."

"Ah! Then you'd better let me know how and where."

Masters explained. Anderson listened gravely.

"I see," he said at last. "You are merely listing a pos-sibility, but at any rate you have foreseen it and reported it to me." He sat back in his chair. "How far has this multihouse transaction gone?"

"Bill Green has got to know this morning how much his house has been valued at and his wife is going along to their solicitor with the surveyor's report today."

"So Bill has still to find a buyer?"

"It is unlikely to take very long."

"How long?"

"From two days to two weeks."

"Then you know how long you've got at your disposal for sorting this Sanders business. No house purchase by you from Carlyle until you've got the answer, George. If and when we know that Carlyle is in the clear, you can steam ahead." As he got to his feet, he said: "Don't worry about it, George. You know what solicitors are like. They can waste more time than Rip Van Winkle had at his disposal. And that over simply making a phone call. When it comes to finalising a deal, they can really hold things up."

"Thank you, sir." Masters moved towards the door. The AC said: "My missus and I will miss our visits to your little house, George."

Masters grinned. "In that case, you and Beryl will have to cultivate the Greens. They're good company, and . . ."

"Out!" commanded Anderson. "An evening's conversation with Bill Green would drive me crackers."

"You don't know what you're missing," smiled Masters as he left the office.

Green and Berger reached the Carlyle home soon after eleven o'clock. Margot Carlyle, in royal blue slacks and white shirt, was busy with a pair of secateurs in the front garden.

"Morning," called Green, as she came across the grass towards them. "Doing the flowers for the house?"

"Dead-heading, actually. But good morning to you, too. Is George with you?"

"Not today," said Green, stretching after the hour's sit in the car. "He's busy."

She laughed. "And you are not, I suppose?"

"Well, now, I have got this and that to attend to. The nicest among the chores being a visit to you."

"Thank you. Now, I've had my midmorning coffee, but you can have some with pleasure."

"There's a bit of talking to do," said Berger, supplying cause for Green to accept the coffee.

"In that case, come through the house. We'll have it by the pool."

As she sat down with them a few minutes later, Margot asked: "Now then, how can I help you?"

"First," said Green, shovelling brown sugar into his cup, "I'd like to mention the letter you gave to Wanda yesterday."

"Ah, yes. Can you do anything about it?"

"The answer to that is, maybe. By that I mean we've lifted a print from it. Not one that's in our records, but should we ever run up against it and are able to link it to its owner, your nameless correspondent will be identified. We should then be able to stop the letters, if they haven't already stopped of their own accord, and then leave it to the courts should you want to take it that far."

"I don't think Hugh would want that." She lifted the plate sitting in the middle of the table. "Do have a piece of shortbread. It's homemade."

"Homemade?" asked Green. "Here? I mean, in this house?"

Margot stared at him. "Of course. Mrs. H. made it. Where do you think it came from?"

Green looked sheepish. "It's Scottish, shortbread is, isn't it?"

Margot, still holding the plate, looked bewildered. "It originated in Scotland, certainly."

Green helped himself to one of the thick, chunky fingers and bit into it. "Jolly good," he murmured.

Margot persisted. "Why the inquisition about where it came from?"

Green wiped a crumb from his mouth. "One of the things George Masters told me to ask you was whether there were any Scots at your husband's birthday party."

"Oh? Why?"

"Some idea he's got. You know George socially, but not how he works. Flights of fancy, he has. His current one was sparked off by that letter you gave us yesterday. He wants to know if you had a Scot at the party."

"You mean he thinks a Scot wrote it."

"Presumably."

"Hang on a moment," said Berger. "I hadn't heard the Chief say this."

"He didn't talk to you this morning, did he?"

"No. But all you told me was that the Chief would like Mrs. Carlyle to give us a guest list of that party."

"That's right."

"But what's that got to do with some letter or another?"

"Sorry, son, you don't know about it yet. His Nibs' little missus produced it from her handbag after you left us last night."

"What sort of letter?"

"Anonymous. Mr. Carlyle's been getting them. Mrs. Carlyle intercepted one and gave it to Mrs. Masters."

"Blackmail?"

"Not exactly," said Margot. "They accuse my husband of stealing other people's inventions."

"I see. They would, wouldn't they, him being in the business he is in? Any threats?"

"Vague ones. 'You'll pay for it in the long run' sort of thing."

Berger grimaced and turned to Green. "And the Chief thinks a Scotsman wrote them?"

"Could have written them," corrected Green.

"Why?"

"How the devil do I know?" growled Green.

Berger shrugged. "If the Chief says a Jock wrote them, then a Jock wrote them."

Margot laughed. "It's like that, is it? What Mr. Masters says, goes?"

"Not quite, ma'am. What Mr. Masters says is right so

152

often that I'd not lay an old ha'penny on him being wrong."

"I see. I knew he had a reputation, but I didn't realise it extended to such limits." She turned to Green. "I can let you have the list. It's very rough. Handwritten with crossings out, with ticks for acceptors, and crosses for nontakers, among whom are Mr. Masters and his wife."

"He was Senior Officer on duty at the Yard that night. There's always one of his rank on every night. He loves it when he gets a traffic problem at two in the morning."

She smiled. "I can imagine. Does he have to deal with sieges when gunmen take hostages and hole up in a building?"

"He could well be in that sort of thing at the outset, but his first job would be to call out the specialists. You know. The ones who use psychiatry to talk these characters into giving themselves up and the marksmen who surround the building. Once the thing was set up, George would retire thankfully."

"I see." She got to her feet. "I'll get the list. It's in my desk."

As soon as she'd gone, Berger asked: "What's going on? Are we here because of an anonymous letter or because Carla Sanders took a bath here in public?"

"I don't know, lad."

"Are we on two cases or one?"

"Again, I don't know, lad. Have you got any fags on you?"

Berger produced his packet. "You don't know, you say, but you were scared of taking a bit of shortbread and that has to be a miracle for you."

"Only because shortbread is Scottish and His Nibs told me to ask if there'd been a Scotsman round here." Green lit his cigarette. "Look at it this way. If His Nibs has got it into his head that a Jock was implicated in writing threatening letters I didn't want to eat a bit of shortbread he might have brought here. And for the same reason I didn't want to take any if His Nibs reckons a Scotsman was implicated in Sanders' death. Get my point?"

"I certainly do. Ah, here's Mrs. Carlyle."

"This is it." She handed Green a sheet of paper. "Can you make head and tail of it? My writing's not the easiest to read."

"Fine," said Green, taking a quick look at the list. "Now, any Scotties here?"

"I think so. If you look down the list you'll see a Mr. McRolfe."

"He sounds Scottish enough."

"Doesn't he? But there's another pair with a not exclusively Scottish name. Carpenter. Ian and Sylvia. I always get the impression he's a Scot."

"Accent?"

"Barely discernible, but he uses words like littly—a littly piece—and factor to refer to an agent. That sort of thing."

Green put a mark beside the name. "Anybody else?"

"There's bound to be, isn't there? You'd never come across a fairly big group of people like that without a number of them having Scottish connections."

"I suppose not. And all these people are friends of your husband?"

"Not all are friends, exactly. For instance, Carla Sanders wasn't. Business acquaintances and colleagues a lot of them. Some are very close friends, of course, some near neighbours."

"Whoever you thought it judicious to invite, in fact?"

"I think it would be fair to say that. There are business considerations to be taken into account as well as friendship when making out a list like that."

"Understood. Now, McRolfe. Is he a friend or a business acquaintance?"

"He's actually one of my husband's business colleagues."

"A director of his company?"

"Not quite. One of the youngish senior heads of department."

"And Carpenter? You must have met him a number of times to know the little vagaries of his speech."

"I've known him for about two years and have met him, I think, on three occasions, probably four."

"So he's just a business acquaintance of your husband?"

"Yes."

"What is he? What does he do?"

"Do you know, I have no idea. But if he does business with my husband I would have thought he must have engineering connections."

"Thank you." Green folded the paper and slipped it into his inside jacket pocket. "I think that's it."

"Just one question, Mr. Green."

Green paused in the act of standing up.

"My husband doesn't know I gave that letter to Mrs. Masters."

"I understand that. He would take no action and you were worried so you acted on your own without telling him."

"Quite right. But I don't like deceiving my husband, Mr. Green."

"I should think not, ma'am." Green finally stood up completely. "But as with most other things there are grades of deceit. If doing a little quiet something for another's good can be called deceit."

"Put like that, it sounds harmless. Which leads me to my question. Would you like me to tell Hugh of your visit or not?"

"Tell him by all means if you would like to, Mrs. Carlyle. But that doesn't mean you have to mention the letter or Scotsmen or anything like that if you don't wish to. We came here to get the party list. You gave it to us and we nattered over a cup of coffee about friends, acquaintances, colleagues and neighbours. In general. Nothing specific about anybody." Green grinned. "I doubt very much whether you could tell us anything very specific about any of them, could you?"

"Only about our close friends."

"And I don't even know which they are, do I?"

She smiled. "No."

"Happy now, Mrs. Carlyle?"

"I think so. I don't like worrying Hugh. I know he always seems cheerful, outwardly..."

"A symptom of his condition, I believe?"

"That's it. It's superficial. He does get a bit worried underneath, you know."

"Who wouldn't, in his condition?" said Berger and reddened under their gaze. "I mean it can't be all that cheerful for an active man in the prime of life to be chairbound."

"It isn't," agreed Margot. "But though he gets a little worried, I don't think there's any clinical depression there, thank God."

"He's still able to work and use his mind," said Green. "That's what'll keep him going."

Tip got back to the Yard some minutes after one o'clock. Masters was not in his office so she left the small sheaf of photocopied documents on his blotter, scrawled a few words on the top sheet of his phone pad, tore it off and anchored it firmly on top of the other papers with the heavy glass ashtray. Masters, she guessed, had gone for lunch, so she then set out in search of Green and Berger. She eventually found Berger in the canteen reading a tabloid whilst eating a wedge of quiche.

"Do you mind if I join you?"

Berger glanced up from, as Tip was pleased to observe, the list of county cricket scores. "I looked for you," he said.

"I've only just got back from the RSM."

"We must have beaten you by a quarter of an hour. Are you going to get some food?"

"Get it for me, will you? A cheese and salad roll. I want to, what in polite circles is known as, wash my hands. Oh, and get me a cup of coffee, too."

So Berger did the queuing up for Tip's lunch. She beat him back to the table.

"What kept you?"

"You can see the rush at the counter, can't you? And that's thirty-five pee you owe me."

As she gave him the money she said: "I meant what kept you down in Kent?"

"Willy P. Green was going on about some anonymous letters that Carlyle bloke has been getting lately. I'd not even heard about them, had you?"

"So that's why you're sounding brassed off, is it?"

"You did know about the letter the Chief got yesterday?"

"No, I didn't. This is the first I've heard of it, but I'm not getting grumpy. You know the Chief. He'll tell us everything. This afternoon, I suspect."

"I hope so." Berger pushed away his plate with the edging crust of the quiche still uneaten. "That stuff's inedible," he grumbled. "They mix the pastry with thistle plaster."

Tip grinned. "Quite right, too. Thistle plaster is for internal use only, if I remember what my old dad used to say."

He stared at her for a moment and then grinned. "Being a bit of a bloody pain, was I?"

"A bit." She picked a few crumbs of cheese from her plate. "But I know how you feel about not being taken into the Chief's confidence. However, we've got to be fair to him. He wouldn't want a conference last night."

He grinned. "Neither would we. We'd got better things to do, hadn't we?"

"If you are asking whether I enjoyed myself walking along the river, the answer is yes, but I didn't like that noisy pub we ended up in."

"I was pleased to get out of it myself."

She finished her roll and drew her coffee towards her. "Now, about the Chief doing things unbeknownst to us. Why don't you do the same to him?"

"Like what?"

157

"Do you remember Carlyle saying the fairy-lights round the pool went out unexpectedly?"

"Yes."

"Why did they?"

Berger sat back to think. "It depends, I suppose, whether the string was wired in series or parallel."

"Don't blind me with science," pleaded Tip. "I've never been able to grasp which was which."

Berger leaned across the table towards her. "Right," he said. "Think of those little sets of Christmas tree lights. One type goes out if one bulb blows and then you are faced with removing each one in turn and testing every socket with a new bulb until they suddenly all come on again. The second type is better because if a bulb blows the others stay lit."

She nodded. "That much I do know."

"I wouldn't think that Carlyle, being the boss of an engineering firm, would have the former type of setup for the lights round his pool."

"He'd certainly have the more efficient sort."

"Quite."

"So why don't you have a ready answer for the Chief as to how those lights went out? And more to the point, why they went out?"

"They'd be easy to put out," said Berger thoughtfully. "If, as we think, Carlyle had a set where one bulb could blow without the rest going out, it means that there were plus and minus poles at each bulb holder. If you remove a bulb or blow it, the current continues to flow. In other words you don't break the circuit."

"So just removing a bulb wouldn't plunge the place into darkness."

"Not if that is all you did. But by taking a bulb out you expose both positive and negative poles."

"The two little spring-loaded plungers that touch the bits of lead on the bottom of bulbs."

"If the bulb-holder is the bayonet type, yes. But most of these strings of lights these days have screw-in bulbs."

158

"I know. With one central blob of lead at the bottom."

"That's right. That's usually the positive pole. The negative one is combined in the holder itself, usually the internal brass screw bit. The screw bit on the narrow part of the bulb picks it up. So, through the business part of the bulb you get the necessary anode and cathode contacts to light the filament. With me so far?"

Tip nodded.

"Right. Now to put the whole string out, you would have to connect across positive and negative, thus short-circuiting the whole lot and thereby blowing the fuse in the plug-top."

"How would you do it?"

"Hide behind one of the bushes carrying the light cable. Surreptitiously remove a bulb. Drop a small piece of metal into the holder so that it would touch both positive and negative. The fuse would blow immediately. While the light is out, shake out your bit of metal, reinsert the bulb, straighten the cable on the bush and do a bunk, quick, before somebody goes indoors and renews the plug fuse."

"Bingo?"

"Bingo."

"Then what?"

"What do you mean, then what?"

"What was your reason for fusing the lights in the first place?"

"There was something I wanted to do surreptitiously. So while the lights were off and everybody was gawping towards the French window, wondering what was happening and who was going to fix it, I did whatever I had to do."

"Which was?"

"How do I know? Spray bugs on Carla Sanders?"

"Was she there by the time the lights fused?"

"Oh, lord, I can't remember. It didn't seem important when we asked Carlyle."

"There you are then. Ask the Chief that."

"You've got something there," said Berger. "If the

lights went off before she arrived, it had nothing to do with her. And vice versa, though not necessarily."

"Very illuminating," said Tip, drily. She looked at her watch. "Come on. We'd better find the DCI or he'll be asking us if we've been on holiday."

"Half past two in His Nibs' office," grunted Green when they had run him to earth.

"Conference?" asked Berger.

"You could say that. Got any fags, lad?"

"Only a couple. I shall want those myself before the afternoon's out. Use your own."

Green sighed. "If I must, I must."

"You shouldn't," said Tip. "And don't forget there's a move afoot to stop people like you smoking in offices and other places of work."

Green grinned. "What about people who aren't like me? Can they go on?"

"You know exactly what I mean," said Tip.

"Yes, I do, love. But I'm long in the tooth and old in sin. I enjoy what I do, otherwise I wouldn't do it."

"And what about other people?"

"Doris hasn't hinted she'll leave me if I don't toe the line." He looked shrewdly at Tip and then across at Berger. "Aye, aye! Have I uncovered some sticking point in what I might call the relationship between you two?"

Neither replied.

"That means I have," grunted Green after a prolonged silence. "I don't know how you are going to resolve it, but I'd advise a bit of give and take on both sides."

"You can't give and take with smoking," declared Tip. "Either you do or you don't."

"It's possible to give and take in attitude, though, petal. You can often achieve things by not being too rabid in forcing your opinions." He looked at them sapiently. "And it's no good for you to say he doesn't love you enough to give up smoking," indicating Berger, "or for you to say she's trying to change you before you get hitched."

"Who is talking about getting hitched, as you put it?" demanded Tip.

"You are, love. Otherwise you wouldn't be worrying. For people you don't want to marry, like me, you actually buy cigarettes. For Sergeant Berger you have nothing but a snarl on the subject."

Tip regarded him for a moment. "I must remember in future I'm consorting with great detectives."

"So you don't deny it," said Green with a grin at Tip.

"I do," said Berger.

"You could have fooled me," grated Green.

"The Chief wouldn't want a married couple in his team," said Tip simply, "and we neither of us want to leave it, yet."

"Got it," said Green with a grin. "The lad has to wait for his promotion board before anything happens. Like young Reed and his little missus."

"Exactly like that," said Tip.

Green shrugged and looked at his watch. "Time we were moving up there."

Masters took the sting from the meeting right at the outset by apologising to Berger and Tip for not keeping them fully abreast of the events of the previous evening. "The DCI and I knew nothing about the letter until after you had left us, and there was no opportunity to break for our usual brainstorming session this morning, because each of us had important jobs to do. However, we can now put matters to rights. The DCI has given me his report over lunch and Tip has very kindly got me some useful medical information from the RSM. Now, you must have some questions, so let us try to get those out of the way before we start trying to get something like a proper picture out of the bits and pieces we've got. Who first?"

"We've heard all about the anonymous letter, Chief, and I was present at the interview with Mrs. Carlyle this morning."

"Yes?"

161

"I was bewildered, Chief. I didn't know whether we went there to discuss the letter or to talk about Carla Sanders. Sometimes I got the impression the two are linked, sometimes that they had nothing to do with each other. We spent most of the time talking about Scotsmen."

"What's your question, Sergeant?"

"Are the two linked?"

"I think there could be a strong possibility that they are."

"But you are not sure?"

"Not as yet. You've got all the information that the DCI and I have."

"Now."

"Admittedly, now. I've already apologised for keeping you in the dark this morning and explained the reasons for that."

"Blame his missus," said Green quickly. "She didn't produce the letter soon enough for you lot to know last night. So get on with what you've got to say, lad."

"How or why do you think a Scotsman is implicated, Chief?"

Masters handed over a photocopy of the anonymous letter. "From that. Study it and see if you come to the same conclusion as I did or simply if you can determine why I came to that conclusion."

"Conclusion sounds pretty final, Chief," said Tip as she moved to look over Berger's shoulder."

"Then it is the wrong word," said Masters. "I should have said that I picked up a hint from the letter by studying it. I won't tell you what it is for the moment because I should prefer to see if you read it the same way as I did."

"And the DCI?" asked Tip. "Did he get it?"

"I can't read," retorted Green.

Tip looked across at him. "If an astute old dick like you can't spot it you can't expect the likes of us to do so."

"Ah!" grunted Green, "but you've had the advantage

of the modern education. You know! The sort that frees the mind and allows it to soar to unknown heights, never mind if you can't multiply two and two and have never heard of punctuation." He took out his cigarette packet. "Have a bash at it, petal," he said plaintively, "we haven't got all day."

Tip stared at him for a moment and then smiled. "Punctuation," she murmured quietly to Berger.

"Punctuation? There isn't any."

Tip studied the letter for many moments before finally saying. "You're right. So the fact that there isn't any must be important."

Masters, who was packing a pipe very carefully with Warlock Flake, said quietly, "The punctuation, or lack of it, is certainly important. But study the import of the letter a little more carefully. And the tone."

"The tone is abusive, Chief," replied Berger. "Ruthless bastard and greedy sod may not be the worst of today's epithets, but they are pretty strong. I mean they leave you in no doubt as to what the writer thinks of Carlyle."

"Quite right. Think on."

"The whole tone is abusive," repeated Berger slowly to himself, "and yet..." He looked across at Masters.

"And yet?"

"In the middle of it he calls Carlyle a washout which is the sort of mild thing I'd have called another lad when I was a little boy at school. Rotter, washout, that sort of thing."

Tip closed her eyes in an agony of thought. And then opened them again and said excitedly: "He didn't call Carlyle a washout, did he, Chief?"

"It's here as plain as the nose on your face," expostulated Berger.

"No, no," said Tip. "Look at the way he has split words at the ends of the lines and then continued on the next line without any hyphen or dash to connect the two pieces. Look at the top line. RUTH it ends with, and the second line starts with LESS. Line four ends with OTH and five starts with ER."

"I can see that," admitted Berger. "But to get back to this washout business."

"Awash," said Tip. "Not A WASH, with or without the out."

Berger stared at her for a moment. "Got it," he breathed. "Out with. Awash outwith your criminal set-up et cetera."

Tip patted him on the arm.

"It took me a long time to spot it," said Masters. "Nobody I've ever known except a Scot, and by that I mean a real Scot, not an Anglo-Scot, has used the word outwith, which means almost the same as without, but not quite. And don't ask me what the real difference is, but there are distinct verbal shades in their usage."

"So you sussed that a Jock had written this letter, Chief?"

"You're quick this afternoon, lad," grunted Green.

Berger looked across at him. "It could be a ruse to put us off the scent."

"It could be," agreed Masters, "but on the whole I think not. And in any case, I couldn't afford to ignore it in case it was put in to mislead."

"Dead giveaway, I reckon," said Green. "It has to be. It couldn't be a ruse if the only bloke to suss it out was His Nibs. None of us others did, without prompting. What's the use of a sign to lead your trackers astray if they can't see the arrow pointing down the wrong way?"

Berger nodded. "I get the point."

"So," said Masters, "to get back to your original question, Sergeant, which was, I think, to ask if the Carla Sanders case and the anonymous letter to Mr. Carlyle are linked."

"That's it, Chief."

"My answer cannot be categorical, but I've begun to think so and as there seemed to be no reason for not considering them in tandem, that is what I proposed to the DCI this morning. Hence his questioning of Mrs.

Carlyle was not clear cut as you have obviously appreciated."

"But why a Scotsman, Chief?"

"I don't understand the question."

Berger sat back and stretched his long legs as he frowned despairingly, searching for the right form of words in which to express his thoughts. Then—

"Chief, I understand why you believe a Scotsman to have written the anonymous note to Carlyle. What I can't understand is why you think the same Scotsman had it in for Carla Sanders."

"He doesn't think that," grunted Green.

Berger sat up, slowly. "I give up, Chief."

"Think, please," said Masters.

"You will pay for it sooner than you think," murmured Tip, quoting from the photocopy of the anonymous letter she was still holding. She said quietly to Berger: "There could be something there."

Berger stared at her for a moment. "That letter reached the Carlyle home shortly before the party, did you say, Chief?"

"Yes."

"So any attack on Carlyle could have been made at the party. It being 'soon' after the letter was written."

"Go on."

"But the attack on Carlyle failed and somehow, Carla Sanders was caught in the crossfire."

"And died from her wounds," said Green. "Go on, lad, you're playing a blinder."

"That's it," said Tip. "The same person was responsible for both Carla Sanders' death and the anonymous note to Mr. Carlyle."

"At last," groaned Green.

Berger turned to him. "And I suppose you worked all that out for yourself, with no help from the Chief?"

"I was having the weekend off," said Green airily. "Once I'd started work again this morning I'd have got it soon enough, but His Nibs had been doing a bit of overtime last night so he was a bit ahead of me at reaching the conclusion."

"You're an awful old fibber," said Tip, giving Green a smile and shaking her head at the same time.

"To be fair to the DCI," said Masters, "he mentioned to me some time ago something you two should always bear in mind, in every case. And that is that the victim of any killing may not have been the intended victim. He told me that he had a strong feeling that Hugh Carlyle had been the target for attack on the night of his party and that somehow Carla Sanders had taken the flak."

"So snubs to you, young Berger, and you, too, Tip," said Green, all but putting his tongue out at them.

"And that was before the anonymous letter came to light, Chief?"

"Oh, yes. The DCI and I were thinking along the same lines, but we had no proof that there had been an attempt on Carlyle's life, so it was going to be very difficult to prove that Carla Sanders had been killed in any way other than accidentally or naturally. Furthermore, we had no clue as to who might be the perpetrator of the act of revenge against Carlyle. As you know, we were asking questions, constructively, I like to think, in the hope that we should be lucky enough to get a hint that proof of what we believed would be forthcoming. That hint came last night in the shape of the letter Tip has in her hand."

"Clear enough now, Chief," said Berger. "And you've concluded a Scotsman is implicated. So what do we do now? Find a Scot and ask him what he did to Carlyle that misfired?"

"There is such a thing as continuation of evidence, Sergeant. We work it all out before we find the Scot. Then we tell him what he did and why we are about to arrest him."

"Sorry, Chief, but have we a clue what he did? I mean the lights went out round the pool. Was that to give him a chance to do something unseen?"

"Answer your own question, please."

Berger glanced at Tip. "The lights went out at the party. That could be suspicious as it could have given somebody the chance to do something surreptitiously."

"Quite right, lad. How was it worked?"

Berger gave an account of his earlier conversation with Tip and then went on to ask: "The point is, was Sanders already there or wasn't she? If she wasn't and the attack on Carlyle went in at that time we know that the attempt was not a momentary effort like, say, a shot with a silenced revolver would be, otherwise it couldn't have harmed a latecomer."

"Right, lad. What if she was there at the time?"

"Then we may have to suppose that it was a quick, short attempt that went wrong."

"There was no shooting there, son. Somebody would have heard or seen something if there had been."

"Would they?"

"Explain, please," said Masters.

"He didn't use a revolver, Chief, but he could have used a pistol. A water pistol. Loaded with liquid containing the leptospirae bugs. All he had to do was create a bit of a diversion by fusing the lights, thereby giving himself a bit more darkness to work in, but not so much that he couldn't see what he was doing. He'd expect Carlyle to wheel his chair over to the ramp into the house to supervise the repair. So he'd know exactly where to find him."

"And there would be shadows on each side of the French window," said Tip. "He could hide there and fire into a target in the overspill of light from the room."

"Thanks," said Berger, looking up at her. "I hadn't thought of that, but it makes things easier to envisage." He turned back to Masters. "He'd fire from the hip, Chief, so as not to be seen pointing the weapon. But water pistols aren't all that accurate, are they! He took a shot at Carlyle who jinked his chair at the same moment. So the spray of liquid missed him and hit Sanders who, as far as I can make out, spent the whole of the party just close by the ramp. So the bugs meant to kill Carlyle killed the girl instead."

There was silence for a moment or two and then Masters said: "It is a most ingenious theory, Sergeant. And could well be right in its broad outline. I suspect the details would need a little revising, perhaps, but the basic idea could be a sound one."

Berger blushed with pleasure and accepted the cigarette Green was offering him. "What's this? A fag from you? It must be my birthday."

"It's a prize for invention," grunted Green. "Like His Nibs, I'm not saying you are right, but it's as good a theory as I've heard to illustrate that point you were making about the attack being a momentary one." He struck a match. "Have a light, too, lad. On me."

Berger looked at him suspiciously. "You're not pulling my leg?"

"Would I offer you one of my fags if I were pulling your old whatsisname?"

Berger accepted the light.

Tip said to Masters: "Do you think that is how it was done, Chief?"

"Without detracting from Sergeant Berger's excellent basic theory, I don't think it was. My reason for saying that is because Hookham—he's Mrs. H.'s husband—wasn't present at the party, though I understand he turned up later, after the pubs had closed."

"Hookham? Where does he come into this, Chief? Is he the Scotsman we've been hearing so much about?"

"He did odd jobs about the Carlyle house," reminded Tip.

"And so couldn't have been within range of the water pistol," went on Masters, ignoring the question about his nationality.

"You still haven't said whether Hookham is a Scot, Chief."

"As far as I know he isn't."

"Then what does it matter whether he was at the party or not?"

"He did odd jobs, as Tip said."

"So?"

"One of his jobs was the emptying and filling of the swimming pool. Remember?"

Tip said excitedly, "He was ill after he'd emptied it that Sunday. Caught flu." Then her voice fell. "But not very badly, Chief. He was just a bit off-colour for a day or two."

"Right, love," said Green. "And that's the clue to the whole business. Remember what the books say about this leptospirosis lark. The infection can vary in intensity from a mild influenza-like illness to a fatal form of jaundice due to severe liver disease. Old Hookham caught the flu, Sanders caught the fatal dose. Or so we believe. Now go on from there."

"Now we know that, it must mean that the pool was the danger spot," said Berger. "It's the only thing that links Sanders and Hookham. She went right in and got the fatal dose, he just pulled the plug, waited for most of the water to drain away and then went in—probably in his wellies—to scrub down and remove the broken glass and food scraps."

"Using a longhandled brush, most likely," added Tip.

"Very good, so far," said Green. "Anything else to add?"

Berger grimaced. "It seems obvious somebody—presumably the Chief's Scotsman—emptied a bottle full of the bugs into the water."

"To kill Carlyle," said Tip. "How horrible! To try to murder a crippled man with a filthy infection like that."

"Don't get emotional, Tip," counselled Masters.

"But, Chief..."

"Save it, petal," warned Green. "You two haven't yet finished the story."

"Oh, you mean about putting the lights out so that he could put the microorganisms in the water without being seen?"

"There's that," agreed Masters, "though at this moment I suspect that point is relatively unimportant. The

169

method will, of course, have to be looked into, sooner or later, as will opportunity and various other little items such as where the bugs came from in the first place."

Tip asked innocently: "Have you any ideas about the source, Chief?"

"Not firm ones. Like Sergeant Berger with his water pistol, I am trying to shape my theories to fit the possibilities." He looked at his wristwatch. "I think it's time we called it a day. But before we go, I'd like you to remember one thing we seem to have learned today, and that is that leptospirae will live in clean water and so, we presume, the infection can be acquired from bathing in clean but infected water. In this connection remember another thing. Because of the danger of infection from chemicals Carlyle was likely to suffer on account of his condition, his swimming pool was always filled with fresh water from the mains, and none of the usual agents for keeping it bug-free, like chlorine, was ever used."

"Good point that," murmured Green. "It means that whoever was out to get him knew enough about the life habits of those little jiggers to realise they would live and move and multiply by the million in Carlyle's pool." He looked across at Masters. "Are we looking for a microbiologist or some such?"

"A Scottish microbiologist who has had dealings in recent years with Carlyle," said Berger. "That should be a fairly easy spec, shouldn't it, Chief?"

"On the face of it, perhaps. Anyhow, think it through." Masters got to his feet.

"Can you give us a few minutes, Chief?" asked Tip.

"Of course. What for?"

"I'd like to take photocopies of the papers you got today, and relevant extracts from the books."

"Highly illegal," said Green.

"Pretend you didn't hear," said Berger.

"Make it snappy," said Masters. "I'm in a bit of a hurry."

The two sergeants left the office.

"Hurry, George?" asked Green. "Going somewhere tonight?"

"All the bits and pieces to do with the house. I can't leave them all to Wanda."

"Packing, you mean?"

"I didn't actually. I meant documentation. I'm going to write all those damn' letters, leaving gaps for dates to be filled in later. Rate rebate, reading electricity and gas meters, phone transfer and so on to say nothing of a few things which I think Wanda will have got from the solicitor. Oh, yes, and there's a chap coming to size up the furniture to give us a removal estimate."

"It's all go, then?"

"Getting up to the start line and pausing on it, waiting for the whistle to proceed."

"Meaning you are waiting for me and my missus to spark."

"I suppose that is the chief thing. But please don't harass Doris, Bill. A few days is neither here nor there. Don't forget Anderson said this present business has to be cleared up before we can make a literal move."

Green stood up. "A few days is all it should take," he agreed. "At least that's what Doris thinks. She's so sure of it she's dragooned Berger and Tip into promising their help with the removal."

"Are they happy about that?"

"Apparently young Berger is going to hire a van and remove us himself. It was his idea. Said it would be cheaper."

"Why didn't I think of that?"

"Too busy thinking about dead actresses, felonious Scotsmen and oast-houses, I suspect."

"That's about the strength of it, I suppose."

The door opened and Tip came back with the papers and books she had borrowed. "Thank you, Chief. We're going to study them tonight."

"We?" demanded Green.

"Sergeant Berger and I."

"You surprise me. Will you let him smoke while he studies?"

Tip coloured.

Green smiled at her. "You'll win, lass. If he behaves himself he won't smoke, and he certainly won't smoke if he starts to misbehave himself. So you win both ways."

Tip grinned at him as she headed for the door. "Yes, I do, don't I?"

7

When they all met early the next morning in Masters' office, Green said to Berger: "Well, lad, did you get anything from your study of those papers last night?"

Berger grinned. "We got to know why the Chief sent Tip to the RSM library yesterday. Or at least one of the reasons."

"Okay, lad, spill it."

"The Chief had suspected that a Scot wrote that anonymous letter to Carlyle."

"I know that," growled Green.

"Then you'll know that when he sent Tip off to get him those papers one of the instructions on the list was to get hold of any printed information about leptospirosis in Scotland."

"That seems a fairly obvious thing to do."

"No, it doesn't," retorted Tip. "The Chief wanted printed information, not just national statistics of the incidence of the disease and stuff like that."

Green sat up and looked across at Masters. "Was that it, George? You wanted some sort of dope specific to Scotland that an interested party up there could read?"

"Roughly that, Bill. I was hoping that there might have been something written by somebody like, say, a microbiologist that pertained so specifically to Scotland that the Scottish daily papers would have picked it up and repeated it as an item of news of some interest up there."

"Where the London dailies would ignore it because it was too local to be national news?"

"That was my line of thought. Lots of bits of interesting parochial news are never seen by the rest of us because Fleet Street filters them out."

"I can understand why they should filter out any reports of leptospirosis anywhere, let alone in Scotland. But it was worth a try, I suppose. And from the way these two kids are acting, I guess it paid off."

"It most certainly did," said Tip.

"How, lass?"

"We learned that Weil's disease had been prevalent in the Aberdeen fish market."

"Interesting."

"Don't be like that. Studies had shown that the disease was not encountered in the Grimsby or Glasgow fish markets, though the sheds in all three ports were equally rat-infected."

Green stroked his chin. "There had to be a reason for that, love."

"There was. In Grimsby the gutting tables were hosed down with sea water, while in Glasgow the workers were using brine and kippering fluid. All those liquids are leptospirocidal. So no Weil's disease. In Aberdeen, however, the washing down was done with ordinary tapwater of nearly neutral pH."

"Meaning it was neither acid nor alkaline?"

"Right. Just right for the bugs to survive in."

"Exactly the same as Carlyle's swimming pool?"

"You've got it."

"Thanks, petal." Green turned to Masters. "And you think that little nugget of information found its way into the Scottish dailies where our unfriendly Scotsman could read it, latch on to it, and decide to infect Hugh Carlyle's pool?"

"Not as quickly as all that, perhaps," replied Masters. "All this information was first discovered by various experts a good many years ago, and matters have been put to rights. More recently another author has gathered all the bits and pieces together in one paper. He is, I believe, a pathologist. At any rate, he has a string of letters after his name, including F.R.C. Path. He wrote a paper on leptospirosis some years ago."

"Did he say anything about prevention?"

"Quite a lot. Washing down tables, floors and fish-boxes in Aberdeen with hypochlorite disinfectant, combined, of course, with strong antirat measures, eliminated the disease. He went on to say that in coal mines the closing down or draining of waterlogged workings, the abolition of pit ponies and so on got rid of that particular danger for miners. Sewage workers and the likes of trout farmers are carefully instructed about the disease and infections among them are unusual nowadays. But the point is, the danger is still there. Measures to prevent trouble are in force, but infected rats still exist. And it is from one or more of such animals that somebody collected the urine for the purposes of fouling that swimming pool."

"The preventive measures don't eliminate the diseased rats?"

"Not possible, Bill. Of course there have to be antirat measures in the workplace, and this means some rats are trapped and killed. But the other measures are protective rather than eliminative. Such things as drainage of waterlogged areas, use of disinfectants, protective clothing, early treatment of skin abrasions and prevention of accidental immersion in water that is likely to be infected are all useful, but they don't eliminate the disease."

Green drew hard on his cigarette and then said: "The last two measures you just mentioned are important to us, I'd say."

"Treatment of skin abrasions and prevention of accidental immersion? I'll say they are important. The whole case revolves round them."

"Carla Sanders' skin abrasions?"

"And her immersion, accidental or otherwise."

"We reckon otherwise, don't we?"

"Yes."

"That's specific, at any rate."

175

"It has to be, Bill. This business was planned. By that I mean the collection of infected rat urine. It could have taken days, or weeks for all I know."

"Not knowing the output of rats, as it were?"

"Exactly. But whatever the statistics, we know the job was planned. And whoever planned it knew the exact date of when he proposed to carry out his operation."

Green grunted. "I get you. Carlyle's birthday. A fixed date on which there was a party at his home every year."

"And a function to which our man was certain he was to be invited."

"That means after Mrs. C. sent out the invites."

"Perhaps. Or perhaps he had been a regular guest at the same function for some years and was fully expecting to be so this year."

Green shrugged. "Not a stone-bonker certainty, was it, though? The guest list could change."

"Of course it could. Neither was it certain that the party would be held round the swimming pool. Had it been raining, for instance..."

"Anybody could make an excuse to go out into a garden like that in any weather, Chief," interrupted Tip. She reddened under his gaze. "Sorry for breaking in, Chief. It just came out."

"Don't apologise, Tip. Give me an example of an excuse you would use for leaving the party in the middle of a rainstorm."

Tip grimaced in dismay.

"Wait until it stopped," said Berger tentatively.

Masters nodded, unconvinced.

"Wait until after dark, certainly," burst out Tip.

"Go on."

"Leave the house on the pretence that I wanted something I'd left in the car."

"Reasonable." He paused for her to continue.

"I think that's it, Chief. It's by no means an unknown thing for people to leave parties surreptitiously. We've all done it from time to time. Gone out

176

for a breath of fresh air, perhaps."

"Fair enough," agreed Masters. "Now to get back to the point at which we digressed. In order to have the necessary supply of leptospirae, the intention to foul the swimming pool must have been planned well in advance of the date of the party. That confirms intent to murder, in my view."

"Hear, hear," grunted Green. "You'll have to tell Edgar Anderson and get this enquiry turned into a case. Then the Kent police can deal with it. It's on their patch."

Masters ignored this. "We know the means, method and opportunity. Now we have to determine who the real victim was to have been, for it is certain Carla Sanders was not intended to die. How do we know that, Tip?"

"It's obvious, Chief," objected Berger.

"For continuation of evidence, we have to spell it out. Something I would like you to pay particular attention to, because I would like you to collate this particular file for the Crown prosecutors. Partly for your continuous assessment and partly because, as you already know, it could be more convenient if the DCI and myself were not to be seen to be too closely associated with the presentation of this case. Certain of the reports have already been typed by Tip, I believe. I feel sure she will do the same for your linking observations and will prepare a duplicate file for consideration by your examiners when the time comes."

"Right, Chief."

"So now, Tip, please. Why do we know Carla Sanders was not the intended victim?"

"Because she was not on the original guest list for the party, Chief, so nobody could know that she would be there. Far enough in advance, that is, to prepare a lethal dose of leptospirae. In fact, the reverse would be thought to be true. She had only just opened in a new West End show and so one could have wagered she would be in the theatre on Saturday evening. As it was, she injured herself late on the Thursday night, and it was only then that the invitation to the party was issued. That left less than forty-eight hours in which to prepare the leptospirae: a time we consider to have been far too short for the collection of a sufficient quantity of rat's urine to pollute a volume of water the size of Carlyle's swimming pool."

"A good point that last one," grunted Green.

"Good," agreed Masters, "but not absolutely valid. Given the right conditions, such as pertained in Carlyle's pool, bugs can multiply by the million in a very short time."

Green grimaced. "Pure, clean water, gently warmed by the sun?"

"Exactly. So make the point but don't stress it too much."

"Right, Chief," said Berger. "Incidentally, how does one collect rat's urine?"

"Doubtless there are a number of ways, including extraction by catheter or forced evacuation by pressure in the right spots on the body, but from what I have been able to gather from a conversation with the pathologist, the easiest way for the layman would be simply to provide a superfluity of liquid food for the rats—some form of broth or syrupy water or whatever they happen to fancy—to cause them to urinate pretty frequently. The urine is then caught on trays of absolutely neutral vermiculite grains on the bottom of the cages. These trays are changed very frequently, and the fouled vermiculite steeped in clean water. The leptospirae are washed off the vermiculite and the water that is used is polluted. The water is than strained to remove the vermiculite and left to stand so that it evaporates at room temperature, getting stronger and more polluted by the hour. It is not, however, allowed to evaporate altogether."

"When you've got enough you fill a litre tonic bottle and push off to the party, I suppose," said Green.

"Something of the sort," agreed Masters, "but a litre bottle would be difficult to conceal on the body, whereas a thin plastic bag . . ."

"I know, Chief," said Tip excitedly. "Just an ordinary see-through plastic bag, sealed at the top. When the lights go out all you have to do is puncture it and drop in into the pool. The pollution is going to escape and the bag will just be an empty bag, either floating just below the surface or on the bottom of the pool and nobody is going to think anything about a single plastic bag in a pool after a party. Lots of little bits and pieces could be there—crumbs, matchsticks, anything."

Masters smiled. "Just what I was about to say, Tip, except that I was going to point out that such a bag could well be a rectangular one that would lie, very flat, probably not more than an inch thick, very neatly inside, say, a man's jacket."

"Make it two smaller bags," suggested Green. "Same shape, but just about right for the two pockets on a jacket. Shoving a hole in two bags would take no longer than puncturing one."

"I like that, Bill. Concealment on the person was going to be a tricky point, that's why I didn't like the tonic bottle. Two flat bags . . . why not? Sergeant Berger, you and Tip will go to see the chap who cleared out the pool . . ."

"Hookham?"

"That's the chap. Ask him whether he found two plastic bags."

"When, Chief?"

"After we've finished here." Masters looked across at Green. "We shall have to interview quite a number of the people at the party, Bill."

Green nodded. "The two Scotsmen for sure."

"There's another bloke, too. Have you ever heard of Slim Piper?"

Green sat up. "Have I not! Stage magician. Seen him many a time in the old days of variety. Could fool anybody with his tricks."

"You didn't happen to notice his name on the list you got from Mrs. Carlyle?"

"Didn't read it, actually. I glanced at it at Mrs. Carlyle's request, just to see that I could read her scrawl, and then pocketed it to give to you, while we went on to discuss Scotsmen."

"I see."

Green looked at him shrewdly. "I know what you are thinking. Piper is a prestidigitator. If anybody could shove a couple of bags into that pool without anybody seeing him do it, it would be Piper."

"It's a possibility."

"He wouldn't need the lights to be put out."

"Not even to hide the bags themselves going down, emptying and gurgling as they went? He'd be able to put them in unseen, perhaps, but he'd have no control over them once they'd entered the water. A few minutes of darkness would help to cover his tracks."

Green nodded glumly. "I suppose so, but would an old trouper like Slim Piper know enough about leptospirosis to realise its potential for harm and the way to milk rats to get at the stuff?"

Masters looked straight at him. "No. I'd bet a large sum of money he wouldn't."

"Why bring him up then, Chief?" asked Berger.

"Simply to show that we don't know what skills were present round the swimming pool that night."

"Two magicians would be a bit much to expect, wouldn't they, Chief?"

"Possibly. But if we substitute a period of darkness as a cover for lack of ability at prestidigitation, then we must look for knowledge of deadly germs, and I wouldn't like to bet that there weren't several people round the pool that night who didn't have that particular accomplishment."

"Coupled with a strong dislike of Mr. Hugh Carlyle?"

"Just so. Or at least one of them with feelings of dislike."

"Somebody he had invited as a guest and so, presumably, regarded as a friend?"

"Or at least not inimical towards him."

"So we have to interview everybody on that list?"

"Perhaps not everybody, but some at least."

Berger scratched his head.

"Careful, lad," warned Green, "or you'll get splinters in your fingers."

"What? Oh, yes." The sergeant looked across at Masters, who waited for the question he knew was coming.

"You said you are going to see the AC (Crime), Chief, to tell him we have established that this was a case of attempted murder where a person, not the intended victim, was killed. Right?"

"Quite right."

Berger went on slowly, feeling his way through his side of the dialogue. "Can we be sure that murder was intended, Chief?"

"Explain what you have in mind, please."

"I've understood all along that Carla Sanders caught her fever because she had open wounds on her leg and the bugs got in that way. I'll go even further and suggest that even so she might have escaped if she'd whipped the bandage off her leg and used a fresh one. What I mean is, she continued to wear an infected dressing which was in direct contact with open wounds, thereby giving the bugs all the time in the world to get to work and enter her system."

"A very good point, indeed, Sergeant. It might account for the attack of fever being so virulent. The bandage would hold millions of the bugs which were—literally—applied to an open wound as a dressing. Small wonder the results were fulminating and rapidly fatal."

"Chalk one up, S'arnt," said Green, "and chuck over one of your fags before you do it."

Berger handed over his packet without a word and without looking at Green. He continued to address Masters. "If Carla Sanders died because she had scratches on her leg, presumably she wouldn't have died if she hadn't had scratches."

"No, no," interjected Tip. "She could have swallowed a mouthful of bug-infested water."

"Would that have been just as serious, then?"

181

"I honestly don't know," supplied Masters. "I imagine it would have been nasty, but at any rate the leptospirae wouldn't have been fed directly into the bloodstream."

"I've been trying to find an answer to that, Chief," said Tip, "but the nearest I could get, and I'm by no means sure it is true or would hold good in this case, is that if Carla Sanders had been drínking a fair amount of alcohol, her mouth and tubes could well have been so antiseptic as to be virtually leptospirocidal or more so than they would have been had she not been drinking alcohol. So if she took in a mouthful of water and spat it out without swallowing any..."

"Immediately on surfacing?"

"Yes, Chief. She could then, perhaps, have avoided a serious nasty by that route. But if she did swallow any, well then I imagine the contents of the inside of her stomach could well have been like one of those broths you mentioned as being culture mediums for bugs. And from then on she would grow her own colonies at a merry rate and so virtually bring about her own destruction."

"With a little help from her friends," murmured Green.

Masters ignored this and said to Berger: "You were making a point, Sergeant, before we got all the footnotes."

"Sorry, Chief," said Tip.

"Nothing to be sorry about. I was simply calling Sergeant Berger back to the point he was making."

"I asked if Carla Sanders would have died if she hadn't had open wounds on her leg. The answer seems to be that she wouldn't have died unless she'd swallowed some of the water. My point is, Chief, that whoever infected that pool would have been most unlikely to kill Hugh Carlyle unless he went into the water with some sort of open lesion on his body or unless he was in the habit of drinking his bath water."

"I don't think you are right, Sergeant. Take Hookham, for instance. He drained the pool and went in, wearing rubber boots, to scrub it out. He got a mild attack of something or other after simply wielding a brush."

"You are sure of that, Chief?"

"Not absolutely. But you have read the medical papers. One of them specifically states that the spirochaete enters the human body through skin abrasions or via the alimentary tract. This latter route was what Tip was referring to when she spoke of swallowing the water. So far, so good. But in the entry in one of the textbooks, under infective diseases, it states that in addition to these other routes, the spirochaete is also able to gain entry through the nasal mucosa. Did you hoist that inboard?"

"No, Chief."

"Ah! But it is a highly important point. I believe Hookham, while brushing the bottom and sides of the pool, got a spray of the liquid in his face thrown up by the action of the bristles. Nothing very much, perhaps. A few minute droplets not big enough to wipe away, as likely as not. If one or two of those particles of water entered his nostrils there is a reason for his mild influenza-like illness, with a little fever, lasting a couple of days. You saw such cases mentioned, did you?"

"Yes, Chief. It said mild cases recover without any specific treatment, most with no treatment at all."

"Right. So far, so good. We believe Hookham got a mild attack. But Hookham, I imagine, is a strong, healthy countryman, used to manual labour, and generally immune to the colds and other febrile diseases which flourish among indoor workers. Hugh Carlyle is very different. Though, apart from the effect on his lower limbs of his particular form of demyelinating disease, he appears to be a fit, strong man, the truth is somewhat different. Any infection, and by that I mean something as slight as a summer cold, can be very troublesome for Carlyle. A severe bout of flu would be very serious. You can imagine what an attack of Weil's disease would do to him."

"Carry him off without a shadow of a doubt," grunted Green. "Not nice." He looked across at Berger. "Were

183

you thinking that whoever dosed that pool only did it to give Carlyle a bout of flu to pay him out for some little thing? If so, you're wrong, lad. Anybody who would go to those lengths to get at a crippled man meant mischief. Real mischief. Like death in agony. In other words, lad, murder with a capital M."

Berger sat quiet for a moment or two, and then said quietly: "That's answered my question, Chief."

"Good. Now I suggest we break off this particular discussion and get about our several businesses."

The AC (Crime) had listened very carefully to what Masters had to report. His reaction was the expected one. The case was now to be upgraded from the mere investigation it had started out as, to a full-blown murder enquiry.

"For me to tackle, sir?" asked Masters.

"Who else? The girl died in the Metropolitan area, so she's your pigeon. In any case you're nine tenths of the way to a solution, so it would be ridiculous to duplicate work by passing it over to somebody else. And I'm damn' sure the Kent people won't want to know about it, though I'll be getting through to them to keep them informed of what has happened."

Masters got to his feet.

Anderson said shrewdly: "Don't let it worry you, George. You've told me all about your business agreement with Carlyle, so there's no chance of any awkward questions being asked. You've been quite open about it and I shall shove a note in my diary to that effect. It will go in today's entry upgrading the Sanders case to one of murder and I'll minute my clearance for you to go ahead with the house-buying."

"Thank you, sir."

"Now don't be long about this business, George. Get it sewn up tight as soon as possible. We've wasted too much valuable time on it already."

*   *   *

Hookham tilted his old trilby hat and scratched his head above one ear.

"Plazzi bags, you say? In the swimming pool that day? Sunday worn't it? Aye, Sunday. Extra clean up I'ad to do. We-ell, there was a deal of rubbish there. Food of one sort or another. Aye, and glass. Two or three glasses not broke, but some were smashed to flinders. And my old woman said to go in in my bare feet! I ask you!"

"Plastic bags," reminded Berger quietly.

"No bags that I remember. I swep' up, of course and had a heap of rubbish, but bags! I can't remember any bags."

"Could you have missed them?" asked Tip anxiously. "Just not noticed them, perhaps."

"Let me see now. I opened up the drain, like. I don't have to go in to do that. Just turn the wheel over there."

"Just a moment," said Berger. "Weren't you a bit worried all the rubbish might block the drain?"

"Not it," said Hookham. "There's a grill to . . ."

"Yes?" asked Berger quietly.

"Now you come to mention it . . ."

"What?"

"It stopped."

"What did?"

"The outflow, of course. When there was still more than two foot of water left."

Berger and Tip said nothing, unwilling to break the slow thread of thought.

"Aye, that's right. I had to go in. There wasn't any depth at the shallow end, of course. Lucky there wasn't or I'd 'ave needed thigh waders at the deep end and I hadn't got them up here with me. It woulda meant going back to the cottage, an' that's a tidy step, there an' back."

Berger just managed to keep his patience as Hookham rambled on. Tip took hold of his wrist and gripped it tightly as a warning against interrupting.

"Were was I? Aye! Even so I had to use a stick to unblock that drain. Clogged it was."

"What with?" asked Berger at last.

"Why, plazzi bags, of course. In't that what you're asking? Glass and stuff doesn't block sinks like them bags. They sit over the grill like a waterproof tent. Glass an' stuff just works like an extra filter."

"What did you do with the bags, Mr. Hookham?" asked Tip.

"Let me see now. Oh, yes. I chucked 'em up onto the side. On to the surround, like. I didn't just want to rake them away so's they could float back an' play the same trick again, did I?"

"And you collected them up later?"

"No, I didn't, now you come to mention it. Forgot all about 'em, I did. Somebody else must 'ave took 'em, because I'd 'ave seen them there since, an' I 'aven't."

Tip went to call on Mrs. Hookham.

"Took some old plastic from round the pool? I should just think I did. Mucky stuff! Where it came from I can't imagine. But there, at a party you get all sorts."

"You've no idea who could have brought it?"

"I put it down to them caterers we had in. Thought it was something they'd had to cover food on the tables and couldn't be bothered to bring it indoors. The breeze took it into the water, I suppose. At any rate, that's where Hookham got it from. I saw him throw it onto the surround, so I picked it up and put it in the outside bin."

"Which has been emptied since then I suppose?"

"Every Tuesday, regular as clockwork. We've got good bin men. I tie the sacks up Monday afternoon and they're here to collect it before eight next morning."

"I see. Did you happen to notice whether the plastic was a sheet or bags?"

"Bags it was. At least there was corners among it. But I didn't count them. Just ordinary see-through plazzi-bags as far as I was concerned."

And with that, Berger and Tip had to be satisfied.

Masters rang Hugh Carlyle at the latter's office. "'Morning, Hugh. No, not about Housmans. I'm leaving all that to Wanda for the moment. I understand she and

186

Doris Green...yes, wife of DCI Green whom you met...are close to some arrangement about taking over our little place. Yes, the Greens appear to have a buyer for their present house, but nothing is certain these days, so we can't go firm for a day or two yet. Business? Yes, I'm calling on a business matter. Interviewing people. We'd like a word with some of your guests. No, we won't upset them. I don't suppose your daughter and her boyfriend will mind answering a few questions, will they? No? Right. If I could have her address. Yes, Rosemary's. And the phone number..."

Green, who had been listening to this conversation, asked, "Does this mean a trip to Cambridge?"

"It might well mean that."

"Today?"

"I shan't know until after I've phoned Rosemary Carlyle. But we can do it fairly easily in a long afternoon if the Sergeants get back with the car."

"They'll be here for a latish lunch," Green forecast.

"In that case, if the girl can see us today I'll make an appointment." Masters picked up the phone. A minute or two later he said: "I thought they'd be living together in that holiday cottage, but they're not."

"Haven't fallen out, have they?"

"No. Young Chesterton goes to see her every afternoon apparently. He's got some sort of mornings-only job for the vacation and is still living in his digs in the city."

"Right. What time did she suggest? I didn't hear her say."

"Anytime we can get there. She gave me instructions for finding the place."

"In that case let's have some lunch while we wait for the kids."

They were on their way by half-past two. Berger took them east to Stratford and then turned north to join the M11. Masters had not asked for a report on the Sergeants' journey to Kent, preferring to let them have lunch and to hear what they had to say during the journey.

Tip had made a full report by the time the Rover was fairly on to the motorway. When she had finished her account of the interviews with Hookham and his wife, Green, who had been paying close attention to all that was said, despite his almost pathological dread of travelling in heavy traffic, said: "It looks as though you guessed right, George. About the plastic bags, I mean."

"No guess, really," said Masters quietly. "Or if it was it was sparked off by your remark about the litre tonic bottle."

"How come?"

"Of late, our tonic has been delivered in plastic bottles. Not glass as formerly. There's an instruction with these new ones. About their disposal. The suggestion is to fill them with hot water. This softens the plastic to a degree that after emptying them you can put your foot on them and they flatten."

"Like disposing of old tin cans."

"Just like that. I found Wanda trying it out one day. Her tread couldn't have been heavy enough. The one she was doing didn't go fully flat."

"You mean it splurged out into a flask shape? Like a half-bottle of whisky?"

"More or less. When I took over they squashed completely flat."

"They would, wouldn't they, with your plates of meat?"

"Quite. But it was the recollection of that which made me think of the bags. Flat, easy to carry bags like the ones you buy frozen shrimps in. Convenient to hide about the person."

Green grunted his understanding and his acceptance of the acknowledgement of his part in the discovery of how the leptospirae were almost certainly introduced into the pool.

"Straight into Cambridge itself, Chief?"

"No. My instructions from Miss Carlyle were to continue along the motorway till junction fourteen, then to take the six-oh-four trunk road for a short way until the turning for a small village called Dry Drayton. On the left. The cottage overlooks a golf course before we reach the village."

"Got it, Chief."

The cottage was easy to find, but it was not a cottage. It was a part of a larger house called Gleaners Hall, a long building almost surrounded by derelict barns, but recently converted into three dwellings for summer letting. As Berger did a hairpin left turn off the minor road, he ran onto a patch of gravel newly laid to provide hard-standing for the three cottages. Before they were fairly out of the car, Rosemary Carlyle appeared at one of the nearby front doors.

"Hello, Mr. Masters."

"Hello, Rosemary."

The two had met, briefly, some years before, when Masters and Wanda had called in on her parents. Then Rosemary had been a grown-up girl. Now she was a personable young woman whom Masters had some difficulty in recognising at first glance.

"You've changed, Rosemary. You're well and truly adult now."

"Am I?" She laughed. "I suppose a year or two at my age does make a difference. How is Mrs. Masters?"

"Very well, thank you. Has your mother told you Wanda is expecting another baby?"

"Oh, yes. Mummy was a bit worried about the lateness. In age, I mean." She reddened. "Oh, I am sorry. I didn't mean..."

"Don't apologise. Wanda and I both know that fortyish is not the best time for a woman to have children, but we have taken the best advice and Wanda is in good hands."

"I'm sure she is." Rosemary looked across to where the other three had congregated. "Can I meet the rest of your team? Mummy told me she has been very impressed by them."

The introductions were made.

"Now come in for a cup of tea," invited Rosemary. "Everything is ready. Or it should be if Tom is doing his stuff properly."

"Is he good in the kitchen, love, this lad of yours?" asked Green as they went through the door which had obviously been newly pierced into this part of the wall.

"Not bad. Do you know what he made for supper last night?"

"Tell me."

"Giblet pie. Have you ever heard of it?"

"Heard of it? I lived on it when I was a kid."

"I thought your staple diet was white stew with bubble-and-squeak," said Berger. "It was the last time the subject was mentioned."

"You mind your own barrer, lad. And if you can't push it, shove it."

Rosemary gurgled with mirth at this verbal passage and went to call Tom from the kitchen into the quite large sitting room of the cottage.

"Glad to meet anybody who can make and appreciate giblet pie," said Green, greeting him. "As long as you take that wrinkled skin out of the gizzards and then chop them small."

"What? The wrinkled skins?" asked Berger.

"The meat," said Tom with a grin. He turned back to Green. "I cut everything very small," he said. "I stew the necks whole—with the chopped livers, hearts and so on—then I strip the meat from the bones so that there's no impediment to easy eating."

"You're a man after my own heart, lad. Can you buy sets easily enough?"

"From the local poulterer. Dirt cheap, because so many of his customers don't want the offal."

"More fools they."

"Tea for everybody?" asked Rosemary loudly.

There was plenty of room for everybody to sit. The owners of the cottage, in addition to a three-piece suite, had added a divan bed to make extra sleeping space for

190

their clients. Berger and Tip shared this, Rosemary and Tom were on the settee. Masters and Green had the armchairs.

The questioning began with Masters asking whether either of the young people had noticed anybody dropping or putting anything into the pool.

Both assured him that they hadn't.

"No unusual movement when the lights went out?"

Rosemary shrugged. "It was almost dark, and I must admit I was more interested in the area of the French windows. I wasn't watching the pool. Not the ends and side away from the house, anyway. And they were in deep shadow. You know how the trees and shrubs throw quite thick patches of black."

"And I went indoors to replace the fuse," said Chesterton.

"Which fuse was it?" asked Berger. "In the plug top or in the box?"

"In the plug, actually. I had to go to the box to get a new fuse. The packets of fuses and electrical screwdrivers hang inside the cupboard, so I took the opportunity, while I was there, to see that the circuit fuse had not blown."

"The lights in the house stayed on?"

"Power and lights are on different ring mains. They have to be, at least in that part of the house, because of the need to plug in certain pieces of massage equipment and the like for Mr. Carlyle. I imagine he didn't want to run the risk of overloading."

"Why not use the outside point?" asked Berger. "There is one there."

"I can answer that," said Rosemary. "Daddy wanted to be able to control the lights from inside the house. Often when they were out there it would start to rain, so he preferred a switch inside. And in any case, Hookham, I remember, was using the outside point for his electric tools after he had rigged the lights which he put up and tested in the morning. I remember him using that strimmer thing round the edges of the grass and under the bushes."

"Thank you," said Masters. He turned to Berger. "Does that answer all your questions about the lights?"

"Yes, Chief. Though I'd like to examine the whole string."

Chesterton looked around at the four detectives. "Before we go much further, can we know what's going on? You've suggested something was put in the pool. What was it? Not a live wire or anything like that, otherwise Carla Sanders would have died in the water, not two or three days later."

"Are you a biologist or anything akin to one, Mr. Chesterton?"

"Good lord, no. I'm strictly on the other side of the fence. Languages, the written word and so forth."

"And you, Rosemary?"

"I'm modern languages. That's how I met Tom."

"I see. So the mention of leptospirae would mean nothing to either of you."

"Not directly," agreed Tom. "But I could work something out. Let me see. *Lepto*, that's Greek for small or slender; *speira* means a coil...yes, it's some minute coil-shaped bug, at a guess. Something perhaps that can't be seen without a microscope."

"Quite correct. A bug. A dangerous bug, a large number of which we believe was dumped in Mr. Carlyle's pool that Saturday night while the lights were out."

"It wasn't all that dark, I seem to remember. For dirty deeds one would need the cover of total darkness, I'd have thought."

"Or a diversion," said Tip. "Like the sudden fusing of the lights."

"I see what you mean. But to tip a bucketful of leptospirae..."

"Why do you say bucketful, Mr. Chesterton?"

Tom looked at Masters. "Sorry. I just sort of assumed they would be in liquid form if they were to go into the

192

water, and you said a large number was introduced. A bucket just came to mind."

"I see. Did you notice any buckets near the pool?"

"Lord, no."

Rosemary asked quietly, "These leptospirae killed Carla Sanders, I suppose."

"Yes."

"But nobody could have known she would go into the water."

"No."

"But everybody at the party would have known my father would be bathing in it the next morning."

"Quite right."

"So Daddy was to have been the victim?"

"We think so."

Chesterton sat forward. "I see now why you are here. Attempted murder."

"Murder, Mr. Chesterton. Not just attempted. The wrong victim, maybe, but still murder."

Tom looked across at Rosemary. "Then we owe Carla Sanders a big vote of thanks for the part she played, because if we hadn't been fooling about just there, with her, I mean, Mrs. H. wouldn't have chucked a trayful of dirties into the drink, thereby ensuring your father couldn't bathe without the pool being emptied and cleaned first."

Rosemary nodded abstractedly at what sounded like the final clearing-up of a sore point in the relationship between the two young people.

"That's one way of looking at things," agreed Masters, "but it doesn't get us any nearer to discovering who meant to do harm to Mr. Carlyle."

"No," agreed Tom, "but I'd say it definitely absolves whoever shoved Carla Sanders and Mrs. H.'s trayload of goodies into the water. That rather saved the day, didn't it?"

"Were you responsible?" asked Masters.

"Unfortunately not. What I mean is . . . oh, hell, the chap who nudged Carla in is indirectly responsible for her death and Mr. Carlyle's life."

"Put like that, it sounds nasty, son," said Green. "But there's no doubt which of the two your girlie here would rather have alive. So let's have the names of all those of you who were crowded round Carla Sanders when she went in, and we can leave you all aside, at least for the time being."

"What? Oh, yes. I can remember there was ..."

Tom and Rosemary between them produced five names which Tip noted for crossing off the guest list.

Masters turned to Rosemary. "Did you know your father had received several anonymous letters during the few weeks before the party?"

"No. Were they threatening ones?"

"Not exactly. Abusive more than anything else. Abusive and accusing."

"Accusing him of what?"

"Unprofessional behaviour. Using other people's ideas for his own advantage."

"Stealing inventions, you mean?"

"I assume so."

"Daddy would never do anything like that."

"He didn't have to, love," said Green. "Only to be thought to be pinching ideas. By a disgruntled and unsuccessful would-be inventor, of course."

"There has never been any scandal like that about Daddy or his firm. It's known for its good reputation. No company like his could operate for a day without absolute honesty and integrity and ... and reliability ... and ..."

Masters cut in gently. "So you have never before heard the slightest whisper of anything that would call the probity of your father's operations into question?"

"Never," said Rosemary vehemently.

"But I have," said Chesterton quietly.

There was a long moment of silence before Rosemary swung round to face him. "Tom! You can't have! Daddy is so honest!"

"It wasn't about your father personally. One of his staff."

"Why didn't you tell me?"

"I wanted to, that Saturday night. But you choked me off about a certain person, remember?"

"Carla Sanders?"

"No."

Rosemary stared at him for a moment or two. Then: "You mean Andrew McRolfe?"

Chesterton nodded. "Old man Carpenter told me."

"Rubbish," said Rosemary. "You're only saying that about Andrew because..."

"Because what, Miss Carlyle?" asked Tip quietly.

"Because the silly fool is jealous."

"Without cause?"

"Just because one of Daddy's managers pays me a bit of attention when he sees me, this silly ass here gets all uptight about him."

Tom shrugged his shoulders in mock despair.

Because the two names mentioned, McRolfe and Carpenter, were the two men known to be Scots, Masters was more than passing interested in this conversation. It was apparent that Green was almost holding his breath in anticipation of something, while Berger was sitting forward in his seat, forgetting he was still holding an empty tea cup in one hand and the saucer in the other. Masters took over the reins from Tip.

"I'd like to hear what you have to say, Mr. Chesterton. Especially whatever it was you wanted to tell Rosemary that night but which you didn't tell her because there was some temporary huff between you."

Chesterton answered. "First off, we were told McRolfe had refused his invitation to the party on the grounds that he was attending some business meeting. Then he turned up. Evidently he'd rung Mrs. Carlyle and said the meeting had been cancelled, so could he come to the party after all. I only got to know this when I saw him there."

"You just disliked him coming," said Rosemary.

"Too true I did. For quite a lot of reasons."

"Tell me those reasons, Mr. Chesterton, please."

"First, I never believed that any man would have a business meeting on a Saturday night, so I reckoned there was something a bit iffy about his first refusal and then his acceptance."

"That's no reason for jealousy," said Rosemary witheringly.

"Please go on," prompted Masters.

"I had intended to ask Mrs. Carlyle about it, but I forgot. However, I do know that Rosemary and I had said at first that we didn't think we could make that Saturday. Rosie had promised to help to look after some mentally ill children who were being taken for a holiday at the seaside and I was working on the Saturday morning."

"But it turned out that you were both free."

"Yes. What we hadn't realised was that the kids' holiday was to finish first thing on Saturday morning. Immediately after breakfast a coach was to pick them up and take them home under the care of their own full-time staff. That meant that Rosemary could get down from Cromer on the Saturday morning so that we would both be here in Cambridge and free to go by lunchtime. As soon as we knew that we rang to say we would attend the party. We couldn't get Mrs. Carlyle at home, so Rosemary rang her father's office and left a message there."

"I see. And it was after that message reached the Carlyle office that McRolfe changed his mind."

"I'm certain of that, but I have no proof of it. Just a damned great suspicion that..."

"Stop it, Tom."

"No fear, sweetie. I'd seen McRolfe nosing about after you."

"He fancied me."

"That's where you are mistaken. He did not fancy you. Not in the way you put it. I told you that Saturday night that McRolfe was an ambitious scug, and what he was after was the Carlyle firm. Not just a good position in it. The whole shooting match. And the best way he could think of doing it was to marry the boss's only daughter."

"Thank you very much."

"Don't get tetchy about it. I told you this on the night of the party and all you did was put your little nose in the air and stalk off."

"Only because you were dancing attendance on Carla Sanders."

"Why not, if my own girl left me in the lurch?"

Masters coughed. "I feel sure that you don't want to come to blows in front of an audience of policemen. Could you continue what you were telling us, do you think, Mr. Chesterton?"

"Sorry. That McRolfe bloke has been on my mind a bit, recently."

"Understandable," grunted Green. "If I'd got a girl like you have to fight for I'd be on red alert for action the whole time."

"Thanks. But to get back to what I was saying. When Rosemary here left me to look for McRolfe that night . . ."

"I didn't go to look for McRolfe specifically."

"No? Well, it damned well seemed like it."

"Children, children!" cautioned Green.

Tom Chesterton turned to Masters. "As soon as Rosemary left me, old Carpenter spoke to me. It was obvious he had overheard every word Rosemary and I had said. I had only met him once before, briefly, but nobody would forget him. Thin and beaky, like a buzzard, he is, with a trace of a Scots accent. I tried to get rid of him, but he said he'd heard us mention McRolfe, and then went on to say that though McRolfe is a highly thought of designer in Mr. Carlyle's company, he was, nevertheless, and here I quote Carpenter's exact words: 'McRolfe is using his position at Carlyle's to further his own ends.'"

"You didn't tell me this," said Rosemary wildly.

"I wanted to but you gave me to understand you wouldn't hear anything against your precious McRolfe."

"Go on, lad," urged Green. "You're winning."

"What? Oh, I told Carpenter that he had made quite an accusation."

"And what did he reply to that?"

"He jabbered something I took to be a Scots expression. 'Maybe aye and maybe hoohaye' was what it sounded like to me. I've remembered it because I'd never heard it before and I took it to mean that maybe he had made a false accusation against McRolfe and maybe he hadn't. So I said that if he had any proof of definite knowledge of professional misconduct on McRolfe's part, he should tell Mr. Carlyle."

"Then what did he say?" asked Rosemary.

"He said something about he thought the hint would be of use to me in making sure you didn't end up in McRolfe's arms."

"How did he know anything about it?" flamed Rosemary. "I suppose you told him."

"I didn't, actually, Roz. I told you he had overheard what you and I had been saying. I don't suppose either of us kept our voices down."

"So what did you say to the nosey old thing?"

"I thanked him for the kind thought and suggested he was making the whole thing up. He then said he was simply trying to help you and me. I'm afraid I lost my temper a bit at that point and said he had only made the accusation against McRolfe in the hope that I would pass it on to your father. I reckoned he wanted your father to know for some purpose of his own."

"To do McRolfe dirt?" asked Green quietly.

"Just that. Then he amazed me by claiming that he had tried telling Mr. Carlyle but he wouldn't listen, which I said was pretty much what I would have expected because Mr. Carlyle is the type of man who is loyal to his staff. Anyhow, that was that. Carpenter said I could take what he'd told me any way I liked, he had spoken merely because he didn't like the idea of McRolfe coming between Rosemary and me."

"That was everything, was it, Mr. Chesterton?" asked Masters.

"Yes. I left Carpenter and looked for Rosemary, to tell her. But she had found McRolfe and was talking to him so I couldn't say anything then, and when I did get Roz alone she didn't give me a chance to bring the subject up. She was too intent on roasting me for hovering around Carla Sanders."

"And since then?"

"I'd forgotten about it. You know, in all the stir over Carla dying and whatnot."

"Really?"

"No, not really," said Chesterton shamefacedly. "I didn't forget it, but once Roz and I were back here and our relationship on an even keel again, I didn't want to rock the boat by bringing up the subject of McRolfe again. If I had done I'd have only got an earful."

"Now I understand," said Masters with a grin. He turned to the girl. "Your young man says you sought out McRolfe at the party."

"Yes."

"Would you like to tell us what was said?"

"Nothing really. I felt a bit of a wimp about it because deep down I knew there was something in what Tom had said, but I couldn't let him get away with it just like that, could I?"

"Certainly not," agreed Tip.

Rosemary glanced at her gratefully. "I knew Andrew McRolfe had made a set at me, but I had a horrible feeling there was no underlying affection in his moves. I mean, I know, even when Tom and I are rowing like cat and dog, that behind it all there's . . . well . . . love, I suppose. On both sides."

Tom took her hand. "Bang on, Roz. Any more little secrets you'd like to let out?"

She turned to him. "You fool. Absolutely nothing went on or was said that night. I invited him to have a drink and he said he'd have a hock and seltzer. I ask you!"

"Seltzer?"

"He wanted white wine diluted with carbonated spring water. I told him to help himself so's to get it

199

right, and told him that if he was as hot as all that he should take his jacket off and put it indoors where it would be quite safe. After all, no other man at the party was wearing a jacket. A couple of old boys had those thin, fawny coloured things . . . what are they called?"

"Alpaca," suggested Green.

"That's the name. But other than those two everybody was in shirts of various shapes and hues."

"What did Mr. McRolfe say to that suggestion?" asked Masters.

"He said he thought perhaps he would keep it on. I wondered for a moment if he was perhaps wearing braces."

"Anything else?"

"I said he could do just as he liked about his jacket, of course, but told him he looked weighed down by it and lest he might just be frightened of catching a chill I pointed out that the evening was gloriously warm. He said he would think about it, and I left him to get his drink while I circulated."

There was a short silence. Masters glanced across at Green, who stared back fixedly. Then Green turned to Rosemary. To her great surprise he asked: "What sort of a jacket was it, love?"

"What sort of a jacket? What does that matter?"

"Please tell me."

"It was a tweedy sort of thing. A sports coat, I suppose."

"A properly tailored jacket, fully lined, with all its pockets, internal and external?"

"As far as I know, yes."

"It was," said Chesterton. "I remember seeing him in it and in my general disgust at his presence there, thought how inappropriate it was. But, in fact, it was a very handsome garment: nice material, long-skirted. You know the sort of thing, judging by the cut of the decent bit of gents' natty you are wearing yourself. It hung well."

"I think I know what you mean," said Masters with a straight face.

"Gussets," said Tip suddenly.

Green looked round at her. "Now what, sweetie?"

"I don't think the pockets were gussetted," said Rosemary. "They weren't patch pockets."

"Sorry," said Tip. "I was thinking and the word just slipped out."

"Oh." Rosemary looked round. "Is that everything?"

"There's very little more I can tell you," said Chesterton. "Not about any reason for Mr. Carlyle being accused of unprofessional conduct, I mean."

"You didn't see McRolfe or Carpenter again at the party?"

"Oh I *saw* them, but I didn't speak to them again."

"Did you speak to either of them later, Rosemary?"

"Yes, I think. In fact, I'm sure so, because I remember saying goodnight to them both."

"Was that before or after Miss Sanders fell into the pool?"

"Before for Andrew McRolfe."

"But not for Carpenter?"

"He went much later."

"Are you sure of those times, love?" asked Green.

"Very sure. Andrew came up and said he was going just about the time I was going to try and get this slob out of the Sanders mob."

"Me?" asked Tom in surprise.

"Yes, you. You must remember. I saw Andrew off and then came back and caught you carrying another plate of food for that woman."

"She had a bad leg, you know."

"And an appetite like a horse, apparently, judging from the number of plates of food all you men collected for her. I remember you told me she wasn't wearing a bra."

"And you said you'd like to push her into the pool and . . ." He looked up, suddenly, aware of what he had said. He sat with his mouth half open as the detectives regarded him wordlessly. At last—

"Go on, Mr. Chesterton," said Masters.

"There wasn't anything more. I merely said we'd all get an eyeful if Carla did go into the pool and came out with just that thin blouse clinging to her contours, and Roz walked away in a huff. She didn't give Carla the old heave-ho, I assure you."

"Despite her stated wish to do so?"

"Yes."

"I believe you, Mr. Chesterton, and even if I didn't I'm not here to investigate an incident such as ducking somebody in a swimming pool."

"Thank heaven for that. For a moment I had myself worried."

Masters reverted to the subject under discussion. "So McRolfe went home early. Before Miss Sanders took her plunge, but after the lights had gone out and been repaired."

"A long time after the lights had been mended."

"Thank you. And Carpenter?"

"After we had sent Carla Sanders home. I remember him saying he would drive her if necessary, but Mummy had already arranged for a young couple to take her. They hadn't been drinking, or something, and I think Mummy thought a couple would be safer than one man alone with Sanders."

"I see. Thank you. That's it unless there is anything else you feel you would like to tell us."

Both the young people shook their heads. Then Chesterton said: "Look, I hope what I've said won't start a witch hunt over what Carpenter said about McRolfe. It could all have been a load of rubbish, you know."

Green said, "Don't worry about it, lad. We don't waste time on witch hunts. But you neither of you told us whether McRolfe ever did get so hot that he took his jacket off."

"I don't think he did," said Rosemary. "As I said earlier, I think he must have been wearing braces. He's the sort that would—at a party like that, I mean."

The next morning the four detectives presented themselves at Carpenter's office. Masters had got the address by the simple expedient of ringing Hugh Carlyle the previous evening. He had refused to satisfy Carlyle's curiosity other than to say he was working his way through most of the guests in an effort to get some sort of lead.

For some reason, Masters was not surprised to hear that Carpenter's office was close to the old Billingsgate Market, tucked away in a narrow little way between Eastcheap and Lower Thames Street, where the buildings still retained some of their original features and where the doors and window bars were still there to fill an appreciative eye.

"I've been expecting a call from somebody," said Carpenter when they had been shown into his office.

"Somebody, Mr. Carpenter?"

"After that lassie died so suddenly."

"Interesting that," said Green, pulling up a chair with one foot and then sitting down. "Fishy, in fact, mate, seeing we only decided yesterday morning that there was something definite for us to look into."

Carpenter pushed his thin beaky face forward on its long neck and grinned at Green, eyes twinkling. "Scotland Yard isn't the sole repository of common sense, knowledge and intelligence you know, Jimmy." It was said with a Scots accent.

Berger and Tip started to grin. Green took it unabashed. "Meaning, I suppose, that the halesome parritch is good brain food."

"As is fish, I understand. And you were the first to mention fish."

"So I did."

"'Who fished the murex up? What porridge had John Keats?'"

"You've beaten me," confessed Green, much to the surprise of the others. "What's murex?"

"It's a sort of sea mussel which gives a purple dye."

"Spill it, all of it. Tell us how you know Carla Sanders' death was fishy."

"As you will no doubt have guessed I have a deal to do with the fish trade which, sadly, is not what it was."

"Common Market and the Icelanders stopping trawlers fishing their old grounds?"

"In a nutshell, yes. And the less fish there is the dearer it becomes and so sales slump even further."

"When I was a lad," continued Green, "there was a decent wet-fish shop round every corner."

"Quite. And a fish and chip shop charged tuppence for the lump of cod and a penny for the potatoes."

"Where is all this getting us?" asked Masters.

Carpenter turned a sharp eye on him. "It means that chaps like me, who inherited a once-thriving business, now have to diversify to scrape a living, while we see our ships rusting out and our deckhands on the dole."

"I try to appreciate the tragedy, Mr. Carpenter."

"You do, eh? Well, perhaps you do, vaguely. But me, I've had to look around, and one of the things I've found I could do, was invent this and that. Just little items connected with my trade, you'll understand, though my father gave me a pretty good education as a grounding for using my brain for something other than providing cod to the makers of fishfingers."

"I understand that bit."

"To spark off ideas I read up everything that's been written about the fishing industry, from the mechanics of belly-and-baitings to..."

"Belly-and-what?" demanded Berger.

"Baitings. It's a type of trawl net."

"I see, sir. Sorry to have interrupted you."

"No matter." He turned again to Masters. "From nets through packing, sales, preservation, right through to hygiene."

"And it is this last which made you suspect that the death of Miss Carla Sanders was far from straightforward?"

"Aye, it was. When I read yon papers talking about

death from uraemia brought on by acute infection it struck a chord in my mind."

"Played a lament on a pigskin piano, did it?" queried Green.

"It did that."

"Now what's he on about?" Tip whispered to Berger.

"Old Greeny always calls bagpipes pigskin pianos."

"Oh."

"Please continue, Mr. Carpenter," said Masters, not in the least displeased at the unconventional form the interview was taking, and realising that Green was as keen as he was himself to hear what Carpenter was leading up to. He could sense the coming confirmation of at least some of their own views.

"I told you I studied the hygiene of the fish trade. And one of the things I read up was the incidence of certain infections common earlier in the century among fish market workers. Some of these were fatal. Much less so now than formerly, of course. The most likely group were the *icterohaemorrhagiae* infections." He grinned at Green. "Now there's a word to go to bed with. Do you think you can spell it?"

"Me?" grunted Green. "Of course. Even our girlie Sergeant here can spell it, can't you love?"

"Quite easily," answered Tip and proceeded to do so.

Carpenter looked at them shrewdly. "You people are ahead of me," he accused.

"Don't forget we have read the postmortem reports," said Masters. "You were telling us of infections in fish markets."

"Aye. Those were the ones that interested me. But I learned all about leptospirosis, because it gave me an idea for a little invention. Quite a simple one. Nothing more than a high-pressure jet that would fit an ordinary garden hose. Handheld and about a yard long, it had a multiadjustable head so that it could get into any corner or crevice where bugs might lurk. But the point is, that ordinary fresh water doesn't kill the bugs. So there had to be a means of introducing a leptospirocidal fluid into

205

the jet. My reading told me that acid—even an acid as weak as acid urine—kills off the bugs. So I incorporated a reservoir in the jet to hold something like weak, watered-down vinegar or any old acid left over from manufacturing processes which could be diluted down and then fed gradually into the jet stream. An addition that would cost little or nothing and yet do the trick. And it worked. I sold—or rather Hugh Carlyle did—quite a large number round the world in docks, mines, sewage works and so on."

"Hugh Carlyle sold them?"

"Yes. I was recommended to go to him with my original plans and he produced the prototypes. He knew what materials to use and he had the plant and the designing expertise. And he knows something about marketing, so he farmed out the large-scale manufacture and the selling. Of course, now, there are quite a lot of jet hoses for cleaning cars and things, with reservoirs for soaps or detergents. More dainty and sophisticated than my original, but I got a deal of satisfaction out of having the idea and knowing that it worked and was effective."

"And a bit of brass, too, no doubt?" queried Green.

"A little. Not much. We didn't sell millions, or even thousands."

"Hard luck."

"We've strayed from the point a little," reminded Masters.

"Aye, so we have. What I was going to say was that when I read how that girl died, suddenly, after an immersion in water at a time when she had severe abrasions on her leg, it rang a bell, because I knew that uraemia is a result of coming into contact with leptospirae and I also knew that ordinary members of the general public do not carry antibodies to leptospirae."

"So you suspected that the girl had died of Weil's disease?"

"I did. But there was nothing I could do about it. The pathologists had discovered it for themselves. I knew

206

that from the newspaper reports after the inquest, as I've just told you. There's one thing I did do, though." He grinned, showing his teeth. "I rang Mrs. Carlyle just to make sure her man's pool had been emptied and scrubbed. Without causing any alarm, you'll understand. It was easy enough to ask in a jocular fashion if they'd scraped the cherries off the bottom and cleared up the broken glass."

"That was good of you, Mr. Carpenter," said Tip.

Carpenter grinned. "I don't want Hugh Carlyle out of the way just yet, lassie. Apart from his being a very nice man, he has one or two little ideas of mine in hand."

"Such as?" asked Green.

Carpenter looked at him cannily. "I'm not for telling anybody my ideas, but if after you leave the police force you become a ship's husband, then you'll be able to buy my wee inventions, maybe."

"Ship's husband? I'm already a husband."

"Let me see," said Masters. "A ship's husband would be the man on shore who sees to making sure that the craft has everything it requires on board before setting sail."

"Right. Trawling fleets and the likes have them. Fuel, nets, food, ropes, ice, salt. Whatever's needed, quartermaster, I suppose."

Masters looked round his team at this point as though urging caution. Then—

"We have established the presence of leptospirae in Mr. Carlyle's swimming pool, Mr. Carpenter. How do you suppose they got there?"

"Infected rats widdling in it."

"That would seem to be the way, but can you see rats going into that pool? There is nothing in the water for them to eat. There are no nesting holes round the sides near the surface. The surround is closely paved and godly clean. Outside that are nothing but shaven lawns. What would cause infected rats—or any rats, even voles—to enter what to them must be an incredibly bleak ambience?"

"They are nosey little devils. One of them could have fallen in."

"A rat, fall in? You, if anybody, should know how they can run up and down ships' mooring ropes with the surest footing."

"Aye, true."

"And, of your knowledge of such things, do you think one rat falling into that pool would or could infect it strongly before climbing out, presumably up an absolutely vertical set of stainless steel tubular ladders?"

"No rat could ever climb those steps," agreed Carpenter. "Once in there, a rat would stay in. It might then pass water a number of times before it drowned."

"True. But if any of the Carlyle household found a drowned rat in the pool, what do you think would happen?"

"They're awful careful folk with Carlyle's health. The pool would be emptied and scrubbed out before being refilled."

"That is my belief, too. So where do you imagine the infected bugs came from, Mr. Carpenter?"

"You're saying they were introduced malevolently?"

"Something of the sort had crossed my mind. Now, Mr. Carpenter, I don't think that many people other than medical men of one sort or another will have read, as you have, all the details of leptospirosis. The clinical picture, its incidence, treatment and prevention."

"I suppose that's right."

"So, if the leptospirae were introduced—as you put it—malevolently into that pool, who would have the knowledge, expertise and opportunity to do it?"

Carpenter stared hard at him for a moment. Then he said quietly: "Are you saying it was me that did it?"

"No, Mr. Carpenter, I am not. But did you?"

"I did not."

Green took out a packet of cigarettes and, surprisingly, handed them round. The gesture broke the tension.

8

"Let us look at the situation logically, Mr. Carpenter," said Masters. "Carla Sanders died of Weil's disease contracted in Hugh Carlyle's pool during a party. You are a confessedly well-read man on the subject of Weil's disease. You are a business acquaintance of Carlyle and you were at the party. We are agreed that the number of people who can know much about leptospirae is very small. Could one of those few, other than yourself, have been at the party and used the opportunity for contaminating the pool? Would you say that such a person was unlikely to be among the guests?"

Carpenter pursed his lips. "Put that way, I'd say the chances were hundreds to one against."

"Are you sure of that?"

"How do you mean?"

"There were certain members of Mr. Carlyle's staff at the party. I believe that all his employees are men with scientific knowledge of one sort or another."

"Engineers, electrics and electronic buffs, mechanics, draughtsmen. Those sorts of men. Not too knowledgeable about biology or microbiology."

"Are you a biologist?"

"Not with any formal qualification."

"But you could learn about leptospirae."

"Given the right papers to read."

"Couldn't somebody else have read those papers? Your copies of them, perhaps?"

"My copies. I take dam' good care . . ." He paused and stared reflectively at Masters. "You're a canny laddie," he said at last. "Everything I had that had any bearing on my jet hose was in one file. Medical papers, my drawings, specifications, everything."

"And?"

"When I approached Hugh Carlyle about the manufacture of the prototype I naturally left the file with him, in his office, for him to read."

"So any of the Carlyle staff could have seen it."

"Carlyle is a careful man. If an idea like mine wasn't actively being worked on, it would be locked away in secure storage. Safe cupboards, they're called. Made of steel with combination locks."

"I'm sure security at Carlyle's is of the highest. It is the foundation stone of a company of that nature. But that doesn't prevent members of the staff learning the secrets, does it?"

"Several of them would have to work on each specification. Designers for instance."

"Ah!"

Again Carpenter thrust his neck out and peered at him. "Now what's biting you?"

Green took up the questioning. "You'll realise we are talking to everybody who went to that party."

"Aye. I'd expect you to do that."

"Yesterday we spoke to Rosemary Carlyle and young Tom Chesterton."

"A bonnie pair."

"We were given to understand you thought so, otherwise you wouldn't have warned the lad against Andrew McRolfe who, you said, was trying to cut him out."

"That's true. I've been thinking about that. Perhaps I shouldn't have interfered. Maybe the lassie was just playing him up to make the laddie jealous."

"Maybe."

"McRolfe is one of Carlyle's designers, I believe."

"A jumped-up draughtsman."

"Whatever he is, did he design your jet spray?"

"Aye, he did."

"And so, presumably, could have read all the papers

in your file. Could have photocopied them, even."

"Aye, he could."

"But as he did so good a job on your jet spray, you will have a high opinion of him, I reckon."

Capenter put his head on one side and glared at Green from under bushy eyebrows. "Since you've had a talk to young Chesterton, you'll know yon's not the case."

"Too true, mate. Young Tom told us you said McRolfe was feathering his own nest by selling Carlyle secrets and that you'd even warned Carlyle about it. Is that true?"

"It's true enough."

"Give us an example."

"One of my own?"

"Yes."

"I'd read up about Lidar."

"What the devil's that?"

"Heard of Radar, haven't you? Well Lidar is along the same lines, but it is Light Detection and Ranging."

"Using what? A laser beam?" asked Masters.

"That's right. Or infrared beams. Both will do. Now I don't know much about the basics of electronics, but I didn't have to for what I wanted. All I had to say was that if they'd put an infrared rotating diode capable of being lowered or raised to the right height on one pole, and a moveable detector on the distant pole, one man could set up his master and then move to the outstation and move his detector until it was dead level with the infrared beam. The detector would give a sound signal when the right height was reached."

"I'm with you. One man operating one of these and far more accurately than two men with dumpy levels."

"You've got it."

"There are such instruments already in use," said Masters.

"I know that. But I had added refinements. A universal swivel at the infrared transmitter so that it could be used in all directions without moving its pole and the incorporation of a clinometer to give slopes upwards or downwards to the nearest half-second of angle. I thought it would be of use in road building and the like where there are rises and falls in surface levels to be measured and laid."

"Too true," grunted Berger. "Even some stretches of motorway switch and curve like nobody's business."

Carpenter ignored the remark. Instead he went on bitterly: "Some, if not all, of my refinements were incorporated in other makes of leveller before Carlyle's company produced a prototype."

"McRolfe was the designer assigned to the job?"

"He was."

"What made you suppose he had sold your ideas?"

"I happened to see him lunching with the designer of the firm who brought out the first leveller incorporating my refinements."

"You knew the man."

"I made it my business to find out who he was when I saw McRolfe had my file on the table and consulted it from time to time as the other chap made notes of the stuff read out to him."

"You know it was your file."

"It had my logo on it." He opened a drawer and produced a hardback file. "Shairny green with a red whiting swallowing its tail to make a circle with my name printed round it. Do you think I could mistake that?"

"I should hardly think so. Shairny green? That's what that sort of indefinite colour is called, is it?" asked Masters.

"That's how we Scots describe it."

"Not it," grunted Green. "Far too bright for shairny."

Carpenter asked: "You would know, would you?"

"I know what shair is. Or shar if you prefer it. It's cow dung mixed with peat, sometimes with coal dust, to make fuel for the fire. And if that rather nice colour is shairny, I'll eat my hat."

"We use it to describe any indefinite green."

"In that case, don't start calling me Shairny, mate.

Or any of you," growled Green, looking round.

"Are there any other examples of McRolfe selling secrets that you know of, Mr. Carpenter?" asked Masters.

"Not definite. Suspicion. On the part of a Mr. Cedric Bush. I met him first at Carlyle's. He's a client there. Has been for some years. Creates things for desks. He told me an executive toy he had designed suddenly appeared on the market before Carlyle had perfected the design. He wasn't best pleased. But he only had suspicions, no proof. But he was unable to convince himself that a second inventor should have hit upon a ball-bearing swinging in an ankh symbol at exactly the same time as he did himself."

Masters nodded his understanding of this point.

"I told Carlyle, you know," went on Carpenter. "Nearly three months ago."

"And?"

"He listened, because he's a courteous man. But he thinks a lot of McRolfe as a designer. Has accelerated his position in the firm, after all. So I don't suppose he did a thing about it. He can't have done, otherwise McRolfe wouldn't still be with the company, let alone at his birthday party."

"That would certainly seem to be the case." Masters got to his feet. "Just one question before we go, Mr. Carpenter. When you saw McRolfe in a restaurant with your file, why didn't you accost him there and then?"

"Because I didn't know at that time who the other man was, and for all I knew, it was McRolfe asking the other man for information he might have wanted to help him with the design. Carlyle's men do have to consult experts in various fields, you know."

"Of course. I should have realised that for myself. Thank you, Mr. Carpenter. Our chat has been very useful."

As they went down to the car, Tip said: "Gussets, Chief."

"Not again," groaned Berger. "You brought that one up yesterday afternoon."

"What is it, petal?" asked Green. "Skirt too tight or something?"

"The plastic bags," explained Tip. "The ones that could have been filled with the contaminated water, but which would have to lie flat to be carried on somebody's person. They would have to be gussetted. Like uniform pockets. To expand but still hold their shape and not just belly out into great spheres."

"Go on."

As they got into the car, Tip said: "I've remembered where I saw just the sort that would do."

"Where, Tip?"

"In Mrs. Carlyle's kitchen. You remember that afternoon we went to talk to Mrs. Hookham, but when I told Mrs. Carlyle I'd loved her kitchen, I meant it. I had actually looked round."

"You saw gussetted bags there."

"Yes, Chief. But a special sort. She has her freezer in an alcove, and on a shelf she has piles of freezer bags and one of those heat sealers."

"Go on."

"The bags were of different sizes, of course. They were all gussetted, but the smallest ones—those about the size of a paperback book—were not only gussetted, they were divided in two down the middle. And they were made of heavy material."

"Two bags in one, you mean?"

"That's it, Chief."

"Why would they be like that, Tip?"

"I don't honestly know, Chief, but have you seen those ice-making bags? They are just one big bag separated into about two dozen diamond-shaped sections. When they're full of water and ready to hang in the freezer they still retain their shape."

"I've seen them. I think Wanda uses circular ones."

"I think heavy plastic, gussetted and divided small bags would hold a lot of water, Chief, but still lie flat enough to go into a pocket without being too notice-able."

"I feel sure you are right, Tip. We shall be going down into Kent to see Mr. Carlyle. Make sure you get a sample of the bags, discover where they are to be bought, and then test them full of water."

"Right, Chief."

"Now that's settled," said Green, "could we get to the Yard so's I can have a cup of coffee? That old Scotsman was too damn mean to offer us one and I'm fair clammed."

"I think he was going to offer us coffee," said Berger from the driving seat.

"Why didn't he then?"

"You brassed him off by calling his file covers the colour of cow dung mixed with peat. And no wonder you're clammed, either, the amount you had to say about it."

Hugh Carlyle had said he would be at home in Kent by four o'clock or soon after that afternoon. Masters and his team arrived before him. Margot, warned of their coming, had tea and buttered scones waiting for them.

"Is it something important, George?" she asked.

He smiled at her. "Please don't worry about it."

"Meaning it is something serious."

"For us, yes, but I hope not for you. Now, Margot, I would like you to take Tip and me into your kitchen."

"Whatever for?"

"I'd like to look at something."

Bewildered, Margot led the way. Mrs. Hookham and Freda were both working, the older woman pressing sheets on a large table-ironer, the younger doing the hand ironing on a board. Both looked up when they saw the newcomers.

"Mrs. H., the Chief Superintendent wishes to have a look round."

"Inspect my kitchen? Whatever for? He'll find nothing here."

215

"Freezer bags, actually," said Masters.

"Oh. Whatever do you want them for?"

"Over here, Chief," said Tip, edging past Freda and being careful to step over the electric lead to her iron.

The alcove was white-tiled to the ceiling. The large chest freezer stood within it, with a foot to spare at each end where, above the height required for opening the lid, shelves had been placed to take plastic lidded boxes, sealer, and two or three heaps of plastic bags.

"These are the ones, Chief." Tip took a couple of the bags from the smallest pile.

"Ask Mrs. Hookham if you could fill one from the tap, please."

While Tip moved away to perform this task, Margot asked: "What is it, George? Are the bags important in some way?"

"They could be, Margot. I'll explain a little later."

Tip came back. "There you are, Chief. Divided down the middle for strength so that they'll hold shape. And apart from the side and bottom gussets they are self-sealing. You just have to press the two top ends together." Tip showed how a single thick line of plastic on one side could be forced between two others that made a crevasse on the other. "I don't think this seal would be quite safe enough, Chief, but a little run of safety glue between the two protruding bits would make it fully watertight."

"Thank you." Masters took the almost flat bag from Tip and carefully slid it, first into a side pocket of his jacket, and then into the inside breast pocket. Tip stood back and regarded him critically.

"Nobody would know, Chief. At least they would only think you'd got a fat wallet in your inside pocket and as for the side pocket, well, it is certainly no fuller-looking than when you are carrying a tin of tobacco in there."

"Good." Masters removed the bag, watched all the time by Mrs. H. and Freda.

"Can you tell me where you buy these particular bags?" asked Masters.

"We don't," said Mrs. Hookham. "Mr. Carlyle keeps us supplied."

Masters turned to Margot. "He buys them in town?"

"No. They come from the office. Hugh carries stocks of all manner of bags and packing materials of very good quality. You see his despatch department has to send out a great variety of machined parts, some quite small, which mustn't be allowed to get rusty or dirty. These particular ones are used for small shafts made of steel, or specially made bolts and their necessary bits and pieces. You'd be quite surprised at what they turn out or have specifically made and each one is, more or less, a one-off item."

"I see."

"Hugh said he couldn't see why Mrs. H. should have to go to the trouble of buying-in freezer bags of a much inferior quality when he was knee deep in them in his store. So he keeps us supplied."

"I use them little 'uns for bits and pieces mostly," said Mrs. H. "Nothing's wasted in this house.. Even a bit of leftover veg, like a few peas or bits of carrot, is sealed in these little bags an' kept for when I'm making soup. In the old days it would have been into the stockpot with them, but this way's easier and cleaner. I even keep the drops of gravy we have left over, don't I, Freda?"

Masters smiled at her. "You blend them all together and get Brown Windsor, do you?"

"Brown Windsor, Green Windsor, Red Windsor, I make them all."

"And very good they are, too," said Margot.

"I'm sure they are. Now, Mrs. Hookham, when you picked up some pieces of plastic that your husband had put on the side of the pool when he was cleaning it out that Sunday morning, could they have possibly been the remains of one or two of these particular little bags?"

"They could have been, but I can't say I noticed."

"Why?" asked Tip, gently.

"All sopping wet and mucky they were."

"Mucky? With bits of food that had fallen into the pool?"

"I don't know what it were, but it was that sticky, I could hardly get it off my hands. The plastic, I mean. Then I had to come in and use the pan scourer to get it off my fingers."

Tip smiled at her. "Thank you. You've been very helpful." She turned to Masters. "All these instant superglues soften in water, Chief."

Masters nodded his understanding of the point she had made. Her idea that the flaps above the closures on the bags would have been sealed with superglue seemed to be borne out. It was also a fair assumption to suppose that since such bags had been readily available on Carlyle's company premises, that was the likely source of the murderer's supply.

Margot led them back to the sitting room.

"Any joy, Chief?" asked Berger.

"'Course there's joy, lad," grunted Green. "Look at that girlie's physog. All smiles. And bright eyes, too, which shows she hit the coconut when she first saw those bags in the kitchen and associated them with the dirty trickster."

"I'm afraid I don't understand anything of what's being said," complained Margot. "Isn't somebody going to enlighten me?"

"Could it wait a bit?" asked Masters. "Until Hugh arrives? Then we won't have to go through it all twice."

"Of course. But I'm all agog to know how freezer bags from my kitchen could possibly cause Carla Sanders to die."

"Not from your kitchen, Mrs. Carlyle," said Tip, by way of comfort. "We are positive they came from your husband's packaging department."

"How?" asked Margot.

"Later, please," said Masters. "If I'm not mistaken, here's Hugh."

*　　　*　　　*

218

They were all sitting round the low table. Margot was pouring tea. Hugh was using a tray clipped onto the arm of his wheelchair to take his cup.

"Come on then, George. Let's have it. Or have you just come down to enjoy Mrs. H.'s scones?"

"Hardly, Hugh, delicious though they are." Masters put down his cup and looked directly at his host.

"Mr. Ian Carpenter is of the impression that, after he had complained to you about unprofessional conduct on the part of Andrew McRolfe, you took no action whatsoever."

"I wouldn't have told Carpenter if I had. It wouldn't do to let all our clients know every time I had to undertake some disciplinary action in the office."

"Not even to satisfy a customer who had a very serious complaint?"

Carlyle laughed. "Very serious? Ian Carpenter had no proof. No proof that would have been accepted in any court of law, for instance, which is where the business might have landed up had I acted on what he told me and dismissed McRolfe."

"So you didn't believe him?"

"I believed him all right. He's a canny Scot and straight as a die. Yes, I believed him. Believed, that is, that he believed what he told me to be true."

"But you were not convinced?"

"I was convinced, actually."

"You were?"

"Yes. I'd been harbouring the odd suspicion against McRolfe, myself. For some little time, in fact. But I had no certain proof, George, nor could I get it. Carpenter's story fuelled my own suspicions, but it wasn't big enough to start a bonfire under McRolfe." He picked up his cup and sipped at it while his listeners waited. Then he continued. "Besides, I didn't want my suspicions to be confirmed, dammit."

"No?"

"For one thing it would have been bloody bad for the firm—my firm—which is based largely on trust. And for another, Andrew McRolfe was as good a designer as I'd ever had. Men as good as he is are hard to come by. I didn't want to lose him."

"Not even at the expense of losing clients?"

Carlyle's mood seemed to change and he again laughed aloud. "I'd never run the risk of losing a client for anybody. Not if I could help it. Desertion by clients could start to snowball. Word soon gets around in the trade, you know."

Masters nodded. "That would seem to suggest to me that you did take some action after hearing Carpenter's complaint, despite trying to give us the opposite impression. What steps did you take?"

Carlyle grinned. "The only ones I could take in the circumstances. I had young McRolfe in and roasted him."

"Bawled him out?"

"Nothing like that. Told him that I was convinced there had been hints of recent security leaks from the Design Department. I didn't accuse him, directly. I didn't accuse anybody specifically. But I left him first in no doubt that if I did discover who was responsible that man would never again get a similar post in British industry. Second, that he, as manager of the department, would carry the can. Third, I left him in no doubt that, though I hadn't said so specifically, I considered he was the culprit and would not only carry the can, but would also, from henceforward, carry his own bloody head under his own bloody arm. After that I kicked him out and told him to get on with his work."

"Darling, you never said anything of this to me," protested Margot.

"Why should I, Mags? Nothing to do with you. Business matters." He laughed. "Besides, it was only a ten-minute storm in the office."

"Which you forgot to mention to Carpenter," said Masters.

"Which I studiously refrained from mentioning to Carpenter. Carlyle's business is Carlyle's business."

"Quite. But that wasn't the end of it, was it, Hugh?"

"What do you mean, George? The subject has never been mentioned again between McRolfe and me and he's still beavering away in my drawing office."

Masters stared at him for a moment.

"When did the anonymous letters start to arrive, Hugh?"

"What anonymous letters?"

"Hugh," said Masters sharply, "stop trying to fence with me. I know you've had a number of anonymous letters recently."

"They've stopped now."

"Maybe they have. I asked you when they started."

"About a week or ten days after Ian Carpenter made his complaint," said Carlyle truculently.

"Was that before or after you had disciplined Mc-Rolfe?"

"Oh, after. I blasted him very soon after Carpenter spoke to me. I just took a couple of days to think how to handle the matter and then I went into action."

"Thank you. Did it occur to you that McRolfe could have been the author of the letters?"

Carlyle was genuinely surprised. "McRolfe? Why the hell should it be he? Dammit, I'd done him a favour by warning him but not kicking him out for the most heinous crime in our particular calendar; and why in heaven's name should he mention my giving away secrets? McRolfe would not want to remind me of that in case it made me remember him and hit on him as the author, by association." He looked carefully at Masters. "Come on, now, George. You've got some bee in your bonnet. What about McRolfe?"

"Let me ask you a question, Hugh. Had you any idea who it was who sent those letters?"

"None."

"Not even though they accused you of using other people's inventions for your own purposes?"

"Oh, that! I told you I had just a hint of suspicion that a few minor ideas were going astray, but I had no certain proof that they were."

"Yet you roasted McRolfe."

"Without specifically accusing him. I was determined to plug the leak if there was a leak, so I told him he was responsible not only for keeping his own mouth shut but also for the integrity of his whole department."

"So you told me."

"Don't sound so bloody sceptical, George. I thought those letters came from one of the scores of minor inventors who apply to us but whom we have been unable to help or, alternatively, one whose ideas had been superseded by somebody else in another set-up altogether."

"So you went through the list of disappointed parties?"

Hugh laughed. "Of course not. It would take weeks to follow that up and I haven't got time to spare for fun and games like that. Besides, I guessed they would stop, and they have."

"After an attempt on your life had been made."

Hugh laughed again. Margot gasped.

"We might as well tell you, Hugh, that in our opinion, your pool was fouled with leptospirae so that you would catch a raging fever which, in your condition, would almost certainly have been fatal. As it turned out, Carla Sanders went into the water before you had an opportunity to do so and, as a result of the melee that caused her immersion, the pool was cleaned and scrubbed before you went in next day. That saved your life."

"Oh, no," gasped Margot.

"Oh, yes, love," said Green, "and it's thanks to you that His Nibs here has managed to fathom the whole business."

"Thanks to me?"

"Yes, love. You gave Wanda that letter to show him, where your old man was throwing them all away." Green turned to Hugh. "Didn't you ever take a close look at those letters and try to find some clue in them that would point to who had written them?"

"I read them, of course."

Green sighed and turned to Masters. "You'd better tell him, George."

Masters accepted the photostat of the letter from the file Tip was carrying and explained how he had come to the conclusion that it had been written by a Scot.

"But don't you see," said Hugh, "that the letters could have been written by Carpenter. He was the one who complained about his ideas being sold and he is also a Scot."

"True. But that was where McRolfe tried to be clever. Somehow he must have become aware of the fact that Carpenter had entered with you a complaint about his leaking secrets about the infrared leveller.

"He is a very ambitious young man, and he wants power, money and position beyond what his own, not inconsiderable, abilities will afford him in the foreseeable future. He grafted for you to get as far as he could, then he saw the chance of selling a few secrets to earn him a bit more money. Finally, and you can judge this for yourselves, he made what I believe is today called a play for your daughter."

"For Rosemary? She wouldn't look at him," said Hugh.

"She did look at him, sir," countered Tip, quietly.

"So she did," said Margot. "I put it down to a man's silly infatuation for a young girl. After all, there was Tom."

"He wasn't very good at it, perhaps," said Tip, "and Mr. Chesterton saw through it very easily. As did Mr. Carpenter. Put quite bluntly, if McRolfe could marry your daughter, he would have the Carlyle company in his pocket. Or so he thought, and that was his aim."

"He never stood a chance," laughed Hugh. "Not with Rosemary."

"I'm sure you are right, sir," continued Tip, "but the situation wasn't quite as straightforward as all that. You see Miss Carlyle, as many young girls will, tried to play up Mr. Chesterton. She paid attention to McRolfe to make her boyfriend not jealous, exactly, but aware that he wasn't the only one who fancied her and to show him he shouldn't take her too much for granted."

"That's absolutely right," said Margot. "I'd noticed it for myself and was a bit amused by it, actually, but I wasn't in the least worried. I was certain nothing would come of it and..." she shuddered, "I had no idea there was anything sinister behind it."

"Well, I'm damned," said Hugh, with a laugh. "And I thought I knew most things that went on round here, but I never saw that bit of byplay."

"Men!" uttered Margot, shaking her head sadly at Tip. "But what had the freezer bags to do with it all?"

"Could we just complete the bit we were on first—" said Masters. "We have told you something of McRolfe's plans and how we think he decided it was Carpenter who had complained about him."

"That's easily explained," said Hugh. "It was because he actually had sold Carpenter's secrets that he guessed correctly who had shopped him."

"Good idea, chum," said Green.

"Whatever it was," said Masters, "because of the roasting you had given him, with the possibility of dismissal looming large and the certainty of no further promotion in the firm as long as you were at its head, Hugh, he decided to kill you. You had bruised his oversized ego and you were blocking his progress. You had to go. I think it took him some little time to come to the decision and think it all through, during which time he had received Margot's invitation to your party. By not telling her of the business about McRolfe and the leakage of secrets, you had not stopped her from including in the guest list somebody who, since the list was first formulated, had become *persona non grata*."

"That's right," agreed Margot.

"But then McRolfe seemed to settle things very nicely by refusing the invitation on what I suspect were false grounds. A business meeting on a Saturday night! Presumably, you, Margot, told Hugh that McRolfe had declined and he, pleased it had turned out so well, still made no mention of the fact that he thought McRolfe to be disloyal."

"Exactly right," said Hugh. "It seemed all was well without need for explanations."

"Quite. Then McRolfe formulated his plans. He would cause you to contract a fatal fever from bathing in your own pool. He had got the idea from Carpenter's file. Weil's disease. He simply had to put contaminated urine from rats surreptitiously into your pool and you would catch a fatal illness from causes which could only be considered natural and would not lay him open to suspicion."

"But as well as nurturing a murderous hatred of you, Hugh, his feelings towards Carpenter were murderous, too. Then, I believe, he saw what he thought was a way of wreaking vengeance on both of you. He would make it seem that Carpenter was implicated in your death should anybody ever come to the conclusion that it was not simply accidental and totally natural.

"Foolishly, he thus complicated matters. Whilst he caught his infected rats..."

"I've been going to ask you, Chief," said Tip. "How would he do that? And know that they were infected, I mean?"

"I cannot, of course, give you the exact steps he took, but you must know from your reading that the reservoir of infection is in an animal population among which are infected individuals who, although healthy, are excreting leptospirae in their urine. Several types of animal are carriers, but up to forty-six or forty-seven percent of rats, in various locations, have been found to harbour these particular bugs. I suspect, therefore, that if you were to set traps in damp, rat-infested places, such as sewage farms, mines, canals, docks, farms, fish houses and so on, you could be pretty certain that almost one in every two would be infected, and perhaps even every one you caught would yield leptospirae."

"As easy as that?" asked Hugh.

"I believe so. There must be some test for infection, of course, but why bother to do esoteric laboratory work when the chances are so high in your favour? However, I am fairly certain McRolfe would grow a culture in a broth of some sort for his own satisfaction, although total failure the first time would be immaterial. He could go on trying with different rats until successful. Theoretically, at any rate.

"So, he was proposing to use information that could easily be linked to Carpenter, but to make sure that link would be spotted should the need arise, he decided to write you anonymous letters, accusing you of malpractice and threatening your life, all with a hidden Scottish flavour to the language used. I say hidden, because obviously the likes of you and Margot did not latch on to it. But should those letters fall into the hands of professionals—among whom I include myself—then sooner or later the Scottish flavour was bound to come to light. Particularly if, Hugh, the recipient had enough common sense to keep the letters so that there were five or six of them to yield their clues instead of just one rescued by his wife."

"Sorry," said Hugh with a laugh. "But you know how it is, old boy. You can't take things too seriously."

"You must, sir," said Tip severely. "They were part of a murder plan. Miss Sanders died, remember."

"You're quite right," admitted Hugh. "I've been a dangerous fool."

"We'll get on," said Masters. "McRolfe's own Scots origins made sure the Scottishness was not too bogus. He was certain the hints would be picked up and Carpenter, a Scot who had complained of having his secrets sold, would almost certainly come under suspicion, particularly as the means used were particularly well known to him. And demonstrably so.

"But now McRolfe realised he had made a mistake in refusing Margot's invitation to the party. He had to have some excuse to come to the house and get near the pool. So he did an almost unheard-of thing. He rang up and asked to be reinstated as a guest. He was in luck's way. Margot, as you hadn't been told of the ill feeling between Hugh and McRolfe, you immediately reissued the invitation. So he came to the party.

"He arrived, we are informed, in a sports jacket in heavy material. It was a warm night and all the other men were in shirt sleeves. According to Rosemary, McRolfe was feeling the heat, and though she invited him to take his jacket off, he declined to do so. Tom Chesterton said that it was a good jacket, but that it seemed to sit heavy on McRolfe's shoulders.

"That information given us by your two young people confirmed something we had already surmised. That was that a fair supply of water, contaminated by leptospirae, had been brought to this house that night in plastic bags carried on somebody's person. A heavily sitting jacket on a very hot night! We wanted to find plastic bags that would suit the purpose. Ones that would not balloon out when filled. We guessed at plastic bags because they would only need to be punctured and put into the water for the bugs to escape—as opposed to pouring a bottleful of the stuff into the pool."

"Much easier," agreed Hugh. "And clear plastic wouldn't be noticed in the water."

"We questioned both Mr. and Mrs. Hookham. Mr. H. had found a load of plastic blocking the drainage hole when he cleaned the pool. Mrs. H. had picked it up and thrown it away. So we knew we were on the right track.

"Tip had the opportunity to look round your kitchen, Margot. In admiration, not looking for clues. But she spotted some strong, gussetted plastic bags by the freezer. Bags divided into compartments so that they would lie flat when filled and fit into the pockets of a man's jacket."

"I saw you try that out."

"Of course you did. And you told me those bags are a standard packing item in Hugh's despatch department. In other words, much easier for McRolfe to get hold of than Carpenter." Masters looked round. "And that is the present situation. We have a case. We now have to complete it. To that end you, Hugh, and you, Margot, will have to make full statements to my two sergeants. Tomorrow morning, please, and I will have to trouble you both to come to the Yard to do it. Can you come straight in, before going to the office? Both of you?"

"Of course," said Margot. "I'll come up with Hugh."

Carlyle grinned. "Don't want us meeting McRolfe before we give the evidence, eh?"

Masters shrugged his shoulders. "I don't think he will be in the office at all tomorrow."

"I see. Arresting him tonight, are you?"

As they drove back to London, Berger, who was at the wheel, asked: "Are you picking up McRolfe tonight, Chief? What I mean is, you didn't deny it when Mr. Carlyle suggested that was what you intended to do."

"Tonight," agreed Masters. "What is the time now?"

"Just gone half-past six," said Tip. "That means McRolfe will be at home now, or will be very soon."

"Just the hammer," said Green. "Better to pick him up at home than create a fuss in Carlyle's office." He turned to Masters. "I know Carlyle said arrest, George, but all civilians talk about arrest when they really mean taking in for questioning."

"Taking in," agreed Masters. "But we must inspect his premises."

"Looking for infected rats, you mean? Thanks very much."

"We shan't do that bit. I've laid on for a Senior Scientific Officer to be on call at Horseferry Road. I'm hoping it will be Harry Moller."

"Dr. Moller who helped us in Ipswich, Chief?" asked Tip.

"The same, petal," said Green, "and don't go making goo-goo eyes at him. He's happily married, remember."

Tip turned and grinned. "But he is handsome, isn't

228

he? All that dark wavy hair and his lean and hungry look. Very sexy."

"If you really think so, Tip, after we get to the Yard you can take the car on and pick up whoever has been told to stand by. You know where the government forensic department hangs out?"

"Yes, Chief."

"And to think I used to like Dr. Moller before we set out on this trip," groaned Berger. "Handsome! Very sexy! It makes you sick."

"See what you've done now, sugar?" said Green. "Upset the lad. You're doing a Rosemary Carlyle on him. Playing him up, and look where that's landed us."

Tip made no reply.

Some forty minutes later, Tip ushered Dr. Harry Moller into Masters' office. The two had worked together on a number of occasions and were, by now, friendly above the cooperation needed in their respective jobs. As Tip had said, Moller, nearing forty, was a man whom most women would find attractive. He was tall and spare, but with good shoulders. He had naturally dark skin, as if permanently suntanned. His dark, wavy hair was beginning to show flecks of grey. The face was handsome, displaying something of his great intelligence and wide knowledge, but with no trace of arrogance. A likeable man, somewhat diffident with strangers, but affable with those he knew.

"Hello, Harry, I was hoping you'd make yourself available when you heard I was asking for forensic help."

Moller smiled as he shook hands. "I never miss a case from your little lot if I can help it, George. They provide a bit of excitement in an otherwise humdrum existence. Even if it does mean staying on at the office till all hours of the night."

"Sorry about that. I'm sure Celia will forgive me for keeping you away from home. How is she, by the way?"

"She's gone bird-watching with a crowd of elderly twitchers. A two-day stint down on the Dart estuary."

"Good. So we are not causing her any domestic problems by keeping you out late."

"None whatsoever. How's Wanda?"

"Doing fine, thank you."

"Doing?" queried Moller. "Has she been ill?"

"The lass is infantising, Harry," said Green. "Hoping to enlarge the Masters' household in six or eight months time."

"I see. Congratulations, George, to both of you."

"Thank you, Harry. Now to work. I'd better tell you what we are about."

"I know it's concerned with leptospirae. My boss told me that much. So I've mugged up on them."

"I told him that much when I phoned to ask for help. Anyhow, here's the problem."

Masters spent some ten minutes briefing Moller. At the end of that time, he said: "You've had a synopsis only, Harry, I know that, but we can flesh it out in the car. Now I'd like to get going. How long will it take to get to McRolfe's address in Teddington, Sergeant?"

"Anything up to an hour, Chief," replied Berger, "but with any luck, half that time."

"In that case, let's get going."

They drew up in front of what had once been a parade of shops set well back from the pavement. Not modern shops. Built, Masters guessed, before the first world war to serve the many streets of smaller houses round about. Now most of them were no longer the shops as originally intended. There was an Indian takeaway, a warehouse-type of establishment selling TV aerials and all manner of batteries, and various offices. It was above one of these that McRolfe had his flat. The upper stories where once the traders and their families had lived were now divided off for sale to young, first-time buyers. To get to the two of which McRolfe's was one, Berger had to shin over a six-foot locked gate. Had he rung the numbered bell on the gatepost, McRolfe, had he been at home, would presumably have come down to let them in. Berger performed this chore. They entered an as-phalted yard, half-covered by an old open-fronted lean-to, once meant for storing boxes of fruit and the like, but now devoted to holding dustbins with large numbers scrawled on them in white paint, odds and ends of timber and a few pieces of disused furniture. The door to the first of the flats was on ground level, opposite this eyesore.

They rounded the end of the building, still in the same yard surrounded by high walls. There was a fire-escape-type flight of iron steps leading up to McRolfe's door. But of greater interest to the team was a row of three or four hutches near the base of the escape. Made of wood, with wire netting fronts, they were obviously purpose-made for their occupants and whatever purpose their owner wanted.

Moller stopped to inspect. Tip, alongside him, said: "No rats, Chief. Not one."

"Are you sure, petal?" demanded Green.

"Perfectly certain. These are guinea pigs. I used to have one when I was a child."

Green scratched one ear. "We've been done, George."

"I don't think so, Bill. What do you think, Harry?"

Moller looked at Masters. "I think I should send Berger up to see if McRolfe is at home."

Masters nodded to Berger, who began to ascend the steps followed by Tip.

"Are you expecting to find the rats up there instead?" demanded Green.

Moller shook his head.

"George?" demanded Green.

"Don't rush me, Bill. Somewhere among all the papers I've read there was mention of guinea pigs in connection with leptospirae, but I can't remember exactly what it was. You see, I was concentrating exclusively on rats. But Harry here seems to be happy to be without rats."

"Perfectly happy, George. In fact, I think the guinea pigs seal your case against McRolfe."

They could hear Berger's voice. "Mr. McRolfe? We are police officers. Do you mind if we come in?"

Masters looked up the stairway. Berger and Tip were

231

disappearing into the flat, presumably behind McRolfe.

"Right, Harry. Put me in the picture, quickly, before Bill and I go up there."

"What you forgot, George, was that the papers you read said that the presence of leptospirae in humans can be tested by inoculating guinea pigs with urine from the patient. If leptospirae are present they grow like billy-ho in guinea pigs. So, briefly, for rats, read guinea pigs in all your calculations except the first one. He obviously caught rats and bought guinea pigs. He inoculated each guinea pig with the blood of one of the rats and cultured the urines of the pigs in suitable media until his tests proved that the organism was present in at least one guinea pig. After that, all he had to do was inoculate all the others with either the blood or urine of the infected rat and he would have a contaminated colony, all members of which would be widdling the organisms for him to collect and keep alive in a culture medium until the time came to transfer them to pure water to add to the swimming pool."

"As simple as that, eh?" grunted Green.

"Not all that simple, Bill, actually. He had to take care in order to get results, and take care that he didn't cause himself harm. But relatively easy in theory, providing he read up the right methods and tests."

"If you say so. Anybody who mucks about with dangerous bugs like that deserves all he gets." He looked up the stairway. "What about it, George?"

"We'll take him in. Harry, you'll look after the animals, won't you?"

"Of course. I'll need to come up and ring the lab to send a carrier-van and a couple of hands."

"Fine. We'll seal the flat and search thoroughly tomorrow. I don't like turning a place over before a suspect has been charged, but we'll just look for samples of those plastic bags and any literature there may be on Weil's disease. Oh, and his jacket of course, to test the pockets."

"Won't he have got rid of everything by now?"

"He hasn't got rid of the guinea pigs."

"I wonder why that is?"

"He likes animals," suggested Green bitterly.

"Two possible reasons," said Masters. "First, he was proposing to try again. Second, he didn't think anybody would link guinea pigs to the disease."

"So he was wrong," grunted Green, setting off heavily up the stairs.

It was after eleven o'clock that night when Masters, accompanied by Green, reached home. Doris Green was already there, keeping Wanda company.

"What's for supper, love?" asked Green anxiously.

"You mean you haven't eaten yet, William?"

"No, sweetheart, we haven't. Don't tell me you haven't provided."

"Doris and I had supper at about eight o'clock."

Green groaned and accepted the gin and tonic Masters handed him. "Thanks, George, but I reckon this will make me kalied on an empty stomach."

"You've always got your forefeet in the trough," snorted his wife. She turned to Wanda. "Would you like me to cut those cold potatoes into scallops and fry them?"

"Yes, please, Doris, but I'll come through and get the salad ready." She turned to Green. "Is a smoked mackerel fillet all right for you, William?"

"Make it two, love, and you're on."

Wanda smiled and left them.

"She's looking bonny, George."

"I think so."

"She'll look even bonnier before the night's out."

Masters said nothing, but refilled the glasses.

It was when the two men were at table and their wives sitting with them for company that Doris raised her glass.

"Toast?" asked her husband.

"Greedy guts. You've got potatoes."

233

Green expired. "I meant were you going to propose a toast?"

"Yes. To all of us." She smiled at Wanda. "We've sold the house, today."

"Good show," said Masters. "Did you get a good price for it?"

Doris blushed. "Enough to enable us to buy your house, George."

"Without too much extra expense, I hope," said Wanda.

"With little or none," said Green. "You see I've raised a bit of capital by promising to sell my memoirs to The Sunday Rag."

"I see. I shall look forward to reading them."

Green smiled. "When you're safely tucked up of an evening in Housmans? With your family round you?"

"It sounds idyllic, William."

"It will be, love. It will be."